I0552903

this time around

International Bestselling Author
Aimee Nicole Walker

This Time Around (Road to Blissville, #4)
Copyright © 2018 Aimee Nicole Walker

ISBN: 978-1-948273-05-3

aimeenicolewalker@blogspot.com

This is a work of fiction. Names, characters, places, and incidents either are the product of the author's imagination or are used fictitiously, and any resemblance to the actual person, living or dead, business establishments, events, or locales is entirely coincidental.

Cover photograph © Christopher John—www.cjc-photography.com
Cover art © Jay Aheer of Simply Defined Art—www.simplydefinedart.com

Editing provided by Miranda Vescio of V8 Editing and Proofreading—www.facebook.com/V8Editing

Proofreading provided by Judy Zweifel of Judy's Proofreading www.judysproofreading.com

Interior Design and Formatting provided by Stacey Ryan Blake of Champagne Formats—www.champagnebookdesign.com

Copyright and Trademark Acknowledgments

The author acknowledges the copyrights and trademarked status and trademark owners of the trademarks and copyrights mentioned in this work of fiction.

dedication

To John,

You are the personification of the phrase "still waters run deep." Always quiet, always observing, always thinking, and so very humble. I am so very proud to be your mother.

one

Andrew "Andy" Mason

COMING HOME ISN'T ALWAYS EASY, ESPECIALLY AFTER BEING gone for twelve years. Times change, and so do people and their attitudes. Sometimes that's good, and sometimes it's not. Growing up in a small town has its highs and lows, but that can be said for all communities. I'd been blessed to live in both small towns and big cities and saw the advantages and disadvantages of both. Neither one was right or wrong; just different. A person had to decide what works for them and not worry about what everyone else thinks.

I left Blissville with big dreams and an even bigger ego. As the first kid from my high school to receive a full ride scholarship to play college baseball, or any sport for that matter, I was certain it would lead to incredible opportunities. In my high school, I was the big fish in the little pond. I was destined for greatness, just ask anyone in town.

When I arrived at my college in Louisville, Kentucky, I became a little fish in a giant pond. The other fish were faster and stronger than I was. I had to make big sacrifices if I wanted playing time on the field, and it came with a price I hadn't been prepared to pay. I had to give up the one thing that was true in my life: Milo Miracle.

I'd heard from my sister, Faith, who's also Milo's best friend, that he and his twin sister, Maegan, had opened a coffee shop in our hometown called The Brew. She'd told me it had fast become one of Blissville's favorite places to hang out, which I saw firsthand after I worked up the courage to stop in when I drove into town mid-morning on a Monday. I figured that Faith would've warned Milo that I was moving back home, but his wide-eyed expression when he saw me said otherwise.

I'd even go so far to say that Milo was furious. His eyes slowly roamed over my body where I stood in the rear of the coffee shop. When Milo's eyes met mine again, the only emotion I saw was cool indifference. He didn't stomp off angrily like he would have when we dated in high school, but I could feel his desire to do so from across the room. I was glad that some things hadn't changed, even if I had to look harder to realize that he hid his passionate nature behind an aloof mask.

Milo's spirit was one of his most attractive qualities, and I would hate to think that time or circumstances had doused his bright flame. Milo buried his emotions and focused on taking care of his customers. I noticed that became harder for him to do the closer I got to the front of the line.

"Long time no see," I said lamely when I stood in front of him.

I saw Milo's jaw clench, but he remained calm. "What would you like today?"

"To talk to you after your shift is over," I said softly. The young, self-confident version of myself that Milo knew would've asked for his phone number or said I wanted to take him to dinner. I lost that swagger years ago when I struck out swinging at the three-two curveball life threw at me. I wanted to see how far I could push Milo. I wanted him to unleash everything he felt so we could get it out in the open and deal with it, but I wouldn't win his forgiveness by embarrassing him in front of his customers.

Milo's only reaction was to blink as he waited for my order.

"Welcome home, Andy," Maegan said, greeting me with a friendly smile. "For good, I hope."

"That's the plan." Did Milo soften slightly when he heard my intentions, or was that wishful thinking on my part? Did it even matter? Twelve years was a long time apart, and what did I know about the man he'd become? I certainly wasn't the same person he used to know. I sure as hell wanted to relearn everything about him though because twelve years did nothing to diminish the way my heart and body reacted to the sight of him.

"Your coffee selection?" Milo asked, irritation creeping into his voice. He nodded to the line behind me, letting me know I was holding things up.

"Uh, yeah. I'll take the chai latte."

Milo raised one perfectly groomed brow. I liked that I surprised him with my drink choice. "Size?"

"Big," I replied, unable to stop myself. "Very big." So maybe I hadn't lost all my swagger, or maybe it was the guy looking at me that made me feel bolder.

Milo's face turned as red as a beet. It seemed he remembered things about me too. "We have a size queen in our midst," he whispered sassily. "Coming right up."

"Don't spit in it," I jokingly said after he turned his back to me.

Milo pivoted slowly, regarding me through narrowed, midnight-blue eyes. "A person would have to feel really strongly about another to evoke such a reaction. I assure you, that isn't the case here. One 'very big' chai latte coming right up." Yeah, he used adorable air quotes and rolled his eyes.

I could see that Milo wasn't going to make my homecoming an easy one, but I wasn't deterred. Instead, I wanted to find ways to rile him up until he lost that cool veneer.

3

two

Milo Miracle

THE MINUTE *HE* WALKED INTO THE BREW, I FELT A CRACKLE IN the air that meant someone special had just entered my life. I glanced up from taking my customer's order in search of the man sent to cure all that ailed me and locked on to familiar light-blue eyes that I had adored for as long as I could remember.

Just great. Andy Fucking Mason is back in town. I shouldn't have cared, but I did. It wasn't like he had never returned home after graduating high school, he just seemed to do it in stealth mode to avoid running into me. It seemed that his days of hiding were over.

Ha! Apparently, *special* was synonymous with a swift kick in the balls, because the man who *reentered* my life wasn't there to *cure* me; he was there to torture me with his sexy presence and remind me of every moment that I had missed him. *Fucking asshole.* He had some nerve to smile like he was happy to see me. Note to self: kill Faith Mason for not warning a bitch that her sexier-than-sin brother was back in town to wreak havoc and turn my world upside down.

I got angrier and angrier with every erratic beat of my heart, but I wouldn't run away from the very public confrontation Andy wanted to have with me. I worked hard to keep my face a mask of pleasantness as my brain spun with so many things I wanted to say, and my body betrayed me with a dick that got happier and harder the closer Andy got to the front of the line. Luckily, the apron I wore hid the way my body reacted to him. I wanted to slug him, demand answers, and ride his cock all at the same time. I'd never hit another person in my life, so that part was out of the question. The other two? Well, they were still viable options.

Then Andy stood in front of me, and all my emotions fled, except anger. How dare he smile and look at me like I was a pastry he could devour with a cup of coffee? Twelve damn years and not a single phone call, text, or email. I could tell he wanted a happy reunion, but I wasn't going to give it to him.

The confrontation that followed was filled with my pissy attitude and Andy's attempt at humor with his laid-back charm. I wasn't interested in a reconciliation until he apologized for being an asshole for twelve years.

I wanted to call Faith and demand an explanation as to why she didn't give me a warning, but I knew the answer. Faith had decided she was Switzerland, neutral and peace-loving, when it came to Andy and me. She loved us both and refused to choose sides or give either of us up. I was grateful for that because I couldn't imagine a world without Faith in it, and I'd never ask her to turn her back on her big brother, no matter how dickhead-ish he was. So, I just let the urge to call her pass and found ways to keep my mind occupied while I internally dealt with the new development.

I held on to that anger long after he left, and it kept me moving for the rest of the day. I stayed after hours to deep clean the shop after everyone else left, hoping to work off some of my frustrations. Maegan and a few others offered to stay and help, but I declined. I just wanted to be alone with my thoughts and rage. By the time I finished, it was pitch black outside, and all the other businesses on the block were closed. I'd finally reached the exhausted, numb state I had craved by the time I stepped into the alley behind the shop where I'd parked my car that morning. The cool spring air kissed my heated skin and revitalized my spirit.

"Milo." *His* voice came out of the darkness and scared me so bad I nearly pissed down my leg.

I gasped and spun around, heart in my throat and anger raging through my blood. "Damn you, Andy!"

He chuckled like it was funny that he frightened me, or maybe it was nervous laughter. Either way, it only made me angrier, and I launched myself at him.

Instead of hitting him with my fists, I used my lips as weapons. Andy was startled at first, but then his mouth softened, and his tongue dueled for dominance with mine. I couldn't seem to stop my hands from roaming all over his broad back, scratching Andy's skin through his thin T-shirt with my nails and yanking his hair while flames of lust lit me up from the inside out. Andy's hands weren't exactly idle either. They mostly mirrored my actions until he firmly gripped my ass with both hands and kneaded the flesh he'd loved so much.

If ever there was a time to call a halt to the madness, it was then. I knew that we were seconds away from fucking in a dark alley, and just couldn't bring myself to care. Where had the anger and mistrust gone? It fled as soon as I felt Andy's lips against mine and his arms around me. It was like no time had lapsed at all, and we picked up right where we had left off. It was wrong, and I'd kick myself for it later, but I just couldn't seem to stop myself. Andy's head wasn't any clearer than mine. Lust was the only thing driving our actions.

The last glimmer of doubt faded when Andy slid his hand beneath the waistband of my jeans to tease the crack of my ass with a long, skilled finger. This man had the hands of a musician, and he played me like a piano, making me rip my mouth from his so I could sing out for more. And he delivered.

Andy spun me around to face the brick wall of the building. The rough brick scratched the palms of my hands when Andy placed them up by my head.

"Keep your hands there," he demanded hotly as he unfastened my jeans and yanked them down with my underwear to my knees. A thrilling shiver worked its way down my spine because this dominant side of him was new.

"Are you going to frisk me?" I asked. "Steal my wallet?"

"I see that mouth of yours hasn't changed a bit, Milo. Maybe you need something to keep it busy."

God, yes! I loved sucking cock, so that wasn't much of a threat. I heard Andy tear open a packet then felt a cool, lubed finger pressing against my pucker.

"Gah," I said when he eased one, probing digit past the tight ring of muscles. I hadn't exactly lived a chaste life since he left town, but it had been a while since I'd had sex. I wasn't about to let Andy know just how eager I was for him to fuck my face. "Busy how?" I prompted. "I use my mouth for many important things. Maybe a... Fuck yes!" I shouted when Andy pegged my prostate.

"I was thinking my cock," Andy growled in my ear. "That mouth of yours always felt so good, but this ass though..." Andy nipped the shell of my ear, making me yelp. "It's even tighter than I remember."

"Stop talking and fuck me already," I groaned when a second finger joined the first. "I'm no delicate flower, Andy."

He chuckled again. "No one would ever accuse you of that. A filthy fuck in the alley is hotter than hell, but causing you pain by ramming my big dick in your tight ass isn't what either of us wants. I need you relaxed and wet."

"I'm going to come," I warned, sounding desperate. I wanted to come around his cock, not his fingers. "Fuck me now, Andy."

He pulled his fingers from my ass then I heard the beautiful sounds of him ripping open the condom wrapper with his teeth. *Now we were getting somewhere.*

My hole felt empty, needy, and deprived. It wanted to be stretched, filled, and mastered. I felt the tip of his cock right where I wanted it, but Andy made no move to push inside me. "Hurry," I urged.

"Just let me add a bit more lube and—" Andy's words became a strangled gasp when I pushed my ass hard against him, impaling myself on his cock.

"Yessss," I hissed between my teeth.

"Fuuuuuuck," Andy said followed by, "Damn you, Milo." He angrily snapped his hips forward, burying his dick deep inside me. "Stay still a fucking minute," Andy demanded, gripping my hips to prevent me from grinding on his cock.

"I like it dirty and rough, Andy."

"It's not you I'm worried about, Milo. I don't want to come already. Kiss me."

"No." Kissing was too intimate, and I wanted to hang on to my anger and sanity.

"Come on, Milo," Andy goaded. "Afraid you won't be able to resist me if you do?"

"So damn sure of yourself," I groused. I was never one to back away from a challenge.

Leaving one hand pressed against the wall, I reached behind me to grip Andy's hair with the other then turned my head and kissed him with twelve years' worth of frustration. After he gathered himself, Andy pulled back until only the tip of his cock remained inside me. The slow drag over my nerve-laden hole was so delicious that it made me shiver with need. I held my breath while waiting for Andy to fill me once more then gasped into his mouth when he punched his hips forward, slamming his pelvis against my ass and driving me up on my tiptoes. *Yes!*

Andy's soft, languid kisses were a contrast to his hard, furious thrusts. He captured my cries as pleasure built inside me. I couldn't take it any longer; I needed to come. I untangled my fingers from his hair and started to reach for my cock, intending to jerk myself off while Andy continued to hammer my prostate.

Andy shoved my hand aside and gripped my cock with his big, calloused hand. The friction was out of this fucking world, and I spurted all over the brick wall after only a few tugs. Andy grunted and filled the condom deep inside me, never pulling his lips away from mine until I collapsed against the brick in exhaustion. If his dick wasn't still in my ass, I probably would've dropped to my knees. It helped that Andy leaned the bulk of his weight against me too.

The emotional and physical turmoil of what I had done caught up to me. I was on the verge of tears, and there was no fucking way I'd let Andy see me vulnerable like that. I swallowed hard to clear all emotion from my voice and icily said, "Kindly remove your dick from my ass."

"Milo," Andy groaned, sensing that the brief truce our hard fucking created was over. I felt his reluctance to pull out, but he did it anyway.

When he turned to discard the condom in the dumpster, I made a beeline for my car. I heard Andy's frustrated sigh when he saw that I was bailing on him, but he didn't call after me. Maybe he wisely knew I needed some space to accept his presence in my life again, or maybe he simply wanted to regroup for the next battle.

I kept myself together for the few blocks to my house and didn't release the torrent of tears I'd felt building all day until I was safely behind closed doors. My rescue kitty, Alli Cat, scowled at me when she entered the kitchen and found me sitting against the door, sobbing my broken heart out. It was hours past her dinnertime, but she put aside her hunger to comfort her pathetic human.

I held her against my chest, and her loud purrs rumbled through me, bringing me comfort. Once I got my crap together, I fed my best girl and took myself upstairs to my bedroom. I wanted to curl up on my bed and sleep away my misery, but there was no way I was climbing between the sheets smelling like Andy Mason.

I took a long, hot shower, eagerly washing away all traces of my shameful behavior. Then fresh tears started up again because I couldn't believe how stupid I was for falling into his arms so easily. Falling? Ha! I launched myself into his arms. *Damn it, Milo. The man disappeared without a trace and you jump his cock without even demanding an explanation? At least make the man work for it!*

By the time I got out of the shower, I had several text messages from concerned people who'd heard that Andy was back in town. I just sent the same message to everyone: *I'm fine. Thank you.* Well, all except Faith, who received: *Some best friend you are! You could've given me a hint that he was coming back home.*

Switzerland, was her reply.

Is he really back for good? I asked.

Um...

Didn't she know, or was she trying to think of ways to soften the blow? I stared at her one-word reply for a few moments, trying to figure it out. If he wasn't going to stick around, she would've said so.

Fuck me! I replied.

Sloppy seconds just aren't my style, Faith fired back. *Love you, Milo. That will never change.*

Love you too. Kinda. Sorta. Maybe.

I set my phone on the wireless charger and turned out the lights. I expected to fall asleep as soon as my head hit the pillow, but instead, my brain regurgitated every memory Andy and I had ever made, including the sexy new one from earlier that evening. I shivered beneath the covers even though I wasn't cold. It wasn't a fever that racked my body either, it was pain. I thought that I was over Andy Mason and didn't anticipate that seeing him, or hearing his voice, would impact me like it used to. I was so fucking wrong.

I also needed Faith to be wrong about Andy's intention of staying in Blissville. While I was happy for his family, who had missed him dearly, I didn't think I could handle the upheaval he brought into my orderly world. My momentary lapse in judgment from that night only served as a taunting reminder of the happiness and pleasure I could find in Andy's arms if only I could trust him again.

Trust wasn't something I gave away; it had to be earned. I might've given my ass up way too easily, but that was a mistake I wouldn't make again, no matter how much he tempted me. That filthy, alley fuck was the last time Andy's dick would kiss my ass until he explained to me where the hell he'd been all these years. *Yeah!* No more angry fucks and mind-blowing orgasms that rocked me to the core.

I woke up the next morning feeling refreshed, revitalized, and ready to resist Andy's charms. It was a tad bit presumptuous of me to think that he would seek me out again, but I didn't exactly discourage him with my slutty behavior the previous night. The Brew was so busy on weekday mornings with the workforce zombies shuffling in to caffeinate themselves before taking on the world that I didn't have time to worry about my reaction to seeing Andy the morning after.

Like the day before, I felt his presence before I saw him. That was enough to irritate me, because I didn't want to *feel* anything for Andy. Not joy from seeing his bright-blue eyes, not lust to feel his arms around me again, and certainly not longing to know who he'd become while he was gone. This ache he created inside me needed to disappear, and fast. The only way to do that was to show him I wasn't interested in picking up where we left off—not twelve years ago when he left town, and certainly not the night before when he fucked the logic and sense right out of me.

Contrary to recent actions, I was no longer the impulsive Milo he used to know. Best he learned that right away.

"Good morning," Andy practically purred when he reached the counter. "I'll have my very big chai latte, but I'd like to get two muffins also. I'm famished this morning."

Don't do it, Milo. Don't take the bait. "What flavors would you like, Andy? Perhaps a chocolate chip with a sprinkling of regret or blueberry with a dusting of that-ain't-ever-happening-again?"

I expected euphoria to flow through my body like endorphins after a good cardio workout when Andy's hopeful smile slid off his face, but all I felt was sadness. A spark of something else flared in Andy's eyes. It wasn't quite happiness or hope; it was something else. A wry grin slowly spread across his face, and I recognized exactly what I saw: Challenge.

Andy's eyes said, "Game on."

three

Andy

MILO THOUGHT HE COULD HIDE HIS ATTRACTION TO ME behind his smart mouth? *Regret and it ain't happening again, huh? We'll just see about that.*

"What's that sprinkled on the lemony muffin? It looks an awful lot like I'll take that challenge. What about this one?" I pointed to one that looked to have cranberries and oranges in it. "I'm thinking it's dusted with I'm-not-going-anywhere." I looked over at Milo's twin sister, Maegan, who was smiling from ear to ear as she joined us. "What do you recommend, Mae?"

"My personal favorites are the banana Milo's-nuts-are-in-a-twist and he's-met-his-match mixed berry," she responded, earning a glare from her brother. "Take your pick, Andy. They're on the house this morning."

I chose the lemon poppy seed and cranberry orange because I'd meant what I said. I accepted his challenge, and I was in town to stay. I wouldn't say that I won our skirmish, but I at least held my own and lived to fight another day. A smart man would've let that be enough, taken his bounty, aka free muffins, and left with a smile on his face. I'd been told I had more brawn than brains plenty of times in my life, so it didn't surprise me when I planted my ass at a small round table where I could keep an eye on Milo.

I tried not to be too obvious that I was watching him from under my eyelashes instead of reading the newspaper I had open in front of me.

"Pssst, you might have a better chance convincing him you're reading if the paper wasn't upside down," Josh Roman whispered sassily.

Sure enough, the paper was turned upside down the entire time. An embarrassed flush crept up my neck, but I didn't let that stop me from standing up and greeting Josh with a hug. "It's good to see a friendly face."

"You too, Andy. How are you really?" Josh asked, assessing me. "What's going on with your hair?"

"What do you mean?" I asked, running my hand over my hair. It was tidy, which wasn't the case the previous night after Milo fisted it while we kissed and fucked.

"It's a little boring, don't you think?" Josh leaned closer, and I could feel Milo's scrutiny from across the room. "Listen, come by the salon this afternoon. I'll work you in for a new haircut and propose an idea I have."

"To win over Milo?" I asked hopefully.

"Oh, honey," Josh said dramatically, placing his hand over his heart. "I'm not a miracle worker. You're going to have to put the time and effort in all by yourself. There will be no shortcuts, or haircuts, that take you to the Holy Land that is Milo's heart." I'd already been to the Holy Land that was Milo's ass. Would it really be that hard to make the leap? "While you're trying to figure it all out, I believe I have a few jobs for you."

I perked up at that idea because I did need to find some

work—either by launching my own construction company or getting hired on someone else's crew. "That sounds good. What time?"

"How does four o'clock work for you?"

"Perfect!" I told Josh loud enough to a glare from Milo. "See you later."

I sat back down at the table, wondering how long it would take before Milo wandered over to ask about the plans I'd made with Josh. I bit my lip to keep from smiling when I saw him wiping down tables that he'd already wiped twice. He worked in a pattern that brought him closer and closer to me. I felt like a fucking spider waiting on his web to pounce on an insect that flew too close. I knew it was only a matter of time before I ensnared Milo, so I would be patient.

"Are you finished with your tea?" Milo asked haughtily.

"Um, yeah. It's empty," I replied calmly without looking up from my paper. I'd stared at the same fucking headline for the past ten minutes and still didn't know what it said. "I can throw it out when I'm ready to leave though."

"When might that be?" Milo asked snidely.

I looked up from the paper then and met his cobalt eyes. They sparkled with a combination of curiosity, jealousy, and anger that made me want to pump my fist in victory. I looked around the café and saw that very few people were milling around, so I wasn't hogging up a table that someone wanted.

"Eager for me to leave? I really don't have any place that I need to be until later this afternoon. I was thinking about getting another cup of tea and one of those banana nut muffins."

"So long as you're paying this time," Milo snarled. "Don't think I'm giving up my muffins every time you decide that you want them."

God, he was so damn cute when he was in a snit. His flushed cheeks, pouty lips, and vibrant eyes reminded me of his post-orgasm afterglow. I didn't really get a chance to see it in the alley before he took off like a bat out of hell, but I recalled it from years ago.

"Do you have some type of customer reward card?" I asked. "Buy so many muffins and you get one for free?"

"No, but that's a damn good idea, Andy," Maegan said from behind the counter. When Milo turned to glare at her, she wiggled her fingers in a wave, completely unashamed that she'd been listening in on our conversation. "We can have cards printed up easily enough. We can mark an X in each box or even punch a hole through it."

"Yeah, Milo. I want you to punch my hole," I whispered to him.

Milo nearly choked on his own tongue before he walked away. The Milo I knew from our youth would've stomped, but the grown man moved gracefully and proud. Everything about him drove me wild, especially his determination that we wouldn't repeat what happened the previous night behind the café.

After waiting a reasonable amount of time to ensure that Milo knew he didn't run me off, I left The Brew instead of ordering more tea. I didn't own a lot of stuff, so there wasn't much I needed to unpack. The movers had delivered my furniture a few days before I arrived, but I needed to sort through the boxes I'd brought with me. Once that was done, I headed to Target for some household essentials and food items. I ended up buying a bunch of crap I didn't really need but had to have anyway. After that, it was time to head over to Curl Up and Dye.

I'd never stepped inside a salon before and expected to feel out of place, but that wasn't the case. It didn't hurt that the receptionist, Chaz, was so friendly and cute. Instead of leading me to his salon chair to cut my hair, Josh took me to a door off the sitting room.

"*Squawk!* Bend me over and spank my ass!" I whipped my head around and saw a vibrantly blue macaw sizing me up. "Hiya, honey."

"Ignore him," Josh said. "He flirts with everyone. What I want to show you is up in my private residence."

"Um," I said uncertainly as I followed him up the steps.

Josh held up his hand to show off a shiny ring. "I'm engaged, Andy. I want your carpentry skills, not your body."

I chuckled.

16

"Gabe and I are getting married this fall, and we're in the process of buying a new home. This space worked great when it was just me, but we need something that is for *us*. My proposal is twofold: I want you to do some updating to the house we're buying, and I'd like to turn this space," he circled in the middle of the living room with his arms out, "into a luxury spa and massage area."

"Sure," I told him. "I just need you to tell me what you want done, any kind of budget restrictions you have, and the timeline. Same goes for the house you're buying."

"Great! Let me talk to Gabe tonight during our final walkthrough of the house, and I'll get back to you with a solid plan." He looked at my hair again and said, "Let's get to work, shall we?"

I had to admit that I felt better when I left the salon with a more modern cut and a follow-up appointment for the next month. I wondered what Milo would think of my haircut, but I didn't dwell on it too much because I was due for dinner at my sister's house. She insisted on having a welcome-back dinner, even though it was a Tuesday night. I'd deliberately timed my return for a weekday to avoid anyone going to any trouble.

I didn't realize how much I missed my family until I walked into Faith's house. Sure, I'd seen them for holidays and special occasions over the past twelve years, but I had slinked in and out of town with as little fuss as possible. I was home to stay, and the relief and excitement they felt was palpable. It was just too bad that *all* the Blissville residents weren't as happy to see me, but I had a plan to change his mind.

I shoved thoughts of Milo aside and enjoyed time with my parents and sister, even though there were a lot of hints that Faith and I needed to start providing grandkids.

"Mom," Faith said in a warning tone. "Is this going to kick off another round of matchmaking?"

"You get a break now that your brother has returned home," my mom said then winked at me. "Milo is still single, Andy."

17

I'd guessed as much when he jumped me in the alleyway, but I didn't share that with my family. "Mom, please don't get your hopes up," I told her, recalling that Milo had basically walked away while my dick was still hanging out of my pants. "Twelve years is a long time for us to be apart."

"I believe in you, Andy," she said sweetly.

"How do you even know that I want Milo?" I asked. Everyone around the table started laughing.

"If you wanted us to believe that then you should've at least stopped by our house and said hello before you went to see Milo. You made your intentions pretty clear," Dad said. "How was your reunion?"

"It didn't go as I had envisioned it," I replied honestly. I didn't expect Milo's hostility that morning when I showed up at the café, nor did I expect him to launch himself in my arms later that night. Milo had always been a walking contradiction, but years ago, I had learned how to decode his actions and understand him. It looked like I would need to refine my Milo-detection skills. "We'll see what the future holds."

"Speaking of future," Dad said, "have you decided if you're going into business for yourself? I think there would be plenty of work to keep you busy around here."

"Actually, a fantastic opportunity came my way." I told them about my conversation with Josh.

"That's what's different about you," Mom said. "I like your new hairstyle."

"I told Josh that I didn't want to mess with gel or mousse or whatever every day, but it does look better."

I was ready to get the conversation away from me and Milo, so I did the only thing I could think to do. I threw Faith under the bus. "So, Faith, how was your date on Saturday night?"

"Date?" Mom and Dad said at the same time.

Faith narrowed her eyes at me, promising retribution. "It was just a work thing," she said nonchalantly.

"On a Saturday night?" Mom asked.

"And who was this 'work thing' with?" Dad wanted to know.

"Just a guy from work," Faith replied. "It wasn't a date. We just met to go over the projected quarterly earnings over burgers and fries." I could tell by the soft blush on her cheeks that it was more than that, but we didn't push her.

"Andy, have you found an NA sponsor and meeting location?" Mom asked. There was no censure or disappointment in her eyes, only a desire to see me stay happy, healthy, and clean.

"I have," I answered her. "My sponsor's name is Oliver and we're meeting for dinner tomorrow night in Cincinnati. I've only chatted with him online and over the phone so far. He seems cool, and he's been clean for fifteen years. Meetings are held at a church north of Cincinnati. I'm not crazy about the drive time or the location, but it's the closest chapter I could find.

"I'm proud of you, Andy," Dad said warmly. "I imagine the struggle to stay clean is especially hard when your order and balance is upset, but we believe in you."

"We do," Mom said, nodding.

Faith reached over and squeezed my hand affectionately, which was more than I deserved after throwing her under the bus like I did.

"Thank you," I said to all of them. "Your support means so much to me. I'm really a lucky man."

It was true. I'd put myself and my family through hell after I left for college. Many families would have turned their backs on someone who embarrassed them as badly as I had, but not mine.

After dinner, I ended up driving by The Brew just for the hell of it. Was Milo working late for a second day in a row? I turned the corner at the end of the block and drove slowly so I could see if his car was parked in the alley. Sure enough, Milo's car was in the same place.

Like the previous night, I parked my truck and waited outside for him to appear. This time, I leaned against his car so he would see me right away. There were many things I wanted to do to Milo, but scaring him wasn't one of them.

"We're not doing this again," Milo said firmly when he locked eyes on me. "When did you start slinking through dark alleys looking to pick up action, anyway?"

"Since last night."

Milo's words said one thing, but his glittering eyes said something entirely different as he stared up at me. I watched him for a few heartbeats then took a risk and reached for him. Milo met me halfway, crashing his mouth against mine just like he had the previous night. My body went up in flames, singeing my common sense and self-preservation.

I didn't want a quick fumble in the dark that would end with Milo walking away from me angrily; I wanted long nights with endless kisses. I would settle for what he gave me while I worked to achieve the ultimate goal. My options were to fuck him on top of his car, up against the brick wall again, or carry him to my truck where I could at least lay him down on the back seat. It was an easy decision to make.

I hoisted Milo up, and he wrapped his legs around my waist. I carried him to my truck while he erotically tongue-fucked my mouth. Milo seemed alarmed when I opened the rear door of my extended cab truck.

"I thought we could use a bit more privacy," I said when I set him on the seat.

I saw the hesitation in his eyes. Was he going to call a halt to this or scoot over and make room for me? "This changes nothing," Milo growled while whipping his shirt over his head. It changed everything, and we both knew it.

Instead of arguing, I said, "Okay, Milo," as I climbed into the truck and closed the door.

I wanted to strip him bare and fuck him while looking in his eyes, but Milo apparently wasn't ready for that intimacy. He quickly pushed his pants and underwear down then got on his hands and knees on the bench seat. Milo looked over his shoulder when I didn't move.

"Second thoughts?" he asked, wiggling his delicious ass.

"Not at all," I replied, reaching into my back pocket. I pulled out the supplies I needed and tossed the wallet to the floor before I shoved my pants down to my thighs.

"You sure are well-prepared for these clandestine fucks," Milo said accusingly. "How handy."

"That's me, Handy Andy."

Milo snorted until I slid a slicked finger inside his pucker. "God, yes. More." So much for his indifference.

I didn't stop to gloat. I kept playing with his ass to get him ready while biting one plump ass cheek then the other. "You still have the sexiest peach I've ever seen."

"Then slick your dick and fuck me before I change my mind," Milo panted, pushing against my penetrating fingers.

He didn't have to tell me twice. Milo wanted it as fast and hard as the previous night, but I showed more restraint. I was rewarded with needy moans and mewling whimpers for more. Milo had resisted my attempt to kiss him once I was fully buried in his ass. Maybe he thought kissing would make our fucking too…intimate. Milo wanted to come, and I wanted a kiss. I kept him on edge until he gave me what I wanted.

"Fine, Andy. Kiss me, damn it."

I placed my hand firmly on his jaw to turn his face and kissed him with everything I had. Milo came apart in my arms the second our tongues met, and I didn't stop until I was filling the condom a few strokes later.

"Same time tomorrow night?" I teasingly asked when he wrestled his clothes back on. "Or do you want to punch my hole next time?"

His eyes widened like he wasn't sure if I was being serious. "Shut up," Milo said, sliding out the other side of the truck. He was back to the distant guy he was that morning. I should've been pissed that he was willing to use my cock to get off, but I was enjoying myself too.

"Hey," I yelled when I stepped out of the truck. "Best way to shut me up is to stick a cock in my mouth. Any takers?"

Milo's steps faltered, but he didn't turn around and flip me off. I took that as progress. I smiled like an idiot all the way home, confident that I'd win him over before too much longer.

four

Milo

"HOW DO I LOOK? EVERYTHING TUCKED IN TIGHT?" I ASKED, popping out my hip and striking a pose for Faith.

"I can't speak to how well you've tucked your balls up inside your body, but from here it looks great." Faith circled her finger in the air indicating that she wanted a three-sixty view. She whistled as I sassily twirled for her. "Can't tell that your cock is taped down so that it kisses your asshole. Wait. It's not tucked inside there is it?"

"Oh, Faith," I said, laughing happily for the first time in weeks. "You're my favorite Drag Hag." Funny how one Mason sibling makes me want to howl at the moon in frustration while the other kept me sane. I slid on a peachy silk robe with my drag name embroidered on the back of it along with juicy-looking peaches that looked very similar to my perky ass.

"I can't believe how much I've missed your shows," Faith admitted. "I love watching you become Madame O-Feel-Ya Peach right before my eyes. It's pure magic!"

"I love you so much, Faith." I pulled her into a hug. "I hate that you're going to miss the show tonight," I told her. "Especially for a work thing on a Saturday night." Her blush made me smile. "When are you going to admit that your 'work thing' with Nathan really isn't work and the only stats you're checking are how many times he makes you come."

Unfortunately for Faith, she'd just taken a drink of Coke. Her cheeks puffed out when she couldn't decide whether to spit her drink and laugh or attempt to swallow it and try not to choke on it.

"Spitters are quitters, Faith," I said, using my Peach voice. "Just relax your throat and let it happen, honey."

Her blue eyes widened in alarm, and I knew I was seconds away from getting doused with soda. The only Mason twin I wanted hosing me down with a sticky substance was her idiot brother. I stepped aside to avoid pending disaster, but Faith turned in the opposite direction. I saw her shoulders shake as she attempted to get her giggling under control. She stilled then swallowed her drink before facing me again.

"Milo," Faith gasped, looking around like a room full of drag queens in various stages of dress, or undress, would judge her. Then her eyes homed in on me and a smug smile slowly spread across her lovely face. "And who are you to lecture me? Are you going to pretend you're not bumping uglies with my brother?"

"I'm not bumping uglies with your brother." *Not right now, anyway.* Whatever madness caused my momentary lapse in judgment had passed. I was on equal footing and no longer tempted to ride Andy's dick. Okay, that was an outrageous lie. The truth was the opportunity stopped presenting itself, or rather, Andy stopped accosting me in the dark alleyway after I finished closing the café.

At first, I thought he'd had his fill of me, but then I found out he was busy remodeling Josh and Gabe's newly purchased home. They were eager to get in before the wedding, so Andy was working long hours. I still saw him every single morning I worked when he

24

stopped in for tea and a muffin. He continued to give me that flirty smile but stopped trying to make small talk after I shut him down for a week. Was he waiting for me to make the next move or was he just tired of my rejection? Even I realized it was shitty behavior on my part to accept the glorious orgasms he'd given me without so much as a thank you. Maybe he'd just had enough. If that was the case, what was I prepared to do about it?

A month or so after he returned home, I realized that there was more going on in Andy's life than just work. I overheard his busy-body neighbor tell her gossip-mongering friend that Andy left every Wednesday night around six o'clock and didn't return until eleven. I wanted to ask how she stayed up so far past her bedtime, but I didn't comment. I was too crushed, even though I should've been happy. Andy had moved on, and I should do the same thing.

Then why was it that Andy still looked hungry and horny when he looked at me? Was his Wednesday-night fuck buddy not getting the job done? Did he leave Andy hungry for more? Was one guy not enough for Randy Andy these days? He was the trifecta of trouble; he made my mind spin, my heart yearn, and my dick hard. Andy was no good for me, and the sooner I accepted it, the better off I'd be.

"Sweetie, I'm not the one putting the extra pep in his step these days. That would be Mr. Wednesday Night giving him a boost with an extra dose of protein."

Faith cringed, and I realized that was probably taking things a tad too far. Then I realized her discomfort had nothing to do with me implying her brother was a cum slut. She looked like she wanted to tell me something about Andy's activities, but I knew she wouldn't. One, she deemed herself neutral, and second, she'd never betray Andy's trust—or mine for that matter. So, even though I wanted her to tell me I was wrong, I knew she wouldn't. She was in a tough spot, and I wouldn't do or say anything that would cost me her friendship. It was time to change the subject.

I clapped my hands excitedly, startling both us and half the queens around me. "Okay, help me pick out the perfect dress for tonight. I haven't performed in more than a year, so I need my return to be flawless."

"What are you performing tonight?"

"There will be two large groups in attendance that have requested performances to entertain the guest, or guests, of honor. One is a birthday party and the other is a bachelor party for two grooms. I'm thinking Marilyn would be perfect for both. I'll sing 'Happy Birthday' to one and 'My Heart Belongs to Daddy' to the other. Of course, I'm going to have a little fun with the lyrics for Daddy."

"I love when you do Marilyn," Faith sighed. "Is someone recording it?"

"Absolutely. I'll make sure you get a copy. So, obviously, I must wear the iconic white halter-top dress for one of the performances. Which one?"

"Definitely the birthday boy," Faith said then began looking through the glitzy dresses hanging on my rack. "Oh, this is stunning and would look amazing with your complexion and beautiful blue eyes."

Faith held up a floor-length, sequined gown that was slit up to the hip and had a plunging bodice that presented an extra challenge for people who didn't have real cleavage. I would take that challenge and master it. The sequins on the dress were various shades of blues, turquoise, and teal, giving it almost a peacock feel. I often preened like a male peacock completely obsessed with its feathers, so it seemed appropriate to me.

"Don't forget the fake diamonds," Faith said. She glanced at her watch and frowned with genuine remorse. "I better go, or I'll be late meeting Nathan for that *work* thing." She hugged me quick and kissed my cheek. "I love you, Peach."

"I love you too, Faith." I waited until she was almost to the door before I yelled, "Work it, girl." Yeah, I knew what she was really working.

Faith turned around and smiled. "Own it," she repeated back to me. *Pretty Woman* was one of our favorite movies, and we tried to fit the lines into our conversations whenever we could.

Once she left, I began putting my makeup on. I started by gluing my eyebrows down, and while that dried, I started dabbing on a thick foundation around my lips, chin, and jawline to cover up any chin hairs I missed with the razor. I'd already shaved once that day, but my whiskers grew back fast. I wanted flawless, ivory skin for my performance. After I was satisfied with the foundation, I started in on my contour and highlighting. It took me longer than normal since I was out of practice, but it was like riding a bike. I was pleased when I started blending all the various shades on my face to form a flawless complexion. My cheekbones looked high and cut, and my nose, forehead, and even the little dip above my lip were highlighted to perfection. I wasn't finished with my transformation though.

I spent another twenty minutes on my cheeks and eyes before I busted out the shimmery powder to accentuate the look I had created with the cream highlighting stick. I turned my head to the left and right, admiring my handiwork in the mirror.

Saving my two nemeses—eyebrows and false lashes—for last, I looked in the mirror to give myself a pep talk. "They just need to be sisters, Milo. They don't have to be twin sisters." I blew out a breath and started in on the left eyebrow. I drew it to perfection, and I danced happily in front of the mirror. I got off to a rocky start with the right eyebrow but pulled it out in the end. After that, it was child's play. Once I had my eyelashes looking amazing, I painted my lips in a daring red color that my drag mother called cock-sucking red. I imagined quite a few guys would imagine my lips wrapped around their cocks by the time I was through performing. The final step was to paint a mole to mimic Marilyn's on my face.

"Almost showtime, Peach," the stage manager, Tony Sopranski, said. "Fifteen minutes."

That sounded like a lot of time, but I needed to manufacture cleavage, put on my wig, and shimmy into my first dress. "Which is first, Tony? Birthday boy or the wedding party?"

"Wedding party."

Double damn because I had to add all the costume jewelry. I released a nervous breath and got my shit together so I could give the future grooms a night to remember. I stood before the full-length mirror with only a few minutes to go. "Fuck, I look…"

"Fuckable," Tony said from behind me. "You'll have them eating out of your palms tonight, Peach. Ready?"

"As I'll ever be," I told Tony as I followed him down the steps and took my position next to the curtain, waiting for my turn to take the stage.

Mistress Dazzle D came off the stage fanning her face and smiling from ear to ear. "Amazing crowd tonight, Peach," she told me. "Knock 'em dead."

I had walked across this stage, and many others just like it, more times than I could count. I could perform these songs in my sleep, but I couldn't deny that I was overcome by nerves as I waited for my introduction.

"We have a very special treat for you tonight," the announcer, Jim, said from his booth high above the action. "Back by popular demand, our very own Madame O-Feel-Ya Peach has returned to the stage at Queen City Divas. Hold onto your hearts and your cocks, and please note that management is not responsible if you jizz your pants." I snickered at that part. "Let's give our Peach a warm welcome."

I waited a few heartbeats as adrenaline raced through my body from the crowd's enthusiastic reaction. Instead of parting the curtains and walking onto the stage, I stuck my long, perfectly toned leg out, knowing that the spotlight was on it. I heard the catcalls when I ran my hand over my stockings and teased the lacy edges of the band around the thigh.

"Peach! Peach! Peach!" the crowd chanted.

I held my microphone up to my smiling lips and winked playfully at Tony. "Who, me?" I asked the crowd in a whispery baby-soft voice, lifting my leg higher against the velvet curtain.

"Peach! Peach! Peach!"

"Quit teasing and give them what they want," Tony told me.

I blew Tony one last kiss and stepped onto the stage. The regulars went wild, and the newcomers seemed to be wowed too. "Hello, my darlings," I said, sauntering to the middle of the stage to take my place. "Have you missed me, lovers?" I turned to the side and ran my hand over the curve of my ass. "Or did you miss my perfect peach?"

"Yes!" they roared.

"I missed you too, lovers," I told the crowd. My nervousness was replaced by excitement and something else, an awareness that I only got when a certain someone was near. *Andy.* With the way the lights hit the stage, it was impossible for me to see into the crowd. I only saw dark silhouettes. I had every intention of going down and working the audience when I came out from behind the curtain, but I was having second thoughts.

I shook it off because it was highly unlikely that Andy Mason was sitting amongst my admirers. Of course, I didn't know jack shit about Andy, other than how good his dick still made me feel. I had no clue what he was into after so many years apart. These fellas wanted to celebrate their big event with a dedicated performance from a queen, so I'd give them a night to remember.

The big band, jazzy music began to play, and I forgot to even think about Andy. I sashayed off the stage singing my revised version of the song, playing to my audience. I stopped at the table for the bachelor party and waved coyly to the grooms.

"Hellooooo, Daddy," I said after the first verse, running my gloved fingers under his chin. I looked to the much younger groom sitting beside him. "You're such a lucky boy."

"That I am, Madame Peach."

I went on to the second verse singing my heart out, making the lyrics as tawdry and dirty as I could. I knew I did well when the audience was laughing and cheering me on. One particular groomsman looked like he wanted to get to know me really well. He brazenly put his hand against my calf and ran his hand up to just above the back of my knee. It had been a month since I'd last had someone else's hands on my body, and I couldn't help getting a little excited. The man was gorgeous and big, just how I liked them. His warm brown eyes promised me a night I'd never forget, but regrettably, I had to keep it moving.

"Unless you're going to stuff a ten spot in my stocking, you might want to remove your hand, darling," I purred.

The hot guy licked his lips playfully and held up a ten-dollar bill. Some men couldn't get past the feminine clothing and were uncomfortable while others easily dismissed the clothing in favor of the fine legs and tight ass beneath it. My brown-eyed admirer had no problem looking beyond the sequined gown. I knew what he was thinking when his eyes drifted down and lingered on my ass.

"Well, okay then," I said sassily, straddling his thigh so he could have access to the lacy, band of my stocking. As I sang the chorus, he boldly traced the smooth skin of my inner thigh, and I allowed the insanity for a few seconds. Loyalty to Andy wasn't on my mind right then but getting an erection when my dick was taped against my taint and ass crack would be painful. I playfully slapped his hand and sauntered away to spend time with the rest of the party.

When I rounded the grooms' table a second time, I glanced over at the group next to them and locked gazes with familiar light-blue eyes. My heart stuttered for a second as Andy checked me out from my stilettos to my blonde wig. Did he recognize me in drag? I was sure no one had told him about this part of my life. I recognized the heat lighting his eyes from within. Andy might not have recognized me, but his body sure as hell did.

I forced my attention away from him and back to the happy couple who grinned and ate up the attention that I and their friends showered upon them. It was obvious to see how much they loved one another when they stared into each other's eyes. It was hard not to get jealous that they'd found their other half while I would most likely become an old, loveless queen.

When the song ended, I kissed both grooms on their cheeks and said breathily, "I wish you many, many years of happiness, gentlemen. May you cling to one another during *hard* times and may all your *ups and downs* be in the bedroom, bathroom, living room, or wherever your hearts desire. Best of luck!" I blew them air kisses then moved to stand beside their table, careful not to look in Andy's direction. I usually liked to flirt with as many guys as possible to maximize my tips, but I wanted to avoid his small gathering as best I could.

"I'll be back a little later for another special performance, lovers," I said to the crowd. "Be sure to stick around."

I sauntered my ass back up the steps with the spotlight following my every move. "Peach! Peach! Peach!" the audience chanted as I made my way to the red velvet curtain.

I felt the intensity of Andy's gaze on me too. Did he know it was me? Was our brief glance long enough for him to recognize my eyes? He wouldn't show up at Queen City Divas expecting to see me, so it wasn't likely. I was nervous as fuck while waiting for my next performance. Maybe he'd be gone. Maybe he'd jump out of his seat and confront me. Maybe he'd bend me over his table and… Nope! Andy Mason wasn't the guy for me.

And what about the guys he was with? I didn't recognize any of them, so how did he meet them? Which one of them did he bury his dick inside every Wednesday? It was the last thought that sent me running for the toilet. I hadn't eaten much, but whatever I had consumed was rejected when I thought about Andy with someone else. I knew that neither of us were abstinent during our twelve years of separation, but I wasn't prepared to come face-to-face with his lover yet.

I brushed my teeth, reapplied my lipstick, and put on my second

Marilyn dress of the night. My pulse hammered in my throat while I stood beside Tony, once more waiting for my name to be announced. The second time around, the crowd was even more eager for me. When I walked out from behind the curtain, a guy was sitting in a chair at center stage. I figured he must be the birthday boy.

"Well, well, well," I said, sauntering up behind him. "What do we have here? A delectable treat for Peach?" I rounded the chair and looked into the eyes of the man who'd sat so close to Andy. Was this him? Wednesday Fuck Guy? Was he the one Andy turned to now? Yeah, I was insanely jealous, and I vowed not to be the only one. He was a sexy guy for sure, and it wouldn't be a hardship to grind up against him for the length of a song. "Are you ready for your one-of-a-kind birthday song, sexy?"

The man squirmed a little in his chair, but he smiled and nodded his head. I stood in front of him blocking his view of the crowd, which might've seemed odd until the small fan hidden in the stage floor blew my skirt up. I struck the iconic Marilyn pose, hiding my crotch from the audience while the birthday boy got an eyeful of my tight ass in silky, white panties. He must've liked what he saw because he literally howled his approval to the delight of the audience. Jim had changed up the stage lighting, which made it possible for me to see the faces in the crowd. I only allowed myself a brief look into Andy's eyes. He wore a crooked grin on his face but didn't look jealous. *Yet.*

I rocked my hips from side to side, allowing the birthday boy to see the play of muscle in my ass and legs. That's right, get your eyeful. I looked over my shoulder at him and bit my lower lip seductively. "Ready, big boy?"

Like the first song, I modified the words because I obviously wasn't singing to the president. I sang it as breathily as I could while straddling his parted thighs. Toward the end, I spun around and pressed my ass to his crotch, grinning when I felt his arousal. Yeah, the birthday boy wanted to split my peach all right, but I was a lady.

When I finished, he looked dazed and a little confused about where he was or even the current year. I kissed his cheek and whispered happy birthday in his ear before I strutted my stuff off the stage. I hung around backstage until the rest of the show was over. We all went out for a bite to eat while reliving some of our fondest performances for the newest queens.

It was well past two in the morning when I stopped for gas as soon as I pulled off the interstate. I was too pissed at myself for not thinking to get gas earlier to notice the truck that pulled in behind me. A flamboyantly gay man couldn't afford to get lost in his thoughts when he was all alone at a truck stop in the middle of nowhere.

"What are you doing out so late?" asked a familiar voice.

I stiffened in shock before I whipped my head around to look at Andy, who leaned against the side of his truck. "Probably the same thing you're doing," I said suggestively. Andy scowled as he thought it over. Score one for the home team. I was so happy when the gas pump clicked off. I replaced the nozzle and took my receipt. "See you around, Andy." I didn't wait for him to respond. I got in my car and drove off.

That night, I dreamed that Andy was the one sitting in the chair getting a special song and dance from me. He wanted to ravish me on the stage in front of everyone, but I led him to the dressing room that was miraculously empty. Instead of rough and physical, Andy loved me slow and tender. Whispering words of love. Unfortunately, it wasn't my name he called out when he spilled inside me.

When I woke up, I was crushed. I couldn't remember the name of the guy Andy called out in my dream, but I knew it wasn't mine. It was then that I became truly convinced that Andy and I were through. I was determined to put our past behind us and move on without him, no matter what it took.

five

Andy

OW MUCH LONGER DOES MILO PLAN TO PUNISH ME? *THWACK thwack thwack.* I knew he'd be a tough nut to crack, but seriously? *Bam.* Two-fucking-years? *Thwack thwack thwack. Bam!* Why couldn't I just give up and find someone new? He wasn't the only single guy around. *Thwack thwack thwack.* Why did just the thought of fucking someone else make me feel guilty? Hadn't Milo proven he didn't want me? *Thwack thwack thwack.* Not even my hammer pounding against lumber drowned out the wild beating of my heart in my ears.

Milo. I needed to do something about, with, or to him so we could get past this stalemate we found ourselves in since I returned home. Two. *Thwack.* Fucking. *Thwack.* Years. *Bam!* I drove the last nail into the stud and dropped the hammer through the loop of my toolbelt.

After our angry, alley sex, I tried showing him that I wanted the opportunity to get to know him all over again, but he continued to shun my every attempt.

Luckily for me, I had a skillset that he and Maegan needed when they bought the rest of the building they had leased for a few years. They wanted to knock down a wall and expand their space to include a bookstore. Maegan also wanted to add a door between the coffee shop and the space on the opposite side so she could open an antique store. There was a fourth space that they wanted to renovate and rent to their cute friend Memphis. I could tell I was the last person Milo wanted to work with, but he sucked it up. After several months of hard work, The Brew became Books and Brew, Curious Things was launched, and Memphis had the perfect setup for Vinyl and Villains, his record and comic book store.

Milo and I had remained civil, but never warmed up beyond the initial coolness of his greeting the first time he laid eyes on me. That is until he thought I might be interested in someone else. I would feel the heat of his gaze on me from across the room but could never catch him in the act when I turned my head in his direction. He wanted me just as much as I wanted him. What the fuck was I going to do about it? Milo clearly had no intention of even meeting me halfway. Did I give up too easily? Two years of craving him and wanting to feel his soft lips against mine. Twenty-four months of not hearing his greedy whimpers telling me he wanted me to fuck him harder. He drove me stark raving mad!

I thought I lost my chance to make inroads with Milo when the renovation projects ended, but Maegan and Milo surprised me with a new project proposal. They wanted to restore the second story above the shops to the apartments they used to be decades ago. Lucky for them, the space was still walled off into four decently-sized apartments, and they were still in reasonably good shape. There were no signs of water damage or anything that could negatively impact the integrity of the apartments or their wallets. It was more labor intensive than anything else, but I had the time and the will to pull it off.

Maegan, unlike Faith, seemed eager to throw her brother in my direction as often as she could. "Milo can pick the flooring," she had said. "He's better at that stuff than I am. I tend to design a space for me where he'll keep things neutral."

Milo was supposed to come up and pick a stain from the samples I brought. We discovered magnificent hardwood floors beneath the ratty, outdated carpet. Maegan and Milo saved a lot of money when I discovered that all the floors needed was a good sanding and fresh stain. Typical of Milo, he seemed to like dragging his feet to make me wait, but I had plenty of other things to do in the other three apartments that weren't as far along as the first one. Still, I ran my hands through my damp hair in annoyance. *Damn Milo!* Why couldn't I just move on from him? Why the fuck did I have to care if he wanted me or not? There were some hot, eligible bachelors in Blissville and the surrounding area, so why did I keep holding out hope? That realtor was sexy as fuck, and that new doctor looked extra bendy. Why couldn't I obsess over someone I stood a chance of having?

"I see you're still listening to the same crappy music," Milo said loud enough for me to hear over the radio. The screaming guitars hadn't drowned out my racing pulse either.

I jerked in surprise then crossed to the radio. Silence washed over the room when I shut it off. Could Milo hear my heart hammering in my chest from across the room? "What's wrong with Guns N' Roses?" I asked him.

Milo rolled his eyes for an answer. It was another reason I shouldn't give a damn about what he thought. Anyone with as poor taste in music as him shouldn't keep me up at night. I will never know what possessed me to do it, but I struck a Britney pose and started singing "Oops, I Did It Again" in a voice I thought sounded pouty and baby soft.

This time, Milo's eyes widened, and his mouth fell open in shock. That lasted for all of two seconds before he doubled over laughing at me. Even more shocking than me busting out my Britney moves and singing was me crossing the room and kissing the smile off Milo's lips when he stopped laughing.

Milo's mouth was stiff against mine, and his body unyielding at first. Then he let out a long sigh, parted his lips, and melted against me. The kiss we shared wasn't soft and sweet, it was long, hard, and angry. Our tongues met and dueled for dominance, my hands gripped his hair tight so that he couldn't get away, and his fingers dug into the muscles of my lower back. Blood rushed to my dick, and I felt the answering need in him. Milo's cock wasn't the only thing that suddenly stiffened against me though.

He broke our kiss and took two big steps away from me. Milo covered his mouth in shock, blinking rapidly.

I took a step toward him. "Milo, I—" I stopped talking when Milo took another step back.

Then he lowered his hand and stared at me in disbelief. "Why'd you do that?" he asked accusingly.

"I don't know."

"What do you mean you don't know? You just walk across the room and kiss someone without knowing why? Is this a regular occurrence with you?"

"It was a kiss, Milo."

"It felt like more than a kiss, Andy. If we were... If you and I were..." He just shook his head, unable to put his thoughts into words.

"If we were dating? If you and I were a couple?" I suggested.

Milo shook his head, but what else could he possibly have said there? "I don't know what I was about to say, but I know what I want to say now. Andy, our ship has sailed. We had our chance when we were younger, and it didn't work out. I see no reason—"

"Bullshit," I snapped out angrily. "Your eyes and body are telling me something completely different."

"I think I heard a serial rapist use that line last night on the ID channel," Milo shot back.

I jerked like he slapped me. *Serial rapist?* That's where I ranked with him. Milo's blue eyes widened from shock and regret over his word choices, but it was too late. The damage was already done. "Don't worry, Milo. It won't happen again."

"Good."

"Great. You want to pick out the stain for the hardwood floors or not?"

"I think I'll leave it up to you," Milo answered softly. "You've made great decisions up to this point."

"Oh, I can think of a recent one I'd really like to take back right about now."

Milo casted his eyes to the floor and swallowed hard. I should've felt guilty, but...*serial rapist.*

"Is that all? I need to get home and cleaned up," I said casually, but watched him closely for his reaction. It was so subtle that I almost missed the way his body tightened like he was bracing himself for a blow. "Night out with the boys." I hoped he didn't ask which boys, because I was totally lying.

Milo met my gaze once more and narrowed his eyes. "What boys?"

In for a penny, in for a pound. I aimed my best, brief-dropping smile at him. "Righty and Lefty, of course."

"You definitely need to go home and shower then," Milo said, crinkling his nose. "You're a little smelly and a whole lot sweaty."

"Can't have sweaty, smelly boys when I hit the club," I agreed.

"Mmmhmm," Milo agreed. "You do know the owner of Vibe lives in Blissville with Memphis's cousin, Emory."

"Yep."

"Well, you and *the boys* have a good night," Milo told me. "I have *big* plans of my own. *Very big* plans."

I watched him leave through narrowed eyes. If he wanted to make me jealous it worked. I had seen him flirting with the silver fox superintendent every morning when he came in for coffee. Romeo. *Snort.* What the fuck kind of name was that? I bet it got the man laid more times than I could imagine.

I should've gone straight home, showered, and drove to Vibe. Finding a willing man to fuck there wouldn't be hard. I didn't need to waste my time on a man who clearly didn't want me, or at least pretended not to want me. Then I worried that Milo might've told me the truth. Did his plans include Vibe too? There was no fucking way I could handle watching him on the dance floor with some douchebag running his hands over his lean body.

I sniffed my pits to see if I really stunk and was happy to find out that Milo was lying about that at least. I headed to Emma and Edson's diner to drown my sorrow in a thick slab of meatloaf, mashed potatoes and gravy, and green beans. If I still had room, I'd eat a piece of peanut butter pie. Better yet, I could take it home and eat it later after I jerked off. Thwacking away my frustration wasn't working, so maybe I needed to do a little more whacking.

I waved and said hello to the people who greeted me and took a seat at one of the empty bar stools at the L-shaped counter in the middle of the restaurant. Why take a table or a booth when it was just me? I sat there minding my own business when suddenly a dark shadow loomed over me. I looked up to see Kyle Vaughn, the town vet, standing beside me. Kyle wore a constant scowl in my presence even though my crime was committed more than a year earlier. I had asked Chaz out on a date, not knowing that the two guys had feelings for one another. Chaz shot me down, and the good doctor never forgave me for asking an unattached man out on a date.

"Hello, Doc." At least I refrained from repeating a cartoon bunny's famous phrase.

"Andy," he said dryly.

"I'm just Andy now, huh? No more Beefcake Andy?" I smiled at his discomfort. At least he had the good grace to cringe. There were much worse nicknames he could've given me though.

"You know about that, huh?"

"Small town."

I'd overheard Milo refer to me as Beefcake Andy when he was talking to his mom and sister. He was waving his hand dramatically in front of his face like he was fanning himself and using a falsetto voice that indicated he was mocking his mother or sister who knew damned well I stood behind him. "I do declare, Milo. I wish you could find yourself a strapping stud for a carpenter. Oh, I know! Beefcake Andy!" he had exclaimed excitedly.

"Strapping stud, huh? It's nice to know that you still notice, Milo," I had teased. "Beefcake Andy is a new one though. It's kinda catchy. I was trying to come up with a slogan the other day. The best I could come up with was Handy Andy, but I like yours much better. Perhaps I should change the name of my business and slap that on my T-shirt."

I blew it off like it was no big deal, but I couldn't help but like the name he'd given me. Later, I learned it was Kyle who dubbed me Beefcake Andy, and the nickname lost its appeal.

"What can I do for you?" I asked Kyle.

"I really appreciate the way you stuck up for Mark and Daniel last week. They told me that you stepped in when some high school boys started bullying them. Mark will face some tough times ahead, and it's nice to know that people in our community will look out for him when Chaz and I aren't there. I know Chaz called and thanked you already, but I wanted to thank you too." Kyle offered me his first genuine smile and extended his hand.

I shook it. "I'm glad I could help."

The waitress, Daniella, set my dinner in front of me, and Kyle surprised me even more when he slapped me on the back. "I won't keep you from your meal. I'm taking home dinner to Chaz and Mark since it was a long day for everyone. Have a good night."

"You too."

That was a pleasant turn of events, but it wasn't enough to overcome the unsettled feelings I had after my confrontation with Milo. I couldn't understand what it was about my high school boyfriend that snagged my attention and wouldn't let go. I heard someone take the seat next to me just as I forked my first bite of meatloaf into my mouth. The hair stood up all over my body, and I knew who it was without looking.

"Thought you had big plans?" I asked.

"I was about to ask you the same thing," Milo said, sounding miserable.

My heart sank when I turned my head and saw the expression in his eyes matched his somber tone. "I lied." I leaned closer and lowered my voice. "I still have plans with Righty and Lefty, but it will just be the three of us." I straightened back in my chair suddenly. "Sorry, I forgot that I stink."

"You don't stink," Milo confessed. "You smell really fucking amazing and that kiss was…"

"Fierce? Fantastic? There are other things that start with an F that two consenting adults could do together."

"I'm tempted, Andy. I truly am." My heart raced as my mind spun with all the possibilities. "There's something I'd need you to do first."

"Buy more condoms and lube?" I asked hopefully.

Milo shook his head sadly, and said, "I need to know why you stayed away so long."

What he really wanted to know was why I stayed away from *him*. "I was a kid out in the world on his own for the first time, Milo. I lost track of who I was, where I came from, and the people who loved me."

I saw in his eyes that he knew the answer was more complicated than that. I also knew that he was jumping to conclusions—most of them were probably right. I was young, unattached, and horny. What right did he have to look at me so accusingly?

Anger flared inside me, but I remained calm outwardly when I said, "You were the one who broke my heart, Milo." That wasn't entirely true; our history was too complicated to blame our breakup on one event. Besides, if I was honest, I'd acknowledge that my actions pushed him into it.

Milo got to his feet. "I broke both of our hearts, Andy." He looked and sounded disappointed—defeated even. Milo knew that whatever my story was, I wasn't ready to share it with him.

My appetite and anger left me as quickly as Milo did. I had wanted him to meet me halfway, and he tried. I was the one who rejected his attempt, so the only person I had to blame for things going south that night was myself. Daniella boxed my dinner along with a huge piece of pie then offered me a sympathetic smile when she returned my debit card to me. "Andy, things worth having don't come easy. Don't give up."

"Thanks, D." I leaned forward and kissed her cheek.

It was a nice thought, but too much time had passed. What Milo and I had when we were younger was all we were meant to have. It seemed silly to wish for anything else. I just needed to convince my heart.

six

Milo

"YOU JUST HAD TO ASK, DIDN'T YOU, MILO? YOU COULDN'T just leave well enough alone," I added, berating myself the next morning after a night of broken sleep.

Andy's answer led me to believe he had found ways to get over his broken heart, or should I say he found guys to help him get over me? I couldn't be angry, because I *was* the one who broke up with him. Andy wasn't the only one who assuaged his misery by finding someone who could help him forget his pain. Unfortunately, my evil brain chose to show me how Andy spent his years away from Blissville, and it looked like a CockyBoys highlight reel.

But then Andy jerked the zebra-striped rug out from under me with his softly spoken rebuke. *"You were the one who broke my heart, Milo."*

I woke up feeling exhausted, angry, and so turned on I couldn't see straight. Eventually, I became Andy's bed partner in my dreams. I ran my hands all over that gorgeous body, lingering on his broad chest. I mean, I hadn't seen Andy shirtless since he returned home, but I could tell he was bigger and stronger than he was at eighteen years old. I had no trouble imagining just how gorgeous his shoulders, pecs, and biceps looked. I was always drawn to men who were a lot bigger than me. Andy had always made me feel vulnerable and safe at the same time. It was something I hadn't felt since we broke up. Sure, I'd dated big guys during his twelve-year hiatus, but I never found that same emotional connection with anyone else, no matter how hard I tried. And boy, did I try. I could've written the book on fake it 'til you make it. *Well, some things a guy can't fake, but you catch my drift.*

I sure as hell wasn't a saint, so I had no right to be mad at Andy. Logic and sensibility had always fled my brain when it came to him though. *Damn it!* He made me so fucking angry, but that didn't stop me from fantasizing about him while jerking off in the shower. Sure, in my spank bank slideshow I called him an asshole while he rimmed mine. I yanked his hair and rode him like he was a prize bull at the rodeo. I'd never had angry orgasms until Andy returned to Blissville, and now I seemed to be addicted to them. I'd become a damn junky looking for ways to piss him off so I could remember the smoldering look in his eyes later when I was alone.

The powerful climax only made me sleepier, which was why I kept dropping shit and burned my hand on the fucking espresso machine again when I opened Books and Brew the next morning.

"Fuck me!"

"Okay," a deep voice said from behind me. Too bad it didn't belong to the man who starred in my dreams. "You shouldn't leave the rear door unlocked. You never know what kind of riffraff will just waltz on in here."

I turned around and pasted a smile on my face. "Tucker, you know that the health department would frown on the kind of icing you'd have me drizzle over these pastries." I gestured to the tray of Danishes I'd pulled from the oven.

Tucker Garrison was the guy I dated in high school after I broke up with Andy. He was as big as Andy, if not bigger, and a gridiron king instead of the baseball star I couldn't seem to get over. I dated Tucker during the final two years of high school but we went our separate ways after graduation. I cared about him, and we had some great times together, but my feelings for Andy prevented me from giving him a real shot. Unfortunately, that hadn't changed even though I saw in his eyes how much he wished it would.

"Maybe some other time," he teased.

Leading him on wasn't something I wanted to do, so I changed the subject. "What's up, Tuck?"

A slow grin spread across his face as he raked his eyes over my body. I had braced myself to hear "my cock" or something similar, but he didn't go there. "On my way home after a long shift. There was a nasty house fire out on Halverston Road early this morning. Luckily, we were able to get the family and their pets out. Their house and everything they owned is gone though." It was then that I saw the exhaustion in his eyes. "I thought a hot chocolate might just be the thing to help soothe me to sleep since I won't have a warm body to cuddle up next to."

I didn't touch that one either. "I'm sorry you had a rough shift. I'll happily make you a hot chocolate," I said, leaving off the *to go* part. "Would you like a pastry too? I just need to ice them."

"Now, we're talking. I'm starting to perk up now."

"No, no," I said. "Let's not perk anything up. I'm talking about the stuff I make from confectioners sugar."

Tucker snorted. "I know that I don't stand a chance in hell with you. I keep hoping though since *he's* been home for two years now, and I still don't see a ring on your finger." I might not wear a ring on my finger, but Andy still had a tight grip on my heart. Even if Andy had never returned, there was no future for Tuck and me. We had our fun years ago, and I wasn't looking to repeat it. Too bad I couldn't say the same about Andy.

I carefully drizzled the icing over the pastries with real blueberries and a lemon tart filling inside. I boxed two of them for Tucker, but I'd have given him the entire pan if it shut him the hell up. I couldn't go anywhere without someone commenting on or alluding to my non-relationship status with Andy. It only added to my misery. Why, if everyone thought we should be together, couldn't I forgive his absence and move forward, either with or without him.

A deep chuckle rumbled from Tucker's chest after I stayed silent for too long. I wished it sent tingles up my spine like Andy's did, but the only thing I could offer him was friendship.

"I hope the two of you sort your issues out soon so the rest of us can stop holding out hope that a certain coffee shop owner could return their feelings."

"Us?" I asked dryly. He made it sound like he was the president of the Milo Miracle Fan Club. I am pretty fabulous, but I suspected that Tuck was grossly exaggerating my appeal to the residents of Blissville. "Tuck, I wish I could feel differently. I really do."

He crossed the expanse of the room and stood in front of me. "Hey, I didn't mean to upset you. I know you can't help who your heart wants, and I want you to be happy. Even if that's not with me." Tuck placed a big hand gently around my neck and pressed a kiss to my forehead. I closed my eyes to keep from crying. *Fuck! Why couldn't I be in love with this guy?*

"You are one of a kind, Tuck," I said when he stepped back.

"That's what my mama says."

"She's right. Someday, you're going to find a guy who deserves all the amazing things you have to offer him." I handed him the box of pastries then made a large hot chocolate to go. Tuck kissed my cheek when I passed it to him. "Get some rest, okay?"

"That won't be a problem. Think about what I said," Tuck told me as he headed for the back door. "Life is precious, don't waste it."

Not long after Tucker left, I heard horrendously loud hammering going on upstairs. Now, Andy had worked on those upstairs

46

apartments for a solid month and had never made that kind of noise. It was almost like he was prodding me to come upstairs and confront him. The longer I stayed downstairs the louder he got. No matter where I went in the coffee shop or bookstore, he seemed to be directly above me, pounding away. Yeah, I was hot-blooded and horny as fuck by the time my last frayed nerve snapped. Luckily, it was midmorning when I'd finally had enough. The early rush was over and both the coffee shop and bookstore were fully staffed when I slammed out of the back door of the shop and let myself in the separate entrance for the upstairs apartments.

The crisp air wasn't enough to cool me down as I tromped up the steps loud enough to alert Andy that I was coming. I found him in the same apartment as the night before when he was putting up new two-by-fours to frame the separate rooms. I was shocked by how much progress he'd made since I was up here the previous night. Andy was down to the last few studs that would create a master bedroom.

"I'm here now, Andy. You can knock it off. Most guys would call or text, but you bang and bang and bang until I can't take it anymore and come up to confront you. That's some passive-aggressive bullshit, Andy."

"You're a self-centered little prick, aren't you?"

Ouch! I had to admit that stung hard. "I am not."

"You think everything is about you, don't you, Milo? Maybe I have other things going on in my life that don't revolve around you. Do you ever think about that? Maybe those issues are what's causing me to take out my frustration on these innocent pieces of wood."

My anger vanished instantly. Had the situation been less serious, and I wasn't so worried about him, I would've offered to let him work out his frustrations on my not-so-innocent wood, but not with a hammer. "What's wrong, Andy?"

"It's not your concern, Milo. Nothing about me should concern you."

I always heard that the truth hurt, and boy, did it ever. "I don't want to be angry anymore, Andy. I want…" I was afraid to voice what I wanted because he had every right to laugh in my face.

Andy's shoulders slumped as the fight drained right out of him. "I don't care what you want anymore, unless it has something to do with this project, Milo. You are a paying customer after all."

His words lashed at my soul and stole my breath away. I could feel my face heat with humiliation. "Just try to keep it down, okay. It's hard for people to cozy up to a book and a cup of coffee with all the banging going on. It hasn't been a problem up until now, so that's why I came up here. I won't bother you again, Andy." I turned and headed back out the way I came. *Don't cry, Milo. Don't cry, Milo. Channel Peach and hold your head up high.* I'd made it through the apartment and almost reached the hallway before his strangled voice stopped me.

"Wait."

I stopped but I didn't turn around. I wouldn't be able to look at him without breaking down. I didn't realize how badly I wanted to bridge the chasm between us until it was too late. Andy had made it very clear that my time to do what was right had passed me by while I was too busy trying to provoke him into making the first move. I was a fucking idiot and had no one to blame but myself. I stood and waited for his final verbal ax blow to strike me down. When the words came, they weren't at all what I had braced myself to hear.

"Are you and Tucker a thing again?"

Like a bad case of herpes, my anger came roaring back. It obliterated my urge to cry and gave me the courage to face him with my head held high. "You're such a liar, Andy. At least you're good at it now. I'm not sure if I should applaud you or be upset. You really had me convinced that you were angry about something besides this *thing* between us, and that I no longer meant anything to you. Oh, I mean a whole lot to you if you're asking me about Tucker."

Andy narrowed his eyes suspiciously. "You're not going to

answer my question, are you?"

"After *this* little stunt?" I asked incredulously. "Hell no. I won't make it that easy for you."

"Nothing about you is easy, Milo. You make me fucking crazy."

"And you're welcome," I said sassily, before I pivoted and returned to work.

I should've felt happy that the hammering was less obnoxious, but my brain was still restless when I joined Maegan for lunch in her small office at the back of Curious Things. Nothing between Andy and me was resolved, we continued circling one another, and I didn't see an end in sight. I poked at my Caesar chicken salad instead of eating it, not unlike how I took a stab at Andy every chance I got instead of kissing him.

"What's going on, Milo?" Maegan asked.

I glanced up and looked into her worried green eyes. "I was going to ask the same about your eyebrows, Mae."

"I'm being serious."

"I am too." I gestured to her forehead with my fork. "I don't think your eyebrows are even related, let alone sisters. I think you should insist on a DNA test."

"I have an appointment with Josh after work. He'll sort them out."

"And maybe he can fix your roots too," I suggested.

"Aren't we a catty bitch today. What's the matter, Milo? Andy won't take the bait and play your silly games?"

"Look who's being bitchy now," I replied with an exaggerated pout.

"Did you guys have a fight?" Maegan almost sounded hopeful. She probably thought we'd kiss and make up afterward and everything would be magical and perfect. That's how it used to be when we were younger, but we were so far removed from the boys we used to be.

"Let's talk about you and the detective instead. I heard that one of your neighbors filed a noise complaint with the police department last night."

Maegan's face turned blood red. "Oh my God!"

"Yes! That's what you were shouting at the top of your lungs when Mrs. Kippert walked by with little Mitzy. Good thing she had her cell phone handy and reported the possible abuse going on inside your house."

My twin sister covered her face with her hands. "I can't believe this," she mumbled. "I should be mortified that they sent a cruiser by to check on me, but they were just doing their job."

"Hopefully it's just your ego that's bruised and not your cervix," I teased. "Are you getting a manicure while you're at Curl Up and Dye? You could get a purplish-blue polish to mark the occasion."

"Milo!" Maegan practically shouted. "Quit deflecting and tell me what's going on with Andy."

"It's nothing," I told her, waving away the concern I saw in her eyes.

"I call bullshit. I've seen every emotion cross your face this morning. That'd be great if you were a mime putting on a show, but I can tell that Andy working so close recently has taken a toll on you. I'm sorry that I pushed the idea of renovating the second floor into apartments. I had hoped it would force the two of you to see how much you still mean to one another."

"Things are really fucked up, Maegan. I don't know what I'm going to do now. I've played this game with him for so long that I'm not sure he would believe me if I suddenly stopped." I told her about my two most recent exchanges with Andy. She just shook her head sadly. "It's not just me though, Mae. I tried to meet him halfway and only asked for him to tell me why he stayed away so damn long, and he wouldn't even tell me that."

"Oh, Milo," Mae said softly. "In case you haven't noticed, Andy is nothing like the proud, arrogant guy who left town fourteen years ago. I suspect his reasons for staying away are the same ones that

50

caused him to become a more humble person." Maegan reached across the table and squeezed my hand briefly. "I would never encourage you to pursue someone I thought was bad for you or didn't want you. Andy wants you, and I know he is the right guy for you. It's time for both of you to stop playing games, take a chance, and be honest with one another. I know you've tried but give him time to accept that you really meant it. Why would he bare his soul to you if you weren't truly vested in hearing it? Don't give up, Milo."

I thought about Maegan's words for the rest of my shift. She was right. Andy and I both deserved better than to live this way with the constant bickering back and forth while trying to make each other jealous. I was the one who broke Andy's heart fourteen years ago, so I would need to be the one who broke the vicious cycle.

Andy's truck was still parked in the alley behind the shop when I finished work for the day. He must've seen Tucker's SUV parked behind the café when he arrived for work and jumped to all kinds of conclusions. I wouldn't be able to repair two years of ridiculousness with a few words, but I could at least set him straight about Tucker.

My second time up to the apartments was a little slower and a whole lot more hesitant without anger and annoyance propelling me up the steps. I rehearsed what I wanted to say, but totally lost my train of thought when I came face-to-face with Andy. More like face to chest. Oh. Dear. God. His bare chest was sexier than I even imagined. I just stood there staring at his masculine perfection, not bothering to ask why he was sweatier than normal. I was just grateful for my blessings.

"I think something is wrong with the thermostat," Andy said. "It just keeps getting hotter and hotter in here." *You could say that again.* "I've called Paul to come check it out. It could be something simple, so don't worry that you'll have to replace the heating system."

"I'm not worried," I said when I could finally speak.

"My eyes are up here," Andy said wryly.

I snapped my eyes up to meet his. He smiled broadly, and I think

I breathed easy for the first time that day. It was the carefree grin I had known and loved so much when we were teenagers. "About Tucker—" I stopped when the smile slid from his face.

"I don't want to know."

"Andy," I said patiently. "Let me finish. There is nothing going on between Tucker and me. He wants there to be, but he knows it won't happen."

Andy snorted. "You sure looked chummy this morning, or do all your early-morning clients kiss you?"

"He kissed me on the forehead and cheek," I explained. "It was a gesture to show he accepted that friendship was all I could offer him."

"Forehead kisses are your favorite, or has that changed?"

I was still a sucker for them. If I thought about it hard enough, I could recall how right Andy's lips felt pressed to my forehead. Of course, his kisses lingered and led to more kisses. That's probably what he thought happened between Tucker and me that morning. Later, I could speak my mind about him jumping to conclusions, but right then I only wanted to assure him of one thing.

I closed the distance between us until I was close enough to smell his intoxicating, masculine scent. "Ask me why Tucker has accepted that he has no future with me, Andy."

"Why? So you can toy with me some more."

"Take a chance. Say the words, Andy."

seven

Andy

COULD TAKE THE BAIT AND SEE WHAT HAPPENED OR PLAY IT SAFE. Trying to figure things out with Milo wasn't unlike managing a damn baseball game. Did I go for a base hit that could tie the game or swing for the fence and win it all? I'd mostly played it safe since my return, and it hadn't gotten me very far. Maybe I did need to take a chance and swing for the fence.

"Why did Tucker accept that he doesn't stand a chance with you?"

"Because I—"

"Hey, Andy, where you at?" a jovial voice asked from the hallway. Paul walked into the apartment and jerked to a stop when he saw me standing so close to Milo. Of course, I wasn't wearing a shirt which gave the impression that he had disrupted something private. "Oh, sorry. I didn't mean to interrupt anything."

I was so close to having Milo admit that his feelings for me were so much more than annoyance and anger. Fuck, I could smell his need rolling off him. Paul's interruption had the same effect as throwing a bucket of ice-cold water on top of him.

"I was just leaving, Paul," Milo said, turning to face him. "Unless you need me to stick around and approve repairs or anything."

"Don't let me hold you up," Paul replied good-naturedly. "I'll have Andy call you if it's something major."

"Fair enough," Milo agreed. "I'll talk to you later, Andy."

I was going to let him leave without saying anything else, but I felt like something had shifted between us, like maybe I'd gained a little bit of ground with him. Not wanting to second-guess my actions all night long, I pulled my shirt on and told Paul that I'd be right back. I caught up to Milo just as he reached his car. I wrapped my fingers around his biceps to stop him from opening his door. Milo spun around, clutching his chest like the time I had startled him in the dark. He apparently hadn't expected me to follow him.

"Because you..." I prompted him to finish what he was going to say before Paul showed up.

"Um, I don't remember."

I blew out a deep breath while I searched for my patience. It was tattered and torn but relatively intact. I backed Milo up against his car until there was no space between us. I saw the way his eyes widened in arousal, and his luscious lips parted just begging for a kiss. Milo placed his hands on my pecs but didn't push me away. I felt like I was in the bottom of the ninth inning in a tied ball game, bases were loaded, I had two outs, and a full count against me. I just needed that perfect pitch to cross the plate so I could knock it out of the park. I considered Milo moistening his lips with the tip of his tongue the pitch I was looking for and swooped in, claiming his mouth with mine.

I captured his little whimper of pleasure in my mouth before I teased his lips further apart, exploring him with my tongue. God, his kisses gave me life. They always had, and I feared they always would. I said fear because there was a good chance that I'd spend the rest of my life alone if we couldn't bridge the gap. I'd never found anyone who made me feel a fraction of what Milo did, and I started to think I never would.

It seemed like Milo was on the same page when he dug his fingers into my pectoral muscles and sucked my tongue into his mouth. I was quickly forgetting what I'd followed him down to his car for beyond kissing him until we both stopped acting stupid. I slid my hands beneath the hem of his light sweater and touched the soft skin covering his tight abs. It must've stunned us both into remembering where we were. I certainly recalled my purpose when I looked into his dazed, blue eyes after breaking our kiss.

"I didn't follow you down here to kiss you," I told him. "I wanted you to finish telling me why Tucker finally accepted that he doesn't have a chance with you?" Milo opened his mouth to answer me, but I covered it with my finger. "No more games, Milo." I removed my finger and held my breath.

"Because I don't return his feelings," Milo told me. "I didn't in high school, and I don't now. I tried then, and my life would be so much easier if I could love him now, but you can't force something that isn't there. Tuck acknowledged that and said he wanted me to be happy, even if it wasn't with him."

Okay, Tucker Garrison was a bigger man than me. I would've engaged the beg, borrow, and steal philosophy to make Milo mine again. "That's mighty big of Tucker."

"Well, he has a big—" My growl cut Milo off, and he slapped my shoulder playfully. "Heart!"

"I bet that's what you were going to say." I ran my thumb over his bottom lip a few times. It was still wet from my kisses, and I wanted to make it even wetter. "Have dinner with me. We can order pizza and um…talk."

Milo snorted. "Talk." He wanted to say yes, I saw it in his eyes. "Are you ready to answer my question from the other night, Slugger?"

My heart raced from hearing the familiar nickname rolling off his tongue, but fear prevented me from meeting his demand. "You're not just willing to get to know the person I am now?" I tried for a teasing tone of voice but failed. I knew that I'd have to tell him someday, but I was hoping to entrench myself deep in his heart so he couldn't easily reject me once I told him about those twelve years.

"The decision you made to basically abandon your family and the community that loved you is part of the man you are now. You're not two different people, and even if you were, I'd need to understand one before I could trust the other."

"What scabs do you plan to scrape off so that you can bleed for me too, Milo? Or am I the only one who has to purge their soul?" I growled in frustration. "Forget I asked. Have a nice night." Our stalemate was still in force, and it didn't look like it would change anytime soon.

I turned back around and focused on putting one foot in front of the other since I could feel Milo's eyes on me. Tripping and falling on my face wouldn't be cool when I was trying to make a dramatic exit. I'd learned a thing or two from him over the years. When I got back upstairs, Paul was packing up his tools.

"The thermostat just needed new batteries," he said.

"Seriously?"

"Yeah, digital thermostats have some cool features, but they have some drawbacks too. A rule of thumb is to change the batteries every sixty days. You want to pass that along to Milo, or do you want me to?"

"I'll tell him. How much do I owe you for a service call?"

"Don't worry about it, kid. I've known you since you were in diapers." Paul and my father had been best friends since elementary school. In fact, for most of my life I had called him Uncle Paul. "So, you think things will finally work out between you and Milo?"

"Why do you ask?" I questioned, narrowing my eyes suspiciously. Was he trying to get details to take back to my folks?

Paul shrugged and said, "I know a guy." He used his best Tony

Soprano voice, which sent mixed signals.

"I don't want to take a hit out on Milo," I replied dryly. My frustration had soared to heights I never knew existed, but I hadn't lost my fucking mind...*yet.*

Paul threw his head back and laughed. "My Tony impression doesn't really fit this situation. I meant that I know a guy you might like."

"To date?"

"Yes, date." Paul rolled his deep-brown eyes and shook his head. "My nephew came out a while back. Good kid, hard worker, and handsome if I do say so myself. He works for me, so you'll probably meet him eventually anyway. I can make that happen sooner, if you like."

"I appreciate it, but—"

"I know, buddy. It's plain to see on your face when you look at him. I hope you guys can work out your differences."

"Thanks, Paul."

I stuck around after Paul left because I had nowhere else I needed to be and no one to spend my evening with. As was my habit, I buried my misery in my work. At least with construction projects, I could see the results of my efforts. Not saying I wouldn't have similar results if I'd chosen to come clean to Milo, but I wasn't willing to risk putting myself out there only to have him reject me. Or worse, pity me. I'd rather him hate me for the rest of his life. I had fucked up in some major ways, but I came out stronger for it.

Work was my therapy, and I fully embraced the physical labor and sweat equity that went into my job. I lost track of how long I hung drywall in the fourth apartment, but my growling stomach told me it was much later than it liked. I was too frustrated to eat at lunch and chose to work through, so I could finish earlier and find some peace away from Milo. What happened? I ended up staying later and was still no closer to getting away from Milo, emotionally or physically.

I thought we were getting somewhere when I walked him to

his car and he confessed why Tucker accepted he had no future with Milo. Now, it might've been arrogant on my part to assume that I was the reason why Tuck kept striking out, but I wasn't afraid to make an ass out of myself. I was immensely pleased to hear Milo say the words when pushed, but it really didn't change anything.

He still wanted to know why I'd been away so long; I wasn't ready to talk about it. Fresh start meant a fresh start. Maybe I was naïve to think I could reinvent myself in my hometown, but that didn't change my desire to be here. I'd faced down my demons and was ready to move forward. I hoped my future included Milo in it, but maybe I was asking for too much. I could understand where Milo's frustration was coming from.

My phone rang, interrupting my latest internal debate. I saw it was the other Miracle twin calling me. "Hey, Maegan."

"Go home, Andy."

"I thought you'd appreciate a contractor that works day and night to get the job done," I replied.

"I do appreciate how hard you work, but I'm more concerned that you're pushing yourself too hard. Did Milo bitch about the project taking too long or something?"

"No," I replied. "Does he think I'm taking too long?"

"Absolutely not, but I know how he likes to push your buttons. Seems you pushed a few of his today too."

"Maybe," I admitted grudgingly.

"Look, I'm not judging you, and Milo probably had it coming. That doesn't mean you work yourself to death. Okay?"

"I appreciate the concern."

"Have you eaten dinner?"

"Um, no. I was getting ready to wrap things up," I lied.

"Uh huh," Maegan said, sounding unconvinced. "Elijah and I worked late too, so why don't you join us for dinner? I have a wild idea, and I probably need you to talk me out of it."

"Umm."

Maegan laughed heartily at my discomfort. "For fuck's sake, Andy. I wasn't proposing a damn threesome or anything."

"Good to know," I replied. If Maegan had an idea she wanted to pitch to me, did that mean Milo would be there too?

"It's just going to be the three of us," Maegan said, answering my unspoken question. "Twenty minutes?"

"I don't know, Maegan, I probably should go home and shower first. I worked up a sweat and probably stink."

"Twenty minutes, Andy." Maegan disconnected the call before I could say anything else.

I packed up my tools, turned off the lights, locked the apartments, and headed to Maegan's house. She and Elijah lived next to one another, but I figured it was only a matter of time before Elijah gave up the pretense of wanting to spend his nights anywhere besides her house.

"Hey there, handsome," Maegan said, when I jogged up the porch. "You're just in time. Elijah brought home some greasy pizza that will cure all that ails us."

"What do you want to drink, Andy?" Elijah asked as he bent over to look inside the refrigerator. "Or should I call you handsome too?"

"I answer to pretty much anything these days," I replied drily. "I'll just have a soda or water."

"We have beer," Maegan offered.

"Nah, I'll pass. Thanks though."

Elijah handed me a Coke and opened a beer for him and Maegan. "I guess you want to know why we invited you over."

"Maegan assured me it wasn't for sex," I teased.

"Freckles, you need to work on your invitation skills if people think that a dinner invite equates a threesome," Elijah said affectionately. "Go ahead and tell the man your idea."

Maegan took a deep breath, held it, and released it slowly. Hell, she was making me a nervous wreck. "You're going to think I'm crazy. He does." She pointed to Elijah.

"Not crazy, just um…" Elijah's voice trailed off as he searched for an adjective that wouldn't send him straight to the dog house. Speaking of dogs, Maegan's Frenchie, Lulu, plopped herself beneath my chair, hoping I would drop a pepperoni.

"Crazy," Maegan whispered. "I want to buy the Bliss House."

I felt my eyebrows rise toward my hairline. "The one the town founder went missing from in 1851? The same house that is reported to be haunted?"

"The same one where Nancy Drew here and The Hardy Boys tripped over a dead body in the cellar," Elijah said wryly.

"We didn't trip over him," Maegan countered, rolling her eyes. "We saw the blood and ran upstairs to call the cops. You solved the homicide, and now the house is up for sale."

Earlier in the year, Maegan, Milo, and Memphis were granted permission by Thom Renzo to look around his deceased parents' home to see if they wanted to buy anything before the house and contents were put in an auction. Maegan always joked that the best stuff was hidden in the dirtiest places—attics, basements, and cellars. I don't think Thom Renzo's dead body was on her list of "best stuff," but that's exactly what was down there waiting for them to find. That night led to a series of events that made it seem like Maegan was in the killers' crosshairs, but no one was prepared for the truth Elijah uncovered when he solved the case.

"You're serious about buying the home?" I asked her.

"I am. I've always loved that house even though everyone else thought it looked like a haunted house from *Scooby Doo*. Something just felt right when I walked through the front door."

"And you want me to inspect it for potential problems?"

"Would you?"

"Sure," I said.

"While you're there," Maegan said, causing both Elijah and me to groan. "Can you give me an estimate on how much it would cost to modernize the big systems and renovate the home to its former glory?"

"I absolutely can do that. I'll need to get an HVAC guy, electrician, and plumber lined up too. I know the basics of those skills, but you want someone more knowledgeable than me looking at the mechanicals. I can make some calls. What kind of timeframe are we looking at here?"

"For an inspection and estimate?" Maegan clarified.

"Yeah. You couldn't start repairs until you owned the home anyway. What do I tell the guys?"

Maegan grimaced. "The lawyer for the estate is giving me ten days to get a conditional approval for the loan, which I can't do until the house is inspected."

I pulled my phone out of my pocket and started to dial.

"Wait!" Maegan's outburst startled me.

"What?"

"Eat your damn pizza first."

I ate two greasy, delicious slices then made some phone calls. Paul thought I was calling for his nephew's number but seemed okay that it was for business. Mike and Chris, electrician and plumber, were a little sketchy about going inside the Bliss House, but they agreed to meet me also. I promised to call them back with a firm date and time once Maegan got us access to the house.

When I left Maegan's house after a third and fourth slice of pizza, I was relieved that I at least made one Miracle twin happy that night. What the hell was I going to do about the other one?

eight

Milo

"I NEVER THOUGHT I WOULD RETURN TO THIS HOUSE AFTER THE way our last visit turned out," I said, looking through the windshield at the large, run-down Tudor home that Maegan wanted to buy. The same sister who conveniently couldn't meet the guys inspecting the house because she had an urgent meeting with an appraiser about a brooch she found the previous week while crawling through cobwebs and dust. This wasn't just some musty, dusty abode either; it was the house where we discovered the dead body of the guy who lured Maegan there with the intent to do ungodly things to her. I couldn't repress the shiver that worked its way through my body. What the hell was she thinking?

"The things we do for your sister," Memphis said.

"You love the thrill of the hunt just as much as she does, Memphis." I pinned my friend with a look that dared him to disagree. Memphis moved to Blissville to help take care of his cousin, Emory, after he had brain surgery to remove a tumor. Memphis fell in love with our small town and ended up staying. Blissville gained a beautiful citizen, and Maegan and I found an amazing friend. "I find it odd that she's not here tonight since this is her *dream* house and all."

Memphis grinned at my air quotes until he looked past my shoulder. His eyes got large like Alli Cat's did late at night when I watched television. She loved to freak me out by making me think a ghost, or the grim reaper, was behind me.

"Don't do that," I told him.

"Um, I think I know why Maegan is suddenly unavailable. Did she tell you who we were meeting?"

My heart sank. I knew without looking who had arrived and made Memphis's eyes widen. I turned and looked anyway. *Why, Mae? Let it go.* "She said a few guys are coming to look at the wiring, plumbing, and heating and air conditioning. She assured me that the realtor, Becker, would also be on site to make sure nothing was overlooked. She didn't tell me that *he* would be here."

Memphis snorted. "He's not Lord Voldemort, Milo. You can say his name." Memphis's eyes got bigger and bigger, which told me that Andy was approaching his car. I would not let him see me rattled. Some might call me vain, but I was glad I had dabbled a little concealer under my eyes to cover the garish, purple bags from not getting enough sleep. I didn't want Andy to see that he'd gotten the best of me.

I opened the door and climbed out of Memphis's car then plastered a fake grin on my face and boldly met Andy's gaze. "I didn't expect to see you here," I said calmly.

Andy's wry smile said that he saw right through my bullshit. He didn't stop walking until he nearly had me pinned against the car. "I could say the same for you, but I'm not disappointed."

I expected things to be awkward between us the next time we met, and I wasn't wrong. It was just a completely different kind of awkward, as in the sporting-a-hard-on-in-broad-daylight-with-no-means-of-relieving-it kind. Andy knew it. I'm sure it was written all over my face, and if not, it was hard to miss the erection that was weeping in my pants for him to put us out of our misery.

"W-w-what's going on?" I asked. Where had the disappointment I saw last night disappeared to? He resembled the cockier Andy Mason I'd fallen for all those years ago instead of the wounded, mysterious man who returned to me—well, Blissville. I hated to admit it, but I missed the swagger. It appealed to my baser needs and made me want to fuck like an animal.

Andy's sly grin spread because he knew it too. "I'm here to do your sister a favor. This home is her dream, and I want it to come true." Andy reached out and rubbed my bottom lip. "Why are you here, Milo?"

"This home is Maegan's dream, and I want it to come true," I repeated, sounding almost as breathy as Peach.

"We're finally in agreement on something," Andy said.

"Hey, Andy," Memphis said cheerfully.

Andy looked away so he could greet Memphis over the top of the car. "How's it going, cutie?" *Cutie?* I had the insane urge to kick him in the balls. "I'm surprised you agreed to come back here. These Miracle twins seem to get you into a lot of trouble."

"I live for trouble," Memphis said suggestively.

Yeah, he was living dangerously talking to my man like that. *My man?* Oh, hell no. "Listen, do you two need a private minute? I could go wait for Becker and the other guys on the front porch."

"Memphis," Andy said, "could you give me a minute with Milo?"

"You got it." Memphis took off so fast I could almost hear the air move.

"Cutie?" I asked when we were alone.

"He's fucking adorable, and you know it. In fact, I thought maybe the two of you had something going on for a while after he first moved here. You seemed to have your heads bent together a lot and kind of existed in a bubble that didn't include anyone other than Maegan."

"There's only ever been friendship between us," I said. A week ago, I would've had a witty comeback, but I was exhausted from circling around him for two damn years. I was done running and playing games.

"Because you were interested in someone else?" Andy pushed.

My pulse pounded in my neck, but I'd come too far to back down. "Yes."

Andy grinned smugly.

"And because Memphis is drawn to bad guys. He likes the edgy, love-them-and-leave-them types. I'm many things, but not that."

"You loved and left me," Andy said.

"I think you know it wasn't that cut and dry, Andy." In the expanse of less than a minute, our conversation took a nosedive into deeper waters than either of us had intended.

Andy leaned forward until his mouth was against my ear. My hands moved on their own volition to grip his waist. It felt natural and right. Andy's hot breath ghosted across the sensitive shell of my ear. I closed my eyes and bit my lip to keep myself from whimpering out loud. I wanted him so fucking bad.

"I tell you what," Andy whispered. "You're not the only one with questions. You tell me why you gave up on us so easily, and I'll tell you why I stayed away." He pulled back and looked into my eyes. "Wouldn't you say that's fair?"

Any other time I would agree, but I didn't want to rehash that time again—not even for Andy. It was just too painful. I saw in Andy's eyes that he understood the struggle. Maybe I was wrong to push him to tell me why he stayed away, but my heart insisted on hearing the truth, even if it hurt me. It was the only way I could trust him enough to move forward.

The sound of other vehicles pulling up diverted Andy's attention. "This conversation isn't over," Andy said. *Or maybe not.* "Are you truly okay with going inside?"

"If Maegan really wants to move here, then I have no choice."

"It looks like everyone else is here except Uncle Paul," Andy said. "Let's go inside and get started."

Andy only introduced Chris and Mike to Memphis and me, since it seemed like Becker already knew the electrician and plumber. Becker unlocked the door, and we all stepped inside, some of us were a little more nervous than the others.

"Is this house really haunted?" Mike asked, sounding hopeful.

"I can't say for sure, but I've never heard or seen anything unusual," Becker said, grinning big enough for the chandelier in the formal entrance hall to glint off his teeth.

"Don't be trying to sell us a Ford Pinto when we are expecting a Cadillac," I told him. After all, realtors were salespeople first.

"I wouldn't dream of it. Do you guys want the guided tour, or do you just want to wander around?"

"Sorry I'm late," said a familiar voice behind me.

"You're not Uncle Paul," I heard Andy say, as he walked past me to greet the newcomer. Fuck, was that appreciation I heard in his voice? If I turned around, would I catch him raking his eyes over Simon Novak from his curly brown hair to his feet? Yeah, Simon was big and brawny—just the way I liked them.

"Uncle Paul couldn't make it, so he sent me. Is that okay?"

"Sure. You must be the nephew he mentioned last night," Andy said.

"Oh man, was he trying to set us up on a date?" *Date? They both called the man Uncle Paul. Didn't that make them cousins? Gross.* "He means well, but it's so embarrassing. I—" His words cut off suddenly. Dread pooled in my gut when I suspected it was because Simon spotted me. "Milo, is that you? I didn't expect to see you tonight."

I turned slowly and pasted a friendly smile on my face. "Hello, Simon. How are you?"

"Better now." Simon walked straight to me and kissed me on the cheek, not caring who was standing around us. "I've been meaning to call you, but—"

"I don't mean to interrupt this charming reunion of hearts, but can we get started?" Andy asked snidely. I smiled inwardly at his jealous tone, more so that he didn't bother to hide it. I thought that was a step forward until I looked in his eyes and saw anger and disgust.

"Yeah, sorry," Simon replied, sounding embarrassed. To Becker he asked, "Which way to the furnace?"

"Um," Becker said, looking back and forth between Andy and me like he was watching a tennis match. "How about I show you, Simon?"

"Sounds good, my man. Lead the way."

"Does this house have fuses or breakers?" Mike asked.

"Breakers," Becker answered. "The electrical system looks to have been updated in the last fifteen to twenty years. The panel is in the same room with the furnace and hot water heaters. Both of you can come with us."

"Deal." The men scurried as fast as they could to avoid the inevitable showdown between Andy and me.

I don't know what Memphis ended up doing because I was too busy following Andy up the wide, curving staircase to the second floor. It seemed like Andy didn't want to discuss what just happened. He'd rather jump to conclusions like he did with Tucker than talk to me about it. Well, too fucking bad. I got angrier and angrier with every step I stomped on.

When Andy reached the second floor, he began looking at the ceiling. I suspected he was searching for water damage but realized I was wrong when he opened a door to reveal a narrow set of wooden steps. "Aha."

"Why are you going up there?" I asked, anger replacing my fear.

"It's just an attic, Milo. The roof is one of the most important parts of a house. I want to make sure it's not leaking. If it is, that's a huge expense to replace the shingles." He was all business again, and I hated that more than his judgment minutes before. At least when he was judging me, it showed he cared one way or the other.

67

"I'm not going up there," I said, crossing my arms over my chest. Yes, I'm aware I sounded like a pouting, five-year-old princess instead of the thirty-year-old princess I was. The lights above the steps went out as if to prove that I was right about the space being creepy as fuck. "See."

Andy pulled out a flashlight from his toolbelt. "See." Then he put it beneath his chin and clicked it on, highlighting parts of his face while others were cast in shadows. His sexy face took on a ghostly appearance. "Boo!" he yelled loud enough to make me jump. Then the jackass laughed and boldly trudged up the steps.

I couldn't be outdone, so I caught up to him by the time he reached the landing or else I'd lose the light when he turned to ascend the next set of steps. I missed a step and crashed headlong into his ass, almost taking him down too. "Careful, Milo. Damn."

"Sorry."

When Andy reached the top of the steps, he found a light switch on the wall. Only one socket had a bulb in it, so it wasn't bright enough for Andy to see anything besides trunks and trunks of stuff stacked everywhere.

I turned my head slightly to the left and saw the outline of a woman's silhouette out of the corner of my eyes. "Ghost!" I yelled, then dove behind Andy.

"Where?" Andy asked, turning in circles and swinging his flashlight to illuminate every corner of the dark, dusty space. "That?" he asked.

I peeked around his broad back and ducked my head under his armpit to see. In the center of the flashlight beam was one of those old-fashioned wire mannequins they used to hang dresses on. In fact, the mannequin sported a flowing, white dress that looked like something a woman wore in the eighteen hundreds. Of course, the white color of the gown in contrast to the dark space gave it a ghostly appearance.

"Seriously, Milo? I nearly pissed myself over a mannequin."

"You almost jizzed yourself earlier."

"Don't pretend I didn't feel your hard-on pressing up against mine, Milo."

"True, but that wasn't what I was referring to."

"Then what the fuck are you talking about?" Andy asked, sounding angry all over again.

"Simon!"

"You want to talk about Simon, Milo? We'll talk about Simon."

"Fine, I'm going first. Since when does your uncle want to fix you up with your cousin? What kind of fuckery is this?"

"Paul isn't my biological uncle," Andy said. "He and my dad are best friends. Uncle was an honorary title I gave him when I was a kid."

"Oh." Yeah, that took the wind right out of my sails. "Are you going to take Simon on a date?"

"Should I, Milo? Is he good in bed?"

I gasped dramatically, of course. "Are you slut shaming me?"

"Are you acting slutty?"

"And if I was?" I demanded to know.

Silence. "You make me fucking crazy, Milo."

"That makes two of us." I realized what I said. "Wait. I meant that you make me crazy too. So crazy that I can't even think. You rob me of my ability to snark."

"You act as if that's a talent," Andy scoffed.

"Those who can, do. Those who can't, bitch."

"You sure do have a type, don't you?"

"Excuse me? Are we back to Simon again?"

"We never left Simon, Milo. You try to divert the topic with your fake outrage."

"I don't *fake* anything, Andy. I didn't like your tone that implied I let any swinging dick have a crack at my ass."

"Just the swinging big ones."

"The thing with Simon happened before you returned home."

His eyes narrowed suspiciously, which made me even madder, if that were possible. "It's fine if you don't believe me, Andy, but I find it amazing that you have the balls to be pissed about my sex life, or lack thereof. What about Mr. Wednesday night? Want to tell me who you've been fucking these past two years?" Andy grimaced and looked away. "People in this town talk, so yeah, I know all about it. You're such a hypocrite. I'm out of here," I said, pivoting on my heels. Although I'm not sure how I spoke at all with that lump of regret lodged in my throat.

"Here, take my flashlight."

"Shove it up your ass." I pulled my phone out of my pocket, slid my thumb up the screen, and clicked on the flashlight. "Got it covered." My anger propelled me down the narrow, sketchy steps. When I rounded the landing, I stared at the bottom of the steps in shock. The door was closed, and I knew I'd left it open when I followed Andy up into the attic.

I didn't panic until I reached the bottom step and twisted the knob. Nothing. It didn't turn at all. "Fuck!" I yelled.

"What's wrong?" Andy called down the steps.

"The damn door is stuck."

"Why'd you shut it?" I heard the heavy sounds of Andy's boots tromping down the steps.

"I didn't shut it." The narrow stairwell wasn't wide enough for both of us, so I turned the knob and banged on the door with my fist. "Come on, you guys. This isn't funny."

"Move," Andy said, nudging me out of the way when he reached the door. He tried to turn the doorknob and didn't have any better luck than I did. Andy jerked and shoved the knob, hoping to break it loose, but it didn't work. "That knob worked just fine when we came upstairs."

"Well, fuck. I thought it would open beneath your magic touch," I said sarcastically. "I didn't think to try the doorknob."

"That mouth of yours is going to get you in a lot of trouble, Milo."

"With who?"

I might as well have waved a red blanket in front of a bull. I found myself pinned between the jammed door and an angry, sexy beast of a man. Andy cradled my head firmly but not painfully and smashed his lips against mine. This was an angry kiss hot enough to singe my perfect eyebrows. I dropped my phone and slid one hand in his hair while I snuck one beneath the hem of his shirt to touch the hot skin at the small of his back just above his toolbelt. It was the place I wanted to rest my heels and urge him to fuck me faster and deeper.

Andy's hands were just as busy. One still held my neck while the other slid beneath the waistband of my jeans to tease my ass crack through my underwear. "We need less clothes," Andy growled against my lips before he switched the angle of his mouth and came back in for more.

I was ready to push him onto the steps and—

The door suddenly opened behind me, and I tumbled backward. Somehow, Andy was able to pull his hand out of my pants and twist our bodies so that he was the one who landed hard on the floor, cushioning my fall.

"Oh, sorry," Memphis said. "I thought when I heard you holler 'fuck' that you were in some kind of trouble, or maybe getting ready to kill each other. I didn't know you were literally fucking."

"We weren't fucking," Andy and I both said at the same time. *Yet,* was the word we left unspoken.

I reluctantly stood up and dusted myself off, while Andy got to his feet a little slower.

"How'd you open the door?" I asked Memphis.

"I twisted the knob."

"Impossible," Andy said in disbelief. "That doorknob wasn't turning, which is how we got locked in when Milo shut the door."

"I. Didn't. Shut. The. Door."

"Then how did it get shut? Magic? The ghost did it! Oh, wait! That was a mannequin."

"You're never going to let me live that down, are you?"

"Fuck no, Encyclopedia Brown."

"Hey, that was a great book series," Memphis said defensively. "Seriously, guys, there's nothing wrong with the doorknob." Memphis reached out and twisted the knob on the outside to show that it worked fine.

Andy reached around to the inside and demonstrated that it didn't budge.

"Fuck!" I said. "I bet they kept someone locked up there."

"Knock it off, or you'll work yourself up again," Andy said mildly. "I'm going back up there to complete my inspection. Don't shut the door again. Unless you want to follow me and finish what we started," he said with a playful wink before he headed back up the steps.

"If you didn't shut the door then who did?" Memphis asked. "Do you smell that?"

I sniffed the air and caught the faintest whiff of pipe tobacco. My eyes got as big as saucers before I hightailed it down the steps and out to the front porch. "It really is haunted," I told Memphis when he caught up to me. "That ghost locked me in the attic with Andy."

"Uh huh. Seems to me the ghost did you a favor."

The jury was still out on that one. My heart raced from fear, but my body burned with need, lust, and excitement. I was fast approaching the point of no return, and I was no closer to finding out what happened to Andy than I was two years ago.

nine

Andy

I T WAS HARD TO PUSH THOUGHTS OF MILO ASIDE TO FOCUS ON MY job with a raging hard-on between my legs. I know, I'm a guy and should be used to working around an inconvenient erection, but the truth is: not all boners are created equal.

A Milo-induced erection, like the man himself, isn't something you can ignore. Milo gets under my skin in ways no one else ever could, and the boners he gave me wouldn't just go away on their own if I worked hard enough. I had two choices: rub one out myself at my earliest convenience or follow him home so we could fuck this physical frustration out of our systems and begin healing the emotional rift. I knew which one I preferred, but it wasn't a decision I could make unilaterally.

I untucked my T-shirt to help hide my erection, but my toolbelt prevented it from giving me full coverage. I felt curious looks, and even some knowing ones, as I ran into the other guys while I made my rounds. Later, I'd marvel over how stunning the house truly was, especially since it was built prior to indoor electric and plumbing, but right then, I only wanted to give an honest appraisal of the condition so I could search out Milo's hiding spot. I hadn't seen him or Memphis since I returned to the attic.

"Milo's outside with Memphis," Simon told me. I guess my thoughts were obvious to anyone who looked at me.

"Look, Simon—"

He held up both hands to stop me. "Say no more. I might not be the most observant man in the world, but I think I know why I never stood a chance with Milo." Simon was the second person to say that in as many days. "That doesn't mean I won't be waiting in the wings in case you screw up once and for all."

Me? Why did everyone always assume that I was the one who ended our relationship? Was it because I stayed gone so long, or was it something that little shit told people after we broke up? I felt my anger returning, which only seemed to make my dick harder. *Damn that Milo.*

"See you around, Simon," I tossed over my shoulder and headed for the door. I should've looked for Becker to say goodbye and thanked Chris and Mike for working me into their busy schedules, but I was beyond niceties.

"All done then?" Milo asked me with forced cheer. "We'll just be going. Come along, Memphis."

"Not so fast, Dimples." It was the first time I used the nickname I'd given him in high school. Many people thought I was referring to the dimples on either side of his mouth or the cute one in the center of his chin. Nope, I was referring to the adorable divots that rested above his ass cheeks. I was obsessed with them when we were younger, and I was eager to get reacquainted with them. "We need to talk."

I saw anger and hunger swirl in Milo's eyes. There would be no talking, not until after we worked off some steam. Was he angry over my assertiveness or because he wanted me so fucking bad? I was about to find out.

"Milo, let me give you a ride home."

"I don't think—"

"Sounds good to me," Memphis said. "I have dinner plans."

"Hot date?" I asked.

"Nah, dinner with Emory and Jon."

"Don't I have a say in who takes me home?" Milo asked angrily.

"Milo, Andy isn't a threat to your safety." *Oh, I wasn't sure about that.* "Of course, I'll take you home if you don't want to be alone with Andy."

I leaned forward and pressed my lips to Milo's ear, loving the slight tremor that shook his body. "Don't be afraid."

"I'm not afraid of you," Milo hissed at me before he turned to his friend. "I'll call you later, Memphis." He trotted down the steps and across the driveway with his shoulders back and head high, not waiting for Memphis to respond or for me to comment further.

"You're going to have your hands full with him tonight," Memphis teased.

"I'm counting on it, cutie. Have a nice night," I tossed over my shoulder as I followed Milo, but at a more leisurely pace. I wanted to draw this out and ratchet up his emotions even more. I took off my toolbelt and tossed it in the back seat of my quad cab.

Milo said nothing when he climbed into my truck, but it would've been hard to hear over my thundering heartbeat anyway. He sat there with his arms crossed over his chest and his lips pursed sexily, but I could tell he wasn't trying to turn me on. He was stewing in his juices, literally and figuratively. Tonight would be the beginning of the end to all the negativity sparking between us.

"You passed my street, Andrew," Milo said feistily. He knew damn well where I was taking him.

"I want to work this out in my bed, Milo. I've wanted you there every single night since I returned."

"You mean on the nights my spot wasn't filled by a different willing body?" he inquired. Was he fishing?

"I haven't hooked up with any guys since I returned home, Milo." I looked over at him when I came to a stop at the intersection down the street from my house. It was clear he didn't believe me, and I realized it was beyond cruel to keep him guessing about my Wednesday night activities. I just didn't want him to be disappointed in me. I'd hurt enough people with my reckless behavior. "Well, there was this one guy."

Milo's lips firmed into a straight line, indicating how much he hated the thought of me having sex with someone else. Good, we were even. The Tuckers and Simons in the world could take a fucking hike.

"We hooked up in the alley behind his business a few times. It was the hottest, raunchiest sex of my life, and I can't get it, or him, out of my mind. He hates me now."

"That's just cruel, Andy," Milo replied, but a crooked smile tilted one side of his mouth. "I could never *hate* you." His confession gave me hope.

"He was all I wanted and craved, and no one else was going to do, even though I would've been well within my right to fuck him out of my system with someone new." I winked playfully to lighten the mood. "It's good that you acknowledge that other pillow belongs to you."

"That's not what I meant, Andy."

"That's what you said, Dimples."

"You'll have to find a new nickname for me," Milo said suddenly. "Kyle is known as Dr. Dimples now. Blissville isn't big enough for two Dimples to be running around."

"What if I call you The Original Dimples?" I asked.

"Nope," Milo said. "You'll need to come up with something new. I'm curious to see what you choose."

"I'm curious to see what you give me to work with," I said, pulling into my driveway.

"You're awfully full of yourself, Andy."

"You're about to be awfully full of my dick."

"Asshole," Milo said as he opened the door and climbed down. He headed toward the front porch after slamming the truck door shut. I called out to stop him.

"I use the back door," I told him.

"I haven't forgotten, Andy." He turned around and faced me. "I love using the back door now too." I didn't know my dick could get any harder, but it did. I didn't want to think about this being a first we didn't explore together, but I planned to make up for all the lost time between us. "Is that going to be a problem for you, Slugger?"

Not giving a fuck what my neighbors might think, I pressed the full length of my body against Milo's. "Does this feel like I have a problem with you putting your dick in my ass?"

"Andy," Milo gasped when he felt how excited I was. "This is probably a big mistake. It's not too late—" I cut him off by briefly pressing a finger against his lips.

"You're right, Milo. It's not too late to have everything we both want. This time around will be different. Have faith and you'll see."

"I need to trust you with my heart before that will happen," Milo reminded me. "But right now, I just want to trust you with my body."

I dropped a quick kiss on his upturned lips then took his hand and led him to the back of my rental house. "It's not much, but it's home sweet home for now," I said once we were standing in the kitchen.

"It's tidy, clean, and cute," Milo said. "Show me to the bedroom."

"Okay, but please don't use any of those adjectives when I take off my clothes. I mean, I am tidy and clean, but cute might be a boner killer."

"Andy, I know it's been fourteen years since I saw your cock, but I'm almost positive that cute isn't a word I would use to—"

"You've seen my dick since I returned," I reminded him.

"No, I've only felt it in my—" Milo's words cut off with a whoosh of air when I hoisted him over my shoulder and carried him to my room. "Fuck, I love when you manhandle me," Milo admitted when I tossed him onto the bed. "I've been looking for someone to make me feel this way since you left me."

"I didn't leave *you*, Milo. I went to college." I pulled my shirt off over my head and dropped it to the floor.

"And never came back," he replied bitterly.

"Who ended our relationship over a text message, Milo?" I asked, renewed anger and frustration rising inside me all over again. That didn't stop me from removing the rest of my clothes until I stood there completely naked and vulnerable while he sat fully dressed on my bed. We were going to have this out once and for all.

"I did," Milo said quietly. "I admit now that I acted hastily."

"Why?" I asked.

"Why didn't you ask me this question back then, Andy, instead of the 'if that's how you feel' reply I got back. You're mad at me for not fighting harder for us, but what excuse do *you* have?" Milo ripped his shirt off and threw it to the floor. I didn't think it was possible for my heart to pound faster or my body to get tighter with longing. Fuck, I was going to die if I didn't have Milo again.

"Honestly?" I asked. Milo nodded. "As hurt and sad as I was, it was easier for me when I didn't have to keep juggling between keeping our relationship a secret from my team and coaches and making you happy too." Hurt flared in his dark-blue eyes, and I regretted that I was the source of pain for him. I only wanted to give him pleasure.

Milo toed off his socks and shoes, then lay on his back to remove his pants and underwear. "You've got me addicted to angry sex. Do you want to have angry sex with me, Andy?" Milo lazily stroked his cock, only stopping to gather pre-cum and smear it as lubricant down his shaft.

I growled as I knocked Milo's hand off his dick and replaced it with my own. I dropped to my knees and released Milo's hard-on long enough to grip his hips and pull him closer to me. He set his feet on my shoulders and spread his legs wider, letting me see all of him. Milo reached between his legs to cup my chin, tugging my face closer to where he wanted it to be. I released his shaft and licked his excitement off my fingers and palm, then gripped the base of his cock before I fell on it like a starving man. I was starving for him—more and more each day we were apart.

Milo arched his back off the bed like a long, sleek cat, hissing his pleasure and digging his nails in my scalp while I gave him an angry blow job. Fuck, I was going to make him purr for me too. I loved sucking cock and knew how to work a man until he was on the edge of blowing his load then pull off before he reached climax. Edge play was my favorite form of torturing a lover, but it wasn't a skill I knew when I was with Milo.

"Andy," Milo growled after the third time I backed him off.

"What's the matter, baby?" I asked, then circled the crown of his cock with my tongue, loving his taste and texture. "You don't like edge play, or are you pissed because I learned how to do this with other people?" Milo's expressive eyes glittered angrily, and I knew I'd hit the nail on the head.

"How pissed are you that your ass won't be the first I fucked?" Milo fired back, his missile hitting its target too.

"Pretty damn pissed," I admitted before I took him back in my mouth and worked him up to the edge a fourth time. Milo was no longer willing to remain idle. Gripping my hair with both hands, he thrust his hips up and fucked my face in earnest. I was too turned on to back him off again, so I swallowed his release when he came with a victorious yell that sounded like a battle cry.

I was feeling damn pleased with myself too when I climbed onto the bed and pulled him up against me so that we lay on our sides facing each other. Milo's midnight eyes were sated, but still a little suspicious about why I hadn't suited up and found my release inside his tight ass.

Milo closed those heavy lids and sighed blissfully when I reached around to cup his ass and trail my middle finger along the

79

crack between his perfect peach. I moved in for a kiss, soft at first, but it quickly grew more passionate as I rimmed his pucker with the tip of my finger. Milo pushed his ass against me, urging me to penetrate him, but I had no intention of fucking him that night. I meant what I said in my driveway. Thinking about him inside me made my dick leak.

I broke our kiss long enough to get my finger wet with saliva before returning to his greedy, pulsing hole. I breached him with just the tip, and Milo bit my lip spurring me on to do more. I hadn't forgotten how much Milo loved having his ass fingered. I recaptured his lips in another searing kiss while working my long digit in and out of his tight clench. Sliding my free hand down between us, I felt that his cock was already getting hard again. Good, I had big plans for it. But first, I cupped Milo's smooth balls in my palm, then massaged them firm enough to drive him insane but not hard enough to hurt him.

Milo broke the kiss and cried out again when I tagged his prostate. "Stop dicking around and shove that big dick inside me!" Now we were getting somewhere; it was too bad for him that I wasn't ready to give in to his demands though. I wasn't guaranteed another night with Milo in my bed, so as much as my cock begged to come, I held off until I didn't think I could take it another second. I crooked my finger up and massaged his prostate in a circular motion, making his dick bounce and drip some more. Almost.

Hunger didn't begin to describe the emotions tearing through my body, lashing at my guts. I stamped down the primal urge to roll him to his back and claim him. Just barely.

"Fuck me, damn it!"

I removed my finger and released his balls to retrieve the condoms and lube from the nightstand.

"No overnight guests, huh?" Milo snarkily asked.

"The lube is for jerking off nightly, and the condoms in the nightstand were a wishful-thinking purchase in case you ever pulled your head out of your ass long enough to stick your dick in mine."

"Like you ever expected me to want to tap that," Milo snorted. His eyes widened when I tossed the condom on his chest.

"Suit up and fuck me already." It was my turn to lazily stroke my cock like I didn't have a care in the world, or I wasn't about to spunk all over myself.

ten

Milo

"**Y**OU'RE SERIOUS?" I ASKED IN DISBELIEF.

"Dead serious. And what about you? Do you really want to fuck me, or were you teasing to get a *rise* out of me?" Andy's mighty cock had arisen all right.

"Dead serious," I said, repeating his phrase, then tore the condom wrapper open with my teeth. "I want inside your ass really bad." *Fuck me!* I sounded like a cheesy porn star, and Peach would be pissed.

Andy didn't seem to notice because he was too busy watching me roll the condom down the length of my dick. His hand was still, gripping his cock tight around the base like he was trying to stave off an orgasm. "It's been a long time though, so lots of lube. Go slow," he added hastily. He sounded as nervous as I felt.

I wanted to go slow and relearn every inch of Andy's cock with my tongue and test the weight of his big, virile balls in my hands. Did he taste as good as I remembered? Did he still love having his sack fondled? I positioned myself between his spread legs, and Andy fisted his cock even tighter. I loved the effect I had on this big, strong man. The bigger they are, the quicker they drop to their knees.

I wanted to shake Andy, to make him regret every second we missed out on the past fourteen years, if only… *Nah, these weren't the types of thoughts to have while licking cock and fingering ass.* Shit, he hadn't been joking about not bottoming often. Andy was tight, and I knew it would be a curtain call for me after only a few strokes inside his tight heat, which meant I needed to make the foreplay even better.

I never forgot a single thing about Andy or the way he made me feel. There in his bed, those lost years were forgotten; it was as if they never existed. He looked at me through the eyes of a man who hadn't known I could break his heart, or mine. Andy touched me with gentle hands even though he had wanted to throttle me just moments prior. Then again, I had that effect on people, and I owned it. What the hell was the point of going through life with a blah attitude? I was passionate about everything I did from sex to picking out fruit at the supermarket. In fact, my ball-massaging technique was very similar to the tactics I deployed to find the right kiwis. Sometimes I rubbed people the wrong way, but sometimes I rubbed them so good they moaned and curled their toes.

I dropped lower and sucked Andy's balls in my mouth one at a time, while continuing to move one, very wet finger inside his ass.

"So good, baby. So fucking good." Andy's guttural cries of pleasure made me bolder, so I worked a second digit inside him, teasing his taint with my tongue. I angled my fingers and tagged his prostate once, twice, then massaged it. "Fuck me now. I'm ready."

"I'm not."

"Milo, I'm going to come. I want to do that with your cock in my ass."

I removed my fingers and moved up his body to position myself between his thighs. My dick wasn't as fat as his, but it was still thicker than two fingers, so I applied a liberal coating of lube on the condom. Locking my eyes on Andy's, I fisted my cock and pushed the head in past the first ring of muscles.

"Oh damn, you're tight," I said between pants. I wanted to shove in and fuck him so bad, but I saw the discomfort on his face. Lowering my lips to hover above his, I whispered, "Kiss me."

Andy cupped my head with both of his hands and pulled me the rest of the way down to crash his lips against his. I reached between our bodies and stroked his cock while his ass adjusted to my penetration. When he was ready for more, Andy raised his hips, and my dick inched forward some more. I wanted to stop and let him adjust, but my cock was so slick, Andy's ass felt so fucking good and tight, and his desperate kisses drove me wild.

I snapped forward and bottomed out, making Andy grunt and gasp into my mouth. I was worried it was too much too soon, but Andy tucked his calves against the back of my thighs to anchor me inside him. I started to move, clumsily at first, but I found my rhythm and loved the musical sound of our bodies slapping together as we groaned and growled for more.

Andy's grip on my hair got tighter, and I felt his dick pulse in my fist at the same time his ass clenched down hard around my cock. Andy broke our kiss so he could pant and grunt as his cum spurted all over his stomach and chest. All the while, his ass milked my second orgasm of the night out of me.

I collapsed on top of his broad chest with my dick still buried inside him. Andy wrapped his thick arms around me and kissed the top of my head. The sound of his heart thumping beneath my ear made me so sleepy. It didn't help when he trailed his calloused fingers up and down my spine.

"This was the best idea I had in two years."

"Maybe fourteen," I challenged, earning a deep chuckle. I was sad when my softening dick slid from his ass, but happy that Andy seemed content to hold me for the time being.

"So much sass," Andy said, his voice sounding far away as sleep claimed me.

Sometime later, I was slowly woken from tender kisses along my spine. I was wide awake by the time he reached the crack of my ass and moaned when Andy dipped his tongue in one dimple then the other.

"God, how I've missed this," I mumbled into the sheets.

Andy crawled up my body and licked the outer rim of my ear. "No more anger or misunderstandings," he avowed.

I wanted to believe that he was right, but I remembered how hot things ran between us. Sure, we were adults instead of kids, but had either of us changed that much? Of course, my ability to think vanished when I felt Andy's finger circling my pucker.

"I meant to wake you up for dinner, but I got a little distracted when your sexy bubble butt was sticking out partway. Seems you got agitated in your sleep and kicked the covers off."

"Habit," I whispered, pushing my ass against him to get that finger where I wanted it. "You made me dinner?"

"I just warmed up some ham and bean soup my mother made over the weekend. I can make a mean turkey club panini if you want one of those too."

It had been several hours since I last ate, but that wasn't the kind of hunger that was spreading through my body like a wildfire. "Later," I replied. "Fuck me, Andy. It's been too long."

"You didn't like fucking my ass?"

"Loved it, but I'm dying to feel you— Oh!" I cried out when Andy's finger pushed in and homed in on my prostate like a heat-seeking missile locked on a target. Andy's free hand kept my ass cheeks spread apart so he could feast his eyes on the activity there. "More," I told him desperately.

"Not yet," Andy said calmly then pulled his finger out of my tight clench. My moaning of discontent turned into whimpers of pleasure when I heard him flip open the cap on the lube. I trembled in

85

anticipation, knowing that soon I would feel his thick cock in my ass again.

"Mmmm," I said when the first slick digit stroked inside me. "Unh," I grunted, pushing my hips against the penetration to signal that I wanted more—more fingers, more depth, more everything. Andy was playing it safe with me, and that just wouldn't do after waiting for *two fucking years*. Another digit joined the first, and I was fast approaching my orgasm. "Fuck me, Andy." I didn't want to come from his fingers.

An animalistic growl rumbled from his chest when he pulled his fingers from my ass. While he rolled a condom on his turgid length, I got on my hands and knees. I grinned because I knew what a pretty picture my ass made up in the air with my hole stretched and ready for him.

"I won't be easy. It's been too long, and you've driven me too crazy."

"Give me all your crazy, Andy. I can take it. I want it." And I did too.

Andy placed one hand between my shoulder blades, holding my head and torso against the mattress while his other held his cock steady as he penetrated me—too slowly.

"That's all you got, Slugger? Where's the passion from the alley when you couldn't sink to your balls fast enough. Fuck. Me. Hard."

The hand between my shoulders slid up to fist my hair the same time he snapped his hips forward, burying his cock to the hilt inside me. "Like that?"

"Not bad," I replied, goading him.

Andy leaned forward and bit the tender spot where my neck curved into my shoulder. "Going to tell me you've had better?"

"Even I'm not that big of an asshole," I replied. "Besides, it would be a lie if I did."

Andy bracketed my body with his much bigger one and began to fuck me in earnest. "Nobody will ever make you feel like I do, Milo."

I loved the sound of our balls slapping together and the groans my greedy, tight ass ripped from his chest. "All mine. Say it, Milo."

"All mine," I repeated, incapable of independent thought when all my attention was focused on the glorious orgasm building.

"Yes, I am yours, Milo. Who do you belong to?"

"Andy!" I yelled as I came again for the third time that night.

"That's right, baby."

Andy rode me harder and faster, then his body stiffened, and he inhaled sharply before he spilled inside the condom. Instead of falling on top of me, Andy rolled over and lay beside me on his back. He threw his arm up to cover his eyes while his chest billowed up and down. His body was covered with a sheen of sweat, and his wet hair stuck to his forehead. He reminded me of a horse that had been ridden hard and put away wet.

He was still for so long that I thought he'd fallen asleep, and I was content to lie there and watch him. After all, I'd fallen asleep on him earlier.

"I supposed now would be an appropriate time to explain to you where I've been going every Wednesday night," Andy said in a soft, hesitant voice. He almost sounded afraid, and that wasn't the Andy I knew.

"Probably, you should've told me before we had sex again," I teased.

Andy moved his arm enough so that he could see me with one eye. "It's nothing sinister, Milo. I'm not living a double life."

"You're not spying for your country every Wednesday between the hours of six and eleven?"

Andy snorted. "Definitely not."

"You're not seeing anyone else?"

Andy moved his arm off his face. "Milo, do you really think I would've brought you here and fucked you if I was involved with someone else?"

"Technically, I fucked you first," I reminded him. "The answer isn't a simple yes or no, Andy. The guy I used to know would never do something like that, but I don't feel like I know you anymore. You're so secretive. If you're not seeing someone else, then where are you going, and why can't you tell me about it? You act like it's something you're ashamed of. Are you?"

"Ashamed?" he asked then thought it over for a second. "No, I'm not ashamed, but I do worry you'll think less of me when I tell you."

I cupped his head in my hands and kissed his forehead like he'd always done for me. Then I kissed the space between his eyes and the tip of his nose before I pressed my lips against his. When I pulled back, I offered the sweetest smile I could muster. "You'll tell me whenever you're ready. I will listen without judgment. Things will be different this time around. Some smart, handsome man told me that a while back, but I wasn't ready to listen to him."

"And now?"

"I'm ready."

The beautiful smile that spread across Andy's face was breathtaking. He was right; things would be different. They would be better, we would be stronger, and we'd appreciate things more than we ever could when we were sixteen and eighteen.

eleven

Andy

MY STOMACH RUMBLED AND GROWLED, REMINDING ME HOW much time had passed since lunch. "I'll tell you everything you want to know, but let's eat first."

"I could eat too," Milo admitted. "That turkey club panini sounds delish."

When we went downstairs, I had every intention of waiting until the sandwiches were done before I started talking, but the gates opened up and words started tumbling out. Maybe because it was easier when I had something to keep my hands and eyes busy so I could avoid the disappointment I was certain to see in Milo's expression.

"I didn't take our breakup as calmly as I indicated in that text message, Milo."

I heard his chair scraping against the linoleum as he scooted back from the table. I didn't feel the air stir when he silently approached me, but I felt him just the same. Milo pressed his hand softly against my shoulder, then slid it down to my waist.

"I was so wrong to push you away, Andy. I should've tried harder and been more patient. I think a part of me expected you to stop me from ruining us, or at least, reach out to me after we had time to miss one another," Milo said softly.

"But I didn't," I replied.

"No, and I realized we were truly over when I didn't hear from you after Maegan was diagnosed with cancer."

I hung my head in shame. That was another one of my bad judgment calls I could never take back or forgive, even if Milo did. I couldn't begin to imagine how hard that was on all of them, especially a twin whose life was intricately woven with his sister's. Just the thought of Faith going through chemo and radiation was enough to break my heart, but Milo lived it day in and day out. Did he feel everything Maegan went through also? I was too afraid to ask him.

"Hey," Milo said softly before he kissed my shoulder. "I wasn't trying to make you feel bad, Slugger."

"I know, but I do."

"I also didn't mean to distract you from what you wanted to say." Milo stepped to the right then hoisted himself up to sit on my counter so he could look at me. "Talk to me, Andy."

His dark-blue eyes were mesmerizing enough to lull me into a sense of comfort that made me feel like I could truly pull it off. I turned the burner down, put the lid back on the soup then stepped between his parted thighs. Milo immediately wrapped his legs around my waist, crossing his ankles behind my back and pressing his chest tight against mine. I couldn't resist grabbing his firm ass, nor was I surprised when my dick twitched even though I'd come twice already. It was the Milo Effect in full force.

I pressed a long, lingering kiss on his lips while searching for the right words to say. Just days before, I wasn't willing to cut myself open and bleed for Milo when he demanded it. Maybe it was because I felt he wasn't ready to hear it, no matter his claims. The moment felt different, and his show of faith and willingness to wait made me want to come clean with him.

It was a story I'd told plenty of times, but only to my family and in my NA meetings. I feared I would destroy our chance at a life together if I wasn't careful, but I also knew we couldn't build a future on a foundation that was missing bricks. I had to fill in all the gaps, and the two of us needed to seal the cracks with mortar. Milo showed he was willing to take a leap of faith, and I wanted to reciprocate.

I reluctantly eased back from our kiss but kept my hands on either side of his neck. I felt the way his pulse vibrated beneath his skin. Was he nervous to learn the truth, excited by our kiss, or both? For me, excitement and dread raced through my body.

"Nothing you say will change what you mean to me," Milo said softly. God, I wanted so much for that to be true.

"I will understand if you change your mind," I told him.

"Not going to happen."

"After we broke up, I went to a very dark place in my head." A look of devastation washed over his face, making me cringe. "None of this is on you, Milo. I mean it. If you want me to continue, I need you to promise me that you'll not try to shoulder any of the blame."

"I can't promise that, Andy. You already told me that I broke your heart. But," he said, covering my mouth with his long, graceful index finger, "I will do my best to remember we were just kids."

What else could I really ask of him? "It wasn't just our breakup though. That's what I'm trying to tell you. It was so many things."

"I have nothing but time for you." Milo stroked his hand over my chest to comfort me.

"It was being away from home and all the people I loved, it was the fear that I wasn't good enough to ever see the field, and I hated being in the closet, Milo. We can't pretend that every person who lived in our small town supported us as a couple back in the day, but we were pretty sheltered from the worst of it by our friends and family. It wouldn't have been that way in college. It was more and more evident each day how I could never be myself."

"I'm sorry," Milo said softly. "I should've known better."

"We were sixteen and eighteen years old, Milo. Mature for our age, but we still couldn't see past the tip of our dicks. It's not like either of us were great communicators. We got mad, fought, then fucked our way past our trouble." I kissed his lips to take the sting out of my words. Our relationship was more than fighting and fucking. I didn't just lose a boyfriend; I lost my best friend.

"At first, I told myself that our breakup was for the best. I decided to put my focus on school and baseball. I have never been the sharpest tool in the shed, so I had to work extra hard to maintain a high enough GPA."

"Andy, stop that," Milo admonished softly. He always hated when I referred to myself as a dumb jock or implied that I was stupid.

"When I wasn't studying, I was in the weight room working out for my first season as a college ball player. It was the one thing that got me through missing my family and you." I dropped a quick kiss on his forehead to smooth out the frown lines. "One night, I pushed myself too hard and tore up my shoulder. I knew Coach would be pissed because I had worked without a spotter, and that was against the rules, so I didn't tell him. I iced the shoulder and tried to stretch it out like I'd seen the trainers do. My shoulder got worse instead of better, but I kept pushing myself because I didn't want to risk my spot on the roster. Unfortunately for me, what might've started out as a minor injury became a torn ligament that needed surgical repair."

"That's what these little scars are from on your shoulder," Milo said then kissed them. "I'm so sorry. Did you miss the entire season?"

I swallowed hard. "My story gets worse from here. Are you sure you're ready to hear it?" Milo looked at me with wide eyes but nodded. "Without baseball, I spiraled into a depression. I withdrew from my teammates, started sleeping longer, skipping classes, and physical therapy for my shoulder." I took a shaky breath then said, "And I became addicted to booze and pain pills."

"Baby," Milo said tenderly.

"I stopped giving a fuck about anything besides getting high enough to forget about my misery." I had to close my eyes because this was the worst part of my story and would hurt Milo the most. When I reopened them, I saw that Milo had mentally braced himself to hear what I had to say.

"Coach called me into his office one day and issued an ultimatum: I could get my act together or he'd personally turn me in to the athletic director himself. My grades were good and fucked by that point, but it wasn't like I could play with my bum shoulder, so he made it clear I had time to get my head out of my ass for the sophomore season. He wanted to call my parents, but I promised him that I would straighten up. Then Coach personally made sure I attended my physical therapy sessions and got me a tutor for the classes I was failing."

"He sounds like a great guy, Andy."

I nodded, but knew he'd be singing a different tune in a minute. "Coach became more than someone who blew a whistle during drills and yelled at me. He became the only person on the planet who knew I struggled and still cared about me. He was my friend. He also became my lover."

Wait for it...

"That fucker," Milo hissed. "He preyed on your loneliness and sadness. You might've been an adult, but that doesn't mean he didn't take advantage of you."

"I know that you and I are not going to agree on Coach's roll in my life, but will you please listen to the rest of the story before you judge him too harshly? He didn't just jump me one day in his office. It was something that gradually developed between us over time."

"How old was he, Andy?"

"What difference does that make?" I asked. "I was a consenting adult."

"He was a person who abused his position of power. As your coach, he held your future in his hands along with your dick. I don't care how old you were, it was wrong. But, I want to know just how creepy this fucker was."

"He was thirty-two."

"You're thirty-two. Tell me, would you enter a sexual relationship with an eighteen-year-old? You know what? It's not even so much about the age to me, Andy. He took advantage of you during a vulnerable time and that really makes me angry."

"Is that part of you listening without judgment?"

Milo bit into his trembling bottom lip. I could tell he was trying to pull himself together. "Baby, I'm not judging you. *He* should've known better. I get that you're sexy as fuck, but he broke the bonds of trust, Andy. This isn't porn where it's hot when the professor and college student get it on. You would face real-life consequences if word got out, and I assumed that's what happened."

I nodded. "We got caught by a teammate who reported it to the athletic director and the dean. Obviously, Coach was fired—"

"As he should've been," Milo interrupted. "They didn't try to expel you, did they?"

"At first, they tried to talk me into leaving the school. They said it was best for me since the rumors had circulated. My parents didn't agree and hired a lawyer."

Milo whistled. "They weren't prepared for Mama Mason, were they?"

I snorted. "Not at all. In hindsight, leaving would've been better for me. No one had the balls to say anything to my face, but they didn't hesitate to leave hateful messages outside my dorm or locker. My roommate insisted on reassignment because I was a pervert who couldn't be trusted. It was my first real run-in with homophobia, and the one person I came to count on was gone."

"Coach abandoned you completely?"

"It was part of the agreement between the attorneys, the school, and me. I was to have no further contact with him. Depression hit me with the strength of a tsunami, Milo. I'd somehow managed to keep my pain pill addiction hidden from Coach while—"

Milo snorted. "Somehow? Honey, it was easy for him to overlook it when he was so focused on fucking up your life and his career. Then abandoned you when things got tough for *him*."

"Milo, you're not being fair to him."

"Let's just agree to disagree about precious Coach," Milo said. "We'll move on, and I'll spend the rest of my life undoing all his mind-fuckery."

I loved that Milo had pretty much agreed to spend the rest of his life with me, but I had barely scraped the surface of my relationship with Coach.

"There's more to the story, isn't there?" he asked hesitantly. I nodded. "Lay it on me, Slugger. I can take it."

"Pain pills and alcohol aren't a great mix. I passed out in a diner about thirty minutes from school. I don't even remember how I got there, Milo. I was fucked up. I don't know why the waitress didn't call the cops, but she called the last number I had dialed on my cell phone instead."

"Coach?"

I nodded. "I apparently called and texted him when I got high. He avoided me. I don't know what finally made him answer my call, but he did. Then he took me back to his house and let me sober up. The next morning, he drove me to an NA meeting and that began my long journey back to sobriety."

"It didn't happen overnight, huh?"

"Not even close," I admitted. "The first thing I did was leave my toxic environment. My parents weren't too excited when I dropped out of college and moved into Coach's guest room. God, Milo, they were so fucking pissed when they first found out about the affair.

They rallied around me when the school tried to fuck me over, but I had disappointed them so much. Our relationship was strained afterward, and it only added to my isolation. They eventually came around when they realized my relationship with Coach was purely platonic by that point. Coach remained my good friend and helped me through the darkest time of my life. He gave me a roof over my head, helped me get clean and stay that way, and he got me a job with his brother who owned a construction company."

"Let's erect a statue to honor his sainthood," Milo said sarcastically.

"Okay, I can see that you're still not a fan."

"Nope, and that's not likely to change. So, moving on," Milo prompted. "Did you stay away for so long because you were ashamed, Andy?"

"Yes," I admitted. "I put so much pressure on myself when I left town to make something big of myself. I was so sure that I was heading to the majors, and the little kids in this town would collect my baseball cards and ask me to sign them when I came home for a visit. There might even be a parade in my honor. And you," I said, lightly poking his chest. "I couldn't wait to make you sorry you broke up with me. I was going to drive into town in my sports car and act like I didn't recognize you."

Milo snickered. "This sounds like a really cheesy rom com, Andy. You couldn't come up with better musings while stoned?"

"It wasn't all that it's cracked up to be," I replied, shrugging my shoulders. "Some people write Pulitzer award-winning novels or songs to change a generation, but not me. I imagined revenge fucks."

"Oh, I see how it is," Milo said, grinning from ear to ear. "Fantasy Milo came up with sexy ways to make you remember him."

"Yes, indeed."

"So, now we've ventured into porn," Milo teased. "Was there cheesy music? Did I show up at your door looking for a cup of sugar?"

"Something like that. Anyway, all I ended up making of myself was a big mess. I disappointed my family, and it hurt to see that in their eyes, so I avoided it by not coming home."

"They might've been upset about the choices that you made, but they would never stop loving you, Andy. They—we—missed you so much." Then, as if to lighten the somber mood, he said, "I'm going to need a demonstration later of what happened when Porn Star Milo showed up at your door asking for *sugar*. For now, let's hear the story about your recovery. Tell me about your local NA chapter and meetings."

"We meet each week for a few hours, and then get a bite to eat afterward. We talk about something other than our addictions and share some laughs. I've made some great friends, and I'd love to introduce you someday if you're willing."

"Any friend of yours is a friend of mine. Except Coach. He won't be getting a Christmas card from Milo Miracle, I can promise you that."

"Fair enough," I agreed.

"About that food..."

I leaned in for one more grateful kiss before I set up my sandwich shop on the other side of the stove from Milo so that he wouldn't get burned from the steam coming from the small griddle. Milo hummed happily as he watched me put together our sandwiches then brown them to perfection.

"You are the panini king," Milo said after his first bite. "And your mom's ham and bean soup is still the best I've ever had. This is so damn good."

"You want another sandwich?"

"Heck no, but I need to get one of those for my house. I bet you can make all kinds of things on there? French toast, waffles, and sausage and egg sandwiches on an English muffin. Yum."

"Still a foodie, I see."

"I haven't changed that much in fourteen years," he said sheepishly.

"You've changed a lot, Milo. I really like what I see too."

"I haven't shown you anything yet, baby," Milo said suggestively.

Oh, but he had. Milo showed me he could be trusted with my secrets and my heart again. Eating panini and soup in my kitchen while wearing nothing but jeans and goofy grins was the happiest I'd been in fourteen years.

twelve

Milo

A S MUCH AS I WOULD'VE LIKED TO SPEND THE NIGHT AT ANDY'S house, I had responsibilities at home that I couldn't ignore.

"Here, pretty kitty. Daddy's home," I called out when I came through the back door. Andy raised a brow at the cajoling voice I used on my cat. "I'm late and she's pissed. Therefore, she'll make me work for it. I'm hoping not to die in my sleep tonight."

"What about me?" Andy asked then flushed with embarrassment from assuming he was spending the night. As much as I wanted to feel Andy's arms around me all night long, he'd revealed a lot of things to me that I needed to process. I preferred to do that alone.

"We'll know more when she decides to come out of hiding and greet you." I walked further into the living room. "Where's my pretty baby? Come let Daddy pet you."

"My dick thinks you're talking to it," Andy said.

"I'll sweet talk it later," I told Andy then went in search of my feline.

"I like your house, Milo," he said as he followed behind me. "It's cozy and inviting." I'd worked hard picking furniture and a color scheme that would make the house feel stylish and cozy. I sure as hell didn't let Peach pick out the décor. There wasn't a disco ball or sequined pillow in sight, much to her chagrin. I chose neutral, light-gray furniture with plum and black accent pieces.

I flipped on the bedroom light switch and saw that Alli Cat was sleeping in a ball on my bed. She raised one eyelid and there was so much attitude in that oddly colored orange eye that I couldn't stop myself from grinning. That cat was born to be mine.

"What the fuck is that?" Andy asked when he saw her lying on my bed. "That's not a cat, that's a…"

"She's part calico and part Maine coon. Her size comes from the Maine coon heritage, but you can see the calico in her black and orange spots mixed in with the stripes." I approached the bed, but Alli Cat paid no attention to me. She raised her head and met Andy's shocked gaze.

Of course, she loved his attention. Alli Cat slowly stood and stretched her big body dramatically so Andy could see how tall and long she really was.

"Amazing," Andy said in awe. "I've never seen a cat like this. She's bigger than a lot of dogs."

"Sassier than any human to ever live too."

Alli Cat pinned me with a glare, making Andy chuckle.

"I see you've met your match, Milo," he said. Then he lowered his voice and said, "Come here, pretty baby. Let me pet you."

I ran over and threw myself on the foot of the bed where Andy waited for Alli Cat. "I'm here." My cat wasn't having any of that crap. She walked over top of me to get to Andy, swishing her big tail in my face and purring louder than a small engine. "Get your furry ass out of my face."

"Well darn, I was hoping you liked to shove your face in a furry ass," Andy said. I raised my head and saw he was wearing a cute pout as he scratched Alli's ears.

"I need to feed the beast then lock her out of the room. I can't have her stealing all your attention," I told him.

"Oh, I don't think that will be a problem."

I rolled out from under the cat and went into the kitchen. I knew as soon as she heard me open the can she'd abandon Andy and come running. I turned and expected her to be at my feet, but she was nowhere in sight.

"I don't believe this," I said, marching back to the bedroom. "She never misses a meal."

"I think your cat has a crush on me," Andy said proudly. "Let's go eat, pretty baby."

He started walking to the kitchen, leaving Alli Cat and me to follow behind him like little pied pipers. I wanted to be called pretty baby too. Fuck, I could purr and arch against him. I'd already done it twice that night, but I'd go a third time if needed.

"How much do I give her?" he asked, taking the can and spoon out of my hand.

"A little scoop of dry food on the bottom, and then a generous helping of the soft food. She's very spoiled."

"You don't say?" Andy asked, gesturing to where the cat wove in and out of his legs. "I'm glad that I won't have to sleep with one eye open." He again eluded to spending the night, and I had to admit that I was warming up to the idea. The last thing I needed to do was get lost in my own headspace.

Andy handed me the can of food, and I placed a plastic lid over the top and set it in the refrigerator. I expected him to grab my hand and drag me back to the bedroom, but he leaned over to pet the cat.

"She doesn't like to be touched when she's eating," I said. "It must remind her of her days at the shelter."

"She doesn't, huh?" Andy said, rubbing a hand over her long back. Alli Cat arched her back like a slut beneath his touch instead of hissing at him.

"That's a first," I announced.

"I was your first in many ways," Andy said, straightening up to look at me. His pale-blue eyes appeared lighter, almost iridescent, the more aroused he became. "You learned to trust me with your body, Alli Cat trusts that I won't hurt her either."

"Now, I just need to trust you with my heart again." I meant that to sound lighthearted and teasing, but I knew it fell short when Andy flinched. Hurting Andy was the last thing I wanted to do. He'd bled his soul for me, and that was a shitty way to repay him for his trust.

"How do you suppose I do that?" Andy inquired as he walked to me.

"Time and patience," I said just as he placed his hand on my waist and pulled me to him.

"You're not the only one afraid to trust again. I think there's more that you haven't told me about why we broke up. Care to tell me now, Milo?"

"All right, fine. Tit for tat, it's only fair." I blew out a nervous breath because I hated to relive this memory. I only dug it out when I felt myself weakening toward Andy after his return home. This time, I was digging it out to hopefully excise the painful reminder for good. "We've already discussed that you turned into an arrogant asshole after you were offered the scholarship." Andy rolled his eyes. Okay, maybe that wasn't the best lead-in, but I wanted to let him know where my headspace was. "You had explained to me that you couldn't be out to your team, and I really did understand your reasons, even if it hurt really bad. You said we would find a way to make it work, but your actions said otherwise."

"What actions?"

"Well, you deactivated all your social media accounts because you were afraid that someone at your college would see our photos and figure out that I was your boyfriend. That made it impossible for me to feel connected to you every day, and I felt cut out of your life. You didn't just delete your social media presence, you deleted my existence," I explained.

"Yeah, I can see why you felt that way." Andy leaned forward and kissed my forehead. "I promise you that wasn't my intent though."

"Hindsight and all that," I told him. "And—"

"There's more?"

"Isn't there always more with me?" I asked Andy.

"Very true. Please continue."

"Do you remember that meet and greet for the baseball team, their families, and the coaches?"

"Of course," Andy replied. "You rode down with my family. It was the last time I saw you for twelve years. I had hoped to sneak off for some alone time, but we never got the chance."

"I'd found a secluded, vacant spot far enough away from the banquet hall where we could've snuck away to talk," I said, earning a smirk. "I mean it, Andy. I just wanted to be alone in the same room with you. Of course, I would've loved the opportunity to kiss you, but I was willing to just hear your voice and look into your eyes."

"So what happened?" he asked.

"I returned to the gathering and went looking for you," I told him. "And I found you."

Andy's brows furrowed in confusion. "Your tone suggests that you caught me doing something wrong."

"It wasn't so much what you did but what you didn't do."

"You're talking in riddles, Milo."

"You were surrounded by your baseball bros having a conversation about me." I knew Andy remembered it when he briefly closed his eyes. He wanted to know why I sent that text ending our relationship in the back of his parents' car on the way home, and I would tell him. "They were too busy making fun of the fairy that came with your family to notice I was standing nearby."

"God, Milo. I'm sorry."

"Them disliking me because I was obviously gay, wasn't the worst part."

"It wasn't?" Andy asked.

"Not by a long shot." I stepped away from Andy needing space. "One of the knuckle draggers asked who I was, and you told them I was Faith's best friend. Even though it was true, and I knew the score, it hurt that you wouldn't even claim my friendship. That's when I knew we were truly doomed to fail. I could've let it play out, or I could end things with you and find someone who was proud of me."

"I was such a dick," Andy admitted.

"Then Maegan got sick, and my whole world shifted. I didn't have time to wallow in misery over our breakup."

"Then Tucker stepped in to save the day. Now he's a firefighter. Always has to be a hero," Andy said. "Tucker the Heroic Fucker."

I snorted. "Tucker does like to save people, even if it's from themselves. I'm sure he'll find the right guy for him. I'm not it."

"Fuck no, you're not." Andy closed the gap I'd put between us. "Tonight was a great start toward building that trust again. I am *very* sorry for hurting you, and not being a friend when Maegan was diagnosed with cancer. I should've put my pride aside and reached out to you. Time and patience," Andy said, repeating my words back to me.

"That's what it will take for us to fully trust one another again. If that's what we truly want. I mean, now that you scratched your itch—"

Andy captured my lips in a long, hungry kiss. "I'll never get enough of you, Milo."

"Why don't you take off your clothes and stay awhile," I suggested, running my hand beneath his shirt to feel his heart pounding in his chest. So much for wanting time alone to process.

"I really want to stay with you."

"But, and I mean the word with one T."

"I have a lot of paperwork to do that I keep postponing, and I need to get my reports together for Maegan. I promised her that I'd have it ready tomorrow since she's working against a tough deadline."

"You really think Maegan should buy the house?" I asked. "It's not a money pit, is it?"

"I think most of the work on my end is cosmetic, but it really depends on what Mike, Chris, and Simon have to say about the mechanicals. That's going to make or break the deal."

"Did they give you an impression one way or the other?" I asked.

"You sound nervous, Milo. Do you not want Maegan buying the house?"

"It's cloaked in so much mystery," I replied. "The founder of our town disappeared without a trace, and then the most recent owner's son gets murdered in the cellar a few months ago. It just doesn't seem like the kind of place you want to build a family in."

"Maegan is a very intelligent woman. She won't let her love of antiques and stories cloud her judgment."

"I know, but it would just be easier if she found a different historic home that didn't have as much tragedy associated with it."

"When has easy ever been the right way?" Andy teased. "Look how hard you made me work for it." He had a point. "Kiss me. I need to get back home."

I pressed my lips to his, thinking it would be a typical goodbye kiss with maybe a little extra heat. It started out that way but got a lot hotter and lasted longer than I anticipated. Andy tugged my bottom lip with his teeth then soothed the sensitive flesh with his tongue. I sucked his nimble tongue into my mouth like I wanted to do with his cock again. When our tongues met, they slowly and seductively swirled around each other like an erotic dance. I could kiss him for days.

I was shaking from head to toe by the time Andy pulled back. "Well," he said then cleared his throat. "That was a kiss to remember."

"Plenty more where that came from," I assured him.

"Milo, can I take you on a date this weekend?"

"That sounds amazing. I work until two on Saturday, but I'm free the rest of the weekend."

"Perfect," Andy responded then gave me one final quick kiss

before he headed to the door. "Having a lazy Sunday with you in bed is exactly how I want to finish off my work week."

It did sound like heaven.

Andy left after promising to call me the next day. Alli Cat looked pissy that I let him get away. "He'll be back," I tried to assure her.

A few minutes later, there was a knock on the kitchen door. My heart sped up with excitement because it meant he changed his mind about staying over. When I opened the door, I found my sister standing on the porch instead.

"Wow, I've never seen you look so disappointed to see me," Mae said.

"I'm not disappointed to see you, I'm just disappointed that you're not someone else."

"Same damn difference," Mae said sarcastically. "Was that Andy's truck I passed coming down the street?" she asked innocently.

"As if you didn't see the magnetic sign on his truck," I replied, rolling my eyes. "Get in here."

"Well, how can I resist with a greeting like that."

"I'm sorry, Your Highness. Would you like a cup of tea?" I asked using an upper crust British accent.

"Actually, a spot of tea would be lovely." Maegan made herself comfortable in the living room on the chaise lounge chair with Alli Cat rubbing the top of her head against Mae's chin. "So, I heard you had a little bit of excitement tonight."

I blinked at her for several seconds. Had Andy's busybody neighbor started calling all over town after witnessing our kiss in his driveway? At least my shouting during sex didn't bring the cops to Andy's front door.

"Oh my God, Milo. I was talking about the ghost encounter at my house."

"Your house, huh? Andy and the others aren't even done writing up reports yet."

"It's going to happen. Ghost and all." She took a sip of her tea, extending her pinky out like a smart-ass. "Besides, Becker got a verbal report from all of them."

"I bet he got an *oral* report."

"I'm just waiting on Andy. I can tell his delay was for a worthy cause, so I'm not upset."

"I'm a 'worthy cause' now?" I wasn't sure I liked being a pet project.

"Milo, you've either smoked a joint, taken a muscle relaxer, or Andy has fucked you blind. I don't need you to tell me which one, or that you've done all three. I'm not here to judge you."

"I've never smoked a joint, and I don't have a prescription for muscle relaxers so that only leaves one other thing. I'm not ready to talk about what's going on between Andy and me." I loved my sister, and she would be the first person I talked to about Andy, but not right then.

"I didn't come here to talk about Andy either."

"Then why *are* you here?"

"I want you to tell me what you really think of the Bliss House."

The truth was, the place creeped me out, but I knew Maegan better than anyone and understood why it appealed to her. And while I believed it was truly haunted, I didn't feel a malevolent presence earlier that night. It felt more playful than dangerous. It would never be the house *I* wanted, but it was everything that *she* wanted. There was only one answer.

"I think you'll create a beautiful life there, Maegan."

107

thirteen

Andy

"YOU'RE THE MAN, ANDY!" MAEGAN SAID AFTER READING my proposal the next morning. She flung her arms around my neck and hugged me tight. "Thank you! Thank you! Thank you!"

"You know, you're not the first Miracle twin to speak those same words to me."

Maegan snorted and released the stranglehold around my neck. "Which ones? You're the man or thank you?"

"All of them." Milo had told me I was the man on more than one occasion and usually followed that up by showing his gratitude. I couldn't wait to elicit that kind of reaction from him again on our date.

"After looking at all the reports, it's obvious that Bliss House needs work and tender loving care, but it's nothing so significant that it changes my mind."

"Be honest, could we have said anything that would've changed your mind?" I asked Maegan.

"No matter how much I loved that house, I would've rescinded my offer if it was deemed a money pit. The structure and major systems are in great shape, so I don't see what there is to lose. Do you?"

"You know that house is most likely haunted, right?"

"Of course. It's part of the intrigue to me."

"You're really okay with that? What if the ghost stands over top of you and watches you sleep."

"Oh my God!" Milo exclaimed as he entered Maegan's office. "I never thought about that." He grinned from ear to ear. "He's going to watch you and Elijah getting it on. He'll knock once if Elijah is doing it right; twice if he needs to work on his technique."

Maegan rolled her eyes. "Knock it off, you guys." She glared at her brother before looking back at me. "I don't see anything in these reports that will prevent the bank from lending me money to buy this house. I'm going to proceed. I know you have a lot going on, Andy, so I won't pressure you to give me a date when you can start working on Bliss House."

"Right now, your apartment project and Bliss House are my only projects. I recently sold a house I bought to fix and flip. I haven't purchased another one yet, so I have time," I told her.

"Wow, you sure like to stay busy," Maegan said.

"It helps me work through my frustrations over a certain someone." I reached out and snagged that certain someone's wrist and pulled him toward me just in case it wasn't clear who I was referring to.

"Milo, do you mind if I go see my loan officer really quick?"

"Nope," he replied. "I can hold down the fort over here because the staff has everything under control at Books and Brew."

"Thank you!" This time she threw her arms around her brother's neck and hugged him. "You guys don't make a mess in here while I'm gone," she tossed over her shoulder.

"Screw that," Milo said, shutting and locking the door. "We're totally making a mess in here."

I thought he meant he was going to shuffle papers on her already messy desk, but he dropped to his knees and unbuckled my belt.

"What are you doing?" I asked as blood rushed to my cock.

"I'm not checking you for ticks, Andy," Milo replied as he went to work on my button fly. "I dreamed about your cock in my mouth and woke up hornier than hell."

"Did you jerk off?"

"No, I decided to save it so I could seduce you at lunchtime. I don't see why I have to wait a few more hours, when I can blow you right now."

I should've kept a cooler head, but it was nearly impossible to think when Milo sucked my glans into his mouth. All thoughts of shutting this down faded, and I pushed deeper inside his mouth. Milo relaxed his jaw and let me fuck his face. In fact, he dug his fingers in my hips and encouraged me to thrust deeper and harder. Once he was happy with my rhythm, he reached between my legs to massage my balls. The thrill of the location and the joy that it was Milo on his knees servicing my cock had me ready to come.

"I'm going to come," I warned, but he didn't pull back. Instead, he buried my cock deep enough in his throat that his nose touched my trimmed pubic hair at the base of my cock. I came on a silent yell. Milo's throat massaging my cock was the most erotic thing I'd ever experienced.

I looked at him in shock when my wet dick slid from his mouth and slapped the front of my jeans. I was so caught up in his cock-sucking skills that I didn't realize Milo had pulled his dick out and jerked off while blowing me until I saw his jizz splattered on the tile floor.

"Grab those tissues for me," Milo instructed. I did as he requested then tucked my cock away while he cleaned up his spunk off the floor and did the same. After he discarded the tissues, I pulled him to me for a long kiss, not caring that his mouth would taste like my cum.

"It doesn't matter to me which Miracle project I work on. It's fine with me if you guys want me to work on the apartments until Maegan's closing goes through then switch to her house."

"The apartments were just Maegan and Mom's way of getting me closer to you. They figured you couldn't resist me if I was near you all day, every day. I guess they just figured I would run upstairs for a quickie during a lull in business."

"Is that a possibility?" I asked. "If so, I need to add condoms and lube to my toolbox."

"I'm really looking forward to our date this weekend, Andy," Milo said, sounding nervous. Did he think I'd changed my mind after the heat of the moment between us passed? I had a newsflash for him. My passions for Milo had intensified, not dwindled.

"I'm looking forward to it too." I smiled down at him, wishing I could stop time and just soak this in. Neither of us had made any kind of serious declaration of feelings, but it felt like we were on solid footing for the first time in fourteen frigging years.

"There's that look again," Milo said softly.

"What look?" I asked.

"The one that shows how much you missed me. I got so angry the first time I saw it."

"When?"

"Your first day back in town," Milo explained. "Some sixth sense told me to look up when you came through the door. You looked hesitant and unsure until our eyes met. Then you looked like you'd found yourself."

"I didn't realize how much I missed you until then. It was a real eye-opening experience, especially when you were so hostile."

"I was more angry with my reaction to you than I was about your happiness to see me," Milo confessed.

"You did eye-fuck me right there in the coffee shop."

"I did no such thing, I—"

"Um, Milo," Maegan said through the door. "I'm back."

"You weren't gone very long," Milo replied, looking around to make sure there was no evidence left on the ground.

"The bank is only at the end of the block. I just signed some application papers and provided the bank with Andy's inspection report. I'm sure they'll hire someone else to complete an independent inspection due to my relationship with Andy."

"You're not sleeping with him. I am," Milo said. He looked back at me and asked, "Right?"

"She did ask me over for a threesome the other night," I confessed to Milo. "I shot her down though."

Maegan burst into laughter. "I did not, lying asshole."

"My sister isn't that kind of girl, Randy Andy."

We both expected Maegan to agree with Milo, but it was quiet enough to hear a pin drop on the other side of the closed door.

"Maegan?" Milo asked.

"You only live once, Milo," his sister replied sassily.

That got his attention, and he hurriedly unlocked the door and yanked it open. "OMG! Are you teasing right now?" he demanded to know. "With who? I don't want to hear any detail about your sisterly parts, but tell me about the dudes."

"Standing right here," I said, sounding disgruntled as fuck.

"You assume it involved two men, huh?" Maegan said, breezing by him. "Tsk tsk, Milo. I'd expect you to be a little more open-minded than that."

Both our mouths dropped open. Milo closely scrutinized his sister to look for any hint that she was lying while I did my best to block my mind from imagining anything at all. I stuck my fingers in my ears and mentally sang *lalalalalalalala* to keep from hearing anything else or conjuring up images.

I was saved when my phone rang. I'd never been so happy to see my mom's name pop up on the screen, although that wouldn't have been the case if she'd called when Milo was on his knees sucking my cock.

112

"I need to take this call," I told Milo and Maegan, stepping out into the store and closing the door behind me. The last thing I needed was my mom to overhear them talking about threesomes. She'd think I was taking on both Miracle twins at the same time. "Hey, Mom," I said with forced cheer.

"Oh, am I interrupting sex?"

"What? No! It's nine thirty in the morning."

"What's your point?" she asked, sounding so confused. "I don't get it. Do you have a medical condition and can't *perform* until later in the day or something? Your dad has some extra blue pills that I—"

"No! Mom, geez. I don't need Viagra for crying out loud. I can get it up just fine." Why couldn't I have a normal mother who wasn't so concerned about my sexual health? "I'm not having sex because I'm on a job site." I said it too loud and the few customers in Maegan's shop looked at me with gaping mouths and bulging eyes.

"Milo's a tough taskmaster, huh?" she teased. I knew by her tone of voice that she'd heard about the kiss in the driveway and the length of time we spent alone in my house. She'd probably heard that I drove Milo home and hung out for a while there also. I wouldn't be surprised if one of Mom's spies was standing on the other side of the door with her brother. "Listen, I'd like you to bring Milo to dinner tonight."

"Well, I can ask if he's available."

"Oh, he is. Faith already texted him this morning to find out what he had going on. He told her nothing that he knew of, which is sad considering that you guys finally patched things up."

"Mom, we didn't patch things up. Well, we sort of did."

"Andy, quit half-assing things when it comes to Milo, and go full ass... Wait, that sounds so wrong."

I was laughing so hard I didn't hear what she said after that. "Oh my God, Mom! You kill me."

"I'm so happy that you're amused at my expense, Andrew."

"I'm sorry, Mom, but it sounded like you were giving me sex

tips. I was waiting for you to tell me to go full throttle or balls deep."

"Andrew, let's not get vulgar."

"I'm sorry again, Mom."

"You can make it up to me by bringing Milo to dinner," she said sweetly. "I'm making barbecue ribs, mashed potatoes, and roasted asparagus."

"Those are my favorites," I told her, trying not to drool. "It's not my birthday."

"Andy, I'm your mother. I'm fully aware of the date I gave birth to my firstborn child." She let out a little impatient huff then continued. "I expect to see Milo Miracle-Mason at my dinner table tonight. Don't let me down."

"Whoa," I said. Her assumptions stole my breath and made my heart race but in a good way.

"You heard me," she said. "You know I don't take no for an answer. I've been patient while you two pussyfooted around. Enough is enough. It's time to make your move."

"Yes, ma'am."

"Six thirty," she told me before she hung up. Not a goodbye or have a nice day. She just told me the time we were eating dinner and *click*.

"Excuse me," a lady said softly. "There's no price tag on this vase, and I'd really like to buy it for my sister's birthday. Can you tell me how much it costs?"

"Um, I don't work here. Hang on a sec." I knocked briefly on Maegan's office door before I opened it. I didn't give the brother and sister enough warning though, because Maegan still had Milo in a headlock. "Mae, there's a lady out here who wants to buy a vase but there's no price tag on it."

"Oh!" Maegan said, releasing Milo fast enough that he stumbled and would've fallen over if he didn't grab the edge of the desk.

"You're lucky I held back because you're a lady," Milo called out after his sister when she walked away with her customer.

Maegan flipped her brother off behind her back.

"What the hell happened in here? One minute she's teasing you about a threesome, and the next thing I know, she's kicking your ass."

Milo scoffed. "She wasn't kicking my ass. I was letting her win."

"Okay, we'll go with that. Why was it necessary for you to let her win, Milo?"

"I got even with her for teasing me about the threesome by recommending that she get an area rug for her office since the tile was hell on knees."

My face turned bright red.

"I tried to play it off like I was joking, but I'm not as good at hiding my emotions as she is." That was definitely true.

"Well, at least she'll have something juicy to report back to my mother," I offered. "Oh, by the way, you're coming with me to dinner tonight at my parents' house."

"Excuse me?" he asked huffily. "What happened to asking me?"

"Look, my mother demanded that I bring you, so I'll hogtie you and carry you in there if I have to."

"No, you won't," Milo scoffed. He was right. I had other ways to persuade him to do the things I wanted.

"She's making that chocolate silk pie you love so much for dessert."

"In that case," Milo said. "What time are you picking me up?"

"Mom said we're eating at six thirty, so—"

"We need to be there by six then," Milo said. I smiled because he remembered.

"Yep. I'll pick you up at five fifty."

"Deal." Milo stood on his tiptoes and gave me a quick kiss. "See you tonight. I need to get back to work before Maegan kicks my ass again."

"Ha! You admit it."

"She's mean as a snake," Milo said dramatically. Then he blew me a kiss and walked away.

I took my phone out of my pocket to text my mom. *He said okay, but only after I promised him one of your chocolate silk pies. Oopsy.*

Atta boy, Andy, she fired back to me.

I chuckled to myself as I went upstairs to get to work. Knowing I would get to spend time with Milo and my family put me in a good mood and made the day go by faster. I wanted to call the whole thing off when I picked up Milo at his house because he looked so handsome in his navy-blue pin-striped dress shirt and dark, denim jeans. In addition to looking good enough to eat, he appeared nervous.

"You wouldn't be so nervous if you knew the lengths my mother went to get you to dinner."

"Does that mean you'd rather I not go?" he asked then worried his full bottom lip between his teeth.

"It means I wish we were both staying home *alone*, but maybe we can duck out early and watch a movie or something."

"Maybe. We'll see how well you behave tonight," Milo teased.

When we arrived at my parents' house, both Milo and I moaned.

"What the hell?" I asked, pointing to the extra vehicles in the driveway. "Both sets of grandparents are here too?"

"What's going on?" Milo asked. "Are they upset with me? Is this an intervention to talk some sense into you?"

"Hardly." I snorted. "My mother called you Milo Miracle-Mason today. I don't think she's trying to scare you off. I think she's going in the opposite direction, and she's brought in the big guns to help her."

"I'm a sucker for your grandparents," Milo said, smiling.

"They still ask me about you every time I see them or talk to them on the phone," I told him. "It's going to be okay. We better get inside before Mom sees the time. I don't want to go last in the food line."

"Always focused on your stomach," Milo teased.

"I can think of an organ that's a lot more demanding at times."

I escorted Milo into my parents' house and smiled as he was hugged and greeted warmly. I was expecting the same greeting, but

Faith grabbed me by the ear and dragged me down the hallway before I could say hello.

"Listen, Andy. Don't fuck this up."

"What happened to Switzerland?" I asked.

"You're my brother, and I love you dearly, but I can't help that we're family. Milo is my chosen family, Andy. If you hurt him again, there will be no place you can hide from him, and our familial DNA won't save your ass from me. Are we clear?"

"Crystal."

I stayed in the hallway grinning like a loon after she left. I truly felt at home for the first time since I returned.

fourteen

Milo

AT FIRST, I WAS NERVOUS AFTER SEEING THAT NEARLY ALL OF Andy's family was present for dinner. Were his aunts, uncles, and cousins on the way over too? But then Andy told me that his mom had tacked his last name onto mine, and I got nervous for a totally different reason.

Andy and I were nowhere close to taking a big step like that. Did I hope that it would happen? I'd been dreaming of the day for as long as I could remember. For the better part of my life, I didn't allow myself to believe it would happen though. Same sex marriages weren't performed or recognized in Ohio until the Supreme Court ruling in 2015 stated that same-sex marriage bans were unconstitutional. I celebrated and cried with my family that day, but there was still a part of me that remained a little sad. The man I had dreamed of sharing a future with had disappeared from my life, so the victory was bittersweet. Little did I know at the time, but his return was right around the corner.

Still, hearing that Andy's family approved of us reconnecting made me feel so much better. Andy's parents, Wendy and Andy Sr., and their parents, Janice, Norm, Dave, and Doris, all smiled happily when we walked through the door. It was like no time had elapsed when I greeted and hugged his parents and grandparents while Faith dragged Andy down the hall for a private chat. I saw the determination in her eyes and knew her decision to be Switzerland was over. It warmed my heart that they truly were happy to see the two of us together.

I thought I had remembered every little detail about Andy Mason, but it seemed that a few things had slipped my mind, such as his love of barbecue ribs. I'm not just talking about a mild passion, I mean he tied a little plastic bib around his neck like you sometimes get in restaurants and went to town. He didn't lick his fingers or act in a disgusting fashion, but he mowed through his plate like he was in a contest. Wendy Mason's ribs were delicious, but they couldn't hold a candle to mine. I decided to bide my time to reveal that particular skillset to Andy.

I ate my dinner at a more leisurely pace and enjoyed a conversation with his family while Andy grunted his responses. Truth be told, his food grunt was very similar to his I'm-gonna-fill-you-up grunt, and my dick started to get ideas.

"Are you still performing, Milo?" Janice asked me. Her big brown eyes looked huge inside her horn-rimmed glasses.

That pulled Andy's attention from his dinner. "Huh?" he asked around a mouthful of food.

"Um, no." Fuck! I didn't expect this to come up over dinner and was ill-prepared.

"That's too bad," her husband, Norm, said. "You were something else, kid."

"Thank you, sir. It was something fun to do while I was in college, but I don't have much time for it now."

"You should make time," Doris added. "You could be on that one show? What's that called, Janice?"

"*America's Got Talent*?" Janice asked.

"Not that one," Doris replied. "The one where there's singing and dancing."

"There *is* singing and dancing on *America's Got Talent*," Doris countered. "Do you mean *American Idol*? They don't really dance on that show, do they?"

"Not that one either. It's on a cable network. I just can't remember the name of it."

"What's this all about?" Andy asked me after wiping his face with a napkin. "Why are you blushing like that?"

"It was nothing, really," I said, trying to discourage his interest. "Just a little something to pass the time and keep me from missing you." Andy rolled his eyes because he thought I was trying to distract him. He wasn't completely wrong.

"The host's name starts with an R," Janice said. "Big tall fella."

Andy's eyes widened and his mouth dropped open when he realized where the conversation was heading.

"Close your mouth, Andy. You have hunks of pork stuck in your teeth," I told him.

Andy covered his mouth with his napkin. "Do not," he mumbled behind the cloth. That's right, Wendy brought out the good napkins, dinnerware, and cutlery that she only used for special occasions like Thanksgiving, Christmas, Easter, and now my return to the fold. I preened just a little bit more but only on the inside, and only for a second, because I needed to avoid a potential disaster.

"I've never seen anyone do a better Marilyn Monroe impersonation than Milo," Dave said proudly.

"Of course, that's the routine you remember," Doris said to her husband. "You still have a thing for her."

"Hey, she was a beautiful woman," Dave countered. "I wouldn't have traded you for her though." Dave leaned over and kissed Doris's cheek.

"Oh, you," Doris said, blushing prettily.

"You might want to take lessons from Grandpa Dave," I said, leaning into Andy. "He's a smooth operator."

"Marilyn Monroe, huh?" Andy asked, smiling from ear to ear.

"Among others," I said proudly.

"I never knew you wanted to do drag," Andy said. He lifted his thumb and wiped something off the corner of my mouth. He held it up to show me a smear of barbecue sauce before he licked it clean. I could only blink at him because my blood was moving south in a hurry. "Milo?"

"Oh, um… It was something that just happened. I had fun doing it while in college, but I got so busy with work that I just kind of lost touch with my friends in the business."

"Who was your drag mother again?" Doris asked. "She was a real hoot."

"Dame Alotta Bang Bang was my drag mother," I answered. "Lady Bea Trix was my drag grandmother. Both of them are retired, but we meet for lunch about once a month."

"What was your drag name, Milo?" Andy whispered in my ear. "Lady Likes Cocksalot?"

"I'm not ready to reveal that to you yet," I replied haughtily. "And none of you will either," I said dramatically pointing my fork at each person gathered around the table. "I'll share that information when I'm good and ready."

"Oh, I bet it was Good-N-Ready."

I leaned forward so that only he could hear me. "Why do you think I had slutty drag names? I was a classy lady, Andy."

He had the nerve to snort.

"Keep it up, Slugger."

"Awwww," Wendy said from the foot of the table. "It's been so long since I heard that cute little nickname."

Andy reached for my hand beneath the table and gave it a firm squeeze before he resumed eating like it could be his last meal.

121

After we finished dinner and cleared the table, I expected everyone to start returning to their homes since it was a work night, but everyone seemed reluctant to leave. I sat close to Andy on the couch while we continued to chat about our lives and get caught up. Andy kept drawing lazy circles on the base of my neck, making me acutely aware of his presence. It was hard to focus on the conversation with him touching me, but I somehow managed.

When it was time to say goodbye, I soaked up all the love and well wishes before following Andy to his truck. He was quiet on the short drive to my house, but I didn't have to wonder where his mind was because I could see the goofy grin on his face in the light from the dashboard.

"Well, thanks for a lovely evening," I said once his truck came to a stop in my driveway.

"Whoa, where are you going so fast?" Andy asked when I reached for the door handle.

"It's getting late and I have to be at Books and Brew at five thirty in the morning," I told Andy.

"Can't I even get a goodnight kiss?"

I released a long, soft sigh because I knew damn well what the goodnight kiss would lead to. I didn't want to go to bed without kissing Andy, but I also knew that he'd end up in my bed for the night if I leaned across that console and pressed my lips to his. Why did I suddenly feel so shy about that?

Andy chuckled and shut off the truck when he saw that he was going to win the battle.

"You're getting awfully brazen, Andy," I said, leading the way up to the door. I tried to sound huffy, but all I heard was horny. Damn him and my pitiful self-control.

We barely had the door closed before he was on me. I knocked my glass tray off the table in my entryway when I tried to drop my keys on it. It shattered, pulling my attention briefly away from the hunk of man trying to peel me out of my clothes.

"Sorry," Andy said.

"No, you're not."

"Okay, I'm not. I'll buy you a new one," Andy offered as he maneuvered me toward the couch.

Meow! Alli Cat heard her new favorite human's voice and came running. I truly loved my cat, but I didn't need her interrupting sexy time. I grabbed Andy's hand and quickly led him to my room. "Hurry before she follows. The last thing I want to do is fight her off while I'm trying to ride your cock."

"This night just gets better and better," Andy said huskily. "First, I get barbecue ribs, and now, I get you."

We stripped out of our clothes fast and met in the center of the bed. I wanted to push Andy to his back and ride him like I said, but he seemed content to kiss me slowly while his hands roamed over my body, making me whimper with want and need.

"There's no need to hurry," he whispered against my lips, as he lazily stroked my cock.

I couldn't help but compare myself to Alli Cat when I first brought her home. She devoured her food so fast that she made herself sick, but she'd learned that eating fast meant survival. How much longer would I have Andy in bed? Would he get bored with living back in small town USA and leave again. Just the thought was enough to have tears burning in the back of my eyes. I wanted to feast on him while I still had the chance.

"I'm not going anywhere, Milo," Andy whispered. He must've sensed that my desperation was stemming from some place other than physical need. "I know it will take time for you to trust me again, but these past two years have taught me that I have limitless patience when it comes to you."

"Why does that feel more like a dig than a compliment?" I asked.

"It's probably a little bit of both," Andy said after careful consideration. "There's nothing wrong with making me work to earn your trust."

"But with one T…"

"But, it might've been a little extreme. On both of our parts," Andy added when I started to argue. "Let's face it, we were both idiots."

A light laugh bubbled up from my chest. "We at least gave the town something to talk about while we sorted this out."

"Let's change the narrative a bit, shall we?" The heat in Andy's eyes made them practically glow. Playtime was over, kids.

There was a notable difference between us in the way we moved, touched, and kissed compared to the other times we were together after he came back. The first two times were hot, angry fucks in a dark alley and the back of his truck. The encounters rocked my world but left me feeling empty afterwards. The previous night, after the run-in with the ghost, was more personal and tender, but still lacked something. Trust, maybe? Not that I worried Andy would physically hurt me in any way. I didn't trust that his feelings for me were more than sexual because he wouldn't confide in me. Trust was a two-way street, and it seemed like we were finally driving in the same direction.

Andy took his time stretching me, kissing my closed eyelids and the tip of my nose before capturing my lips in a long kiss that made my toes curl. Even when I was good and ready for his cock, he didn't stop. He kept alternating between teasing circles around the crinkled rim and gentle strokes deep inside that made my eyes roll back inside my head.

"I forgot how much I love having my ass fingered," I confessed.

"I didn't."

"I think I forgot how much I love your cock inside me too. Better remind me," I teased.

Andy rolled to his back, and I got my turn at ramping up his desire when I straddled his thick thighs and took my time massaging his balls and stroking his dick. I loved the way Andy's body shook beneath mine before I rolled the condom on and lubed him up for the main event.

Performing as a drag queen taught me many valuable lessons, and I used them on Andy that night. I was confident when I positioned Andy's dick at my eager entrance, I mastered him like I did the stage when I sank down on his length, and I moved my hips gracefully and seductively as I drove us both to the brink of pleasure then shoved us over the edge.

Andy was there to catch me when I fell, wrapping his arms around me and holding me safely against his chest. I forgot sex could be like this—a meeting of something spiritual rather than a random exchange of body fluids.

"Do you want me to go home?" Andy whispered in my ear as I started to drift to sleep.

"Hell no." I lifted my head up and looked into his drowsy eyes. "Do you want to go home?"

"Hell no." Andy lifted his head and kissed my lips really quick. "I need to clean up though. Someone made a mess all over my chest and stomach."

"Which I'm wearing too after lying in it these past few minutes."

"Hey, at least we won't have to argue about who's sleeping in the wet spot."

I stiffened against him, because that wasn't an argument I'd had with Andy since we'd never spent the night together. "True," I said, hoping I sounded calmer than I felt. I tried to shake off my jealousy, but I felt it growing stronger instead.

Andy's eyes registered regret when he saw my reaction, but I didn't want my pettiness to ruin our night. I gingerly eased myself off his still semi-erect penis and smiled as brightly as I could. "Shower with me?"

It was another first, running soapy hands all over his gorgeous body and having him do the same for me. Our kisses were steamier than the hot water, and we realized we weren't quite as tired as we first thought.

Once we finally tumbled into bed, Andy spooned up behind my

body. Instead of worrying how many other guys he'd shared after-sex cuddles with, I focused on how warm and content I felt. "I could get use to this," I whispered in the dark.

"Mmmmhmmm," Andy said drowsily.

I slept harder that night than I could ever recall in my life, and I knew it was mostly because of the human furnace pressed up against me. It wasn't just because of the amazing orgasms either, it was a sense of rightness and belonging.

I woke before Andy since I had to be up at four thirty. I wasn't sure if I should wake him up or let him sleep. It wasn't like he had to show up at our job site by a certain time, so I let him sleep. I took a quick shower to wake up, and then hoped for the best when I got dressed in the dark. I loved my job, but leaving Andy naked and alone in my bed was the hardest thing I'd ever done.

Maegan arrived about an hour after I did. She stopped in her tracks and did a double take when she spotted me pulling a huge tray of muffins from the oven.

"What?" I asked. Could she see a difference in me after one sappy night?

"Did you get dressed in a hurry or in the dark?" she asked, pointing to my feet.

I looked down and saw that I'd put on a black and gray sneaker on my right foot and a silver and navy sneaker on my left. I looked up at Maegan and smiled. "Both."

I was prepared to wear them the rest of the day rather than wake Andy up to ask him to bring the other two shoes. Luckily for me, Andy saw the mix-matched pair of shoes by the dresser, guessed what I'd done, and brought both shoes with him so I could change.

"Thank you," I said appreciatively.

"I was going to run them by sooner then go home and get ready for the day, but someone's cat was pissed about getting locked out of the bedroom and took her revenge on my work boots."

"Oh no," I said. "Let me replace them for you."

"Don't worry about it," Andy said good-naturedly. "It was a really old pair." He looked over at my tray of goodies. "Can I get a muffin and tea to go?"

"Sleeping with the owner has its benefits," I teased, snagging three muffins for Andy to take with him.

"Least of which is the muffins and tea," Andy said. "I want to see you again tonight, Milo."

"I'd like that too."

"We'll sort out our plans later," Andy replied. "I need to get a jumpstart on my day so I can finish earlier." Before he left, Andy placed a lingering kiss on my forehead that turned into a longer French kiss.

"That's the good morning kiss I wanted to share with you this morning in bed," Andy told me. "I missed you."

"I'm sorry. I didn't want to wake you up when you were sleeping so soundly."

"Wake me up next time." Andy dropped another quick kiss and disappeared upstairs.

As I was changing into shoes that matched, I heard Maegan hiss and curse out the espresso machine. It was about damn time that evil bastard took its vengeance out on someone other than me. Oh, it was shaping up to be a fabulous fucking day.

fifteen

Andy

THE REST OF THE WEEK PASSED ALONG IN REMARKABLE BLISS. Milo and I weren't frustrated or fighting, but we sure were doing a lot of fucking. It seemed like we were trying to make up for lost time, and perhaps we were. I wanted to leave my mark on him, and he seemed just as eager to do the same to me.

When I first asked Milo out on a date, I didn't anticipate spending every single night in his bed leading up to it. I had to admit, it felt kind of ass backwards to be screwing before our official date. It wasn't like I wanted him to have some lame-ass, three-date rule when it came to me, but I didn't want him to think I only cared about sex. I even said as much to Milo. I expected brownie points for being sensitive. In typical Milo fashion, he gave me the exact opposite.

"Andy, are you still allergic to peanuts? Do you still break out in hives when country music starts to play? Are you still a switch hitter? At the plate," he clarified when I raised a brow.

"Yes, but—"

"Well, I still hate green peppers and onions, I still love to sing 'Does He Love You' at the top of my lungs." He paused and looked at me seriously. "Just so you know, I'm Reba, the heartbroken wife, and Faith is still Linda, the cheating whore."

"Is that the video where Reba blows up the husband and his mistress on the boat at the end of the video?" I asked.

"Hey, I said I was heartbroken. I never said anything about being a saint." Milo mumbled something that sounded an awful lot like "they had it coming," but I couldn't be sure. "Anyway, we still know many things about each other. I still adore your family, and they feel the same about me. You still love my family, and they think you hung the moon. I see nothing wrong with what we're doing. Are you unsatisfied?"

"What exactly *are we* doing, Milo?" I wanted him to say the words. I needed to know he thought of me as his boyfriend, and that we were in a relationship. I needed him to throw me a bone.

"How about you tell me what this is all about, Andy?" Milo crawled onto my lap, pressing his dick against mine, slowly grinding his hips and making me forget what I was saying. The only thing I could focus on was the sensuous way Milo moved. He removed his shirt and tossed it on the floor behind him.

I loved running my hands all over his smooth, toned chest while he arched his back and purred like a kitten. My shirt came off next, then our shorts and briefs. Milo slid the condom on my erection then coated it with lube before he lined it up to his honey hole and sank down onto my cock.

"Fuck me," I yelled when Milo demonstrated how fucking flexible he was by bracing his hands on my knees and arching his back.

He *overrode* my concerns about us not spending enough time doing something besides sex. He overrode it so damn good that it was another hour before I remembered what I was trying to say when he distracted me with his smoking hot and oh-so-limber body.

"Milo, I just don't want you to get the impression that I'm here because sex with you is convenient."

He looked up from the bowl of ice cream he was eating. Even the way he licked his spoon made me want to shove him down and crawl on top of him. "Andy, no one would ever accuse me of being convenient." Milo snorted then went back to deep-throating his spoon.

"I'm being serious, Milo," I said in mild annoyance.

The way he dropped his spoon inside his bowl and set it on the coffee table with a *clunk* was as dramatic as the sigh he released from his lips. "Why are you making this out to be a big deal? We didn't just meet, we've known each other since we were kids. Sure, both of us have changed somewhat, but we're still the people we used to be. I'm just more flexible and you have bigger muscles."

"I'm an addict, and you're a retired drag queen," I added. "Don't forget those important details."

"Andy, your strength of character only makes you that much more appealing to me." He leaned over and kissed me softly when he saw that I wasn't buying it. "It takes a lot of courage to battle those demons, Andy. A lot of people either don't try or don't care. You cared enough about yourself and your family to want a better life. No one gets to look down their noses at you. Ever."

"What about your secret drag queen life?" I asked.

"Oh my! That would make an excellent reality television show," Milo said excitedly. "Blissville has come a long way in acceptance since we were younger. I rarely hear any comments about my 'sinful sexuality' any longer, but I'm not sure they'd be as accepting of Ma—" He stopped talking just as he was about to reveal his drag name to me. I was dying to know and see the performances.

I'd only been to a show once with Oliver and a few other guys from my support group. We were the only ones drinking soda instead of beer, but we had an amazing time. Ollie especially liked the happy birthday dance he got from that sexy queen. What was her name? Peaches-N-Cream? Split My Peach? I couldn't remember her name, but that ass…

130

I wanted Milo to feel comfortable enough with me to talk about his queen days. Maybe that's why I worried we were having too much sex. *Said no dude ever.* Yeah, it was the way he avoided talking about his performances that made me edgy.

"Fair enough, but why won't you talk to me about it?"

"It's not who I am anymore," Milo said with a well-practiced, casual shrug.

"Okay, will you at least tell me how you got started?"

"I did it to entertain Maegan while she was at the hospital. It was accidental at first. Mom, Dad, and I put on a show and modeled wigs for her when she lost her hair." A sad smile formed on his handsome face, and I could tell the memories were bittersweet.

"Hey," I said softly, wrapping my arms around him and pulling him tight against my chest. "I didn't mean to bring up such painful memories."

"No, it's a fair question for you to have, Andy." Milo seemed to shake off his sadness and kissed my cheek. "Maegan giggled so hard when I strolled into her room with a long, flowing wig. It was the first time I heard her laugh in weeks, and I vowed to find a way to make her smile every day."

"Were you at the hospital a lot with her?"

"I left long enough to sleep and go to school. I hated being apart from her that much, but Mom insisted it was healthier for me to keep as normal a schedule as possible under the circumstances." I knew my parents were looking out for me, but all it did was make me feel isolated. "Next thing I knew, I was wearing costumes and performing concerts for Maegan and the other kids undergoing treatment. I kept my routines G-rated, of course."

"And then?"

"I just fucking loved it," Milo replied with another shrug. "I became someone else in those moments and my problems disappeared. They always came rushing back, but I enjoyed my momentary escape."

"I bet you were amazing," I said softly. "Maybe someday you'll trust me enough to share some videos or something. Give me a private performance."

"We'll see," Milo replied noncommittally.

"Are you worried that I'll judge you or find you unattractive?" I couldn't understand why he was so hesitant to share this part of his life with me.

"You say it won't turn you off now, but it's different when you realize your boyfriend has shoved his nuts up inside his body and taped his cock between his ass crack."

I couldn't keep from grimacing, but then I realized what word he'd just used. "Well, I want my *boyfriend* to be happy, so if wearing makeup and gowns does that for him, then I'll find a way to deal with it."

"You're so adorable," Milo said. "I see what you did with tricking me into saying we were boyfriends."

"I did nothing of the sort," I denied. "But I admit that I love hearing it."

"Is that what's bothering you, Andy? You don't know where you stand with me?"

I tipped my head to the side then gave a little nod.

"You didn't just wear me down, Slugger. I've wanted you right here all along. It took us a ridiculously long time to reach this point, but here you sit beside me. Tonight, I'll lay my head on the pillow next to yours and thank God that you're alive and healthy. Tomorrow, I'll wake up and thank him that I get another day to love you."

"Wow," I said breathlessly. "That's an incredibly sweet thing for you to say."

"Then, I'll show that appreciation by fucking or sucking your cock."

"There's my guy," I said then threw my head back and laughed. "Where do you see this thing going between us?"

"We'll know when we get there, won't we?"

He had an excellent point. We could write down a list of every-thing we expected to happen between us, but we had no idea if they'd come true. Besides, isn't the journey the best part?

"So, where are you taking me?" Milo asked when I picked him up for our date.

"We'll know when we get there, won't we?"

"You've waited all week for that chance, haven't you?"

I shot him a smirk before answering. "Yep, I was prepared to wait longer if I had to though." It was so much fun being the person who had the answers instead of the one who had to guess. "Would you like a hint?"

"Nah," Milo replied casually. "I like surprises."

Okay, his easy acceptance was a little bit of a letdown. I was kind of hoping he'd at least offer up sexual favors if I held out. Obviously, I'd gotten over my concerns that Milo thought I only wanted him around for sex.

Milo laughed when I pulled into the parking lot of Gemini's Burgers and Fries. It looked like a run-down dive in the middle of nowhere between Blissville and Cincinnati, but they had the absolute best burgers I'd ever had. I brought Milo here on our first date in high school.

"Kicking it old school, huh, Slugger?"

"I thought it might be fun," I said with a sly grin. The place was always hopping, no matter the day of the week. Saturdays were even nuttier. "It looks really busy, so we can go somewhere else if you want."

"I don't mind waiting," Milo said. "Do we need to be at a certain place at a specific time?" I saw what he was doing. He wasn't nearly as cavalier about our destination as he wanted me to believe.

"Yes, but we have plenty of time to get there." I nodded to the

133

restaurant. "If you're game, I am too."

When we walked through the door, I was amazed how little things had changed since my last visit fourteen years ago. I'd craved the food but couldn't seem to talk myself in to going without Milo since it became "our place" when we were dating. The layout was the same, the pictures of sponsored softball teams from the eighties still hung on the wall. Man, those guys wore some serious shorty shorts back in the day. The waitresses were different, of course, because Carl liked them young and pretty, even though he was the furthest thing from it.

"I see Carl still likes to sing along with country music at the top of his lungs," Milo said to me. The kitchen was open for people to watch Carl cook their food and the waitresses assemble their baskets. It was kind of an odd setup, but it made Carl's cooking and singing part of the dining experience.

That was my least favorite part since I couldn't get into the music. "You want to sing a duet with him?" I asked.

"You mean again?" Milo asked with a raised brow. "Don't tell me you forgot about the Garth Brooks and Trisha Yearwood performance?"

"How could I ever forget the look on Carl's face when you just joined in?" I started laughing then I realized what Milo had said. "So, you haven't been here in a while?"

"Not since our last date," Milo said. "It didn't feel right coming here without you."

"Same here. Mom and Dad wanted to come here as soon as I got home, but I told them I wanted to go somewhere else. I could tell by their sympathetic glances that they knew why."

"Yep, my parents stopped mentioning it to me also."

The wait time wasn't as long as I anticipated, but then again, Carl had added picnic tables behind the restaurant so people could dine outside during nice weather. When given the opportunity to pick, we chose the picnic table outside so we could hear each other speak.

Even if I loved the music, it would've been too loud for me. I felt like I was yelling in Milo's ear while we waited for a table.

There were a couple of horseshoe pits and cornhole sets outside for people to enjoy before and after they ate, along with several video arcade games and a few pool tables inside. There was plenty to keep people happy while they waited for their food. When it arrived... drool city.

"Oh my God!" I mumbled around a mouthful of burger.

"You sound like me when I have your cock in my mouth," Milo whispered across the table, nearly making me choke.

He lost his smug look when he sank his teeth into his juicy double cheeseburger. "Oh my God!" he moaned. And yeah, he made me want to stuff something entirely different in his mouth. I wanted to feel the vibrations of his words, hums of pleasure, and groans bouncing along my cock and zapping my nuts like little bolts of lightning. Milo swallowed his bite of food and wiped his mouth with a napkin, but not before I got to see how wet it was from the grease. I wanted to see a different kind of wetness on his lips, spread it around with the tip of my dick. "I know what you're thinking," Milo told me.

"You wouldn't be wrong."

"Are you sure you don't want to take this back to my place after we're finished eating?"

"We'll get there eventually," I replied.

"Sounding awfully smug."

"I'm just basing this on the fact that I've spent every night in your bed since we reconnected."

"You make a good point." Milo swirled his French fry in ketchup. "So, what are we going to do between food and sex to entertain ourselves?"

"I thought you liked surprises," I countered.

"I lied. I want to know what devious plans you have in store for me."

"Us," I corrected. "You'll just have to wait and see."

135

After dinner, Milo expressed concern again about his sister buying Bliss House during the drive to Cincinnati but admitted he'd never seen her so happy. "She deserves it too. Life has dealt Mae some disappointing blows. She's earned the happiness she's found with Elijah, and the chance to build a life with him. But that house?"

"It truly is an exceptionally built house, Milo. I'm looking forward to working there because you just don't see craftsmanship like that anymore."

"Ghosts and all?"

"It adds to the ambiance."

"Well, I need to get over my aversion then since I have a feeling I'll be there a lot."

"You can start out easy by bringing me dinner a time or two. Get used to the place when it's just the two of us," I suggested.

"That's not a bad idea," Milo said, tipping his head as he considered it. "That way only you see me freak out if the ghost appears, or I stumble across more mannequins. Maybe I can make friends with the ghost so I don't choke from fright during our next Thanksgiving meal."

"Here we are," I said, slowing to turn into the parking lot of our next destination.

"Bowling!" Milo had never really been that good at it, but he seemed to enjoy it back when we dated. Okay, mostly he liked teasing me with his perky little ass.

"Confession," I said softly when I put the truck in park. "There's some people I want you to meet."

"Oh, so this is like a double date?" Milo asked.

"Not really. You'll see when I make the introductions," I answered vaguely.

I paid for the shoe rental while Milo searched for a bowling ball that fit him. "I hate having big knuckles and skinny fingers," he mumbled when I approached him with the ugly-ass shoes. "It means I have to get a much heavier ball than I prefer."

After a few more minutes, Milo found the sapphire-blue ball he was looking for, and I grabbed the first one that accommodated my knuckles. Milo followed me to the lane that my friends had already rented for a few hours.

"There he is," one of the guys said jovially. "We were starting to think you were ditching us. Again."

"Nah," I said. "Milo and I stopped for dinner first." Milo stepped up beside me with a pleasant smile on his face.

"Hello," he said, sounding shy.

"Guys, this is my boyfriend, Milo." I started introducing the guys from right to left. "Milo, this is Oliver, or Pastor Ollie to his congregation. He's my NA sponsor. I thought it was past time you two met."

I glanced over at Milo, whose eyes had widened. Surprise? Lust? What was up with that weird look on his face? He swallowed hard then extended his hand to Ollie. "It's nice to meet you."

Ollie shook his hand while scrutinizing Milo's face through narrowed eyes. "Man, I feel like I know you from somewhere."

"I don't think so," Milo said in a squeaky voice, running his finger nervously under the collar of his shirt. Was it Ollie's stark white clergy collar against the black shirt that made Milo feel uncomfortable? Did he think Ollie would judge us? Something was going on here, and I would get to the bottom of it before the night was over.

sixteen

Milo

TRIED TO HIDE MY SHOCK, BUT I KNEW I'D FAILED MISERABLY when I felt Andy staring at me. "I doubt we run in the same circles, Father." *Oh, but we did.* He was the birthday boy I gave a lap dance to while I tried to make Andy jealous. He sure as hell wasn't wearing a collar when he popped wood against my ass. I had to be wrong; it couldn't be the same guy. I recognized those big brown eyes as the ones that looked at me with unbridled lust. *Holy shit.* I must've broken at least a hundred commandments.

"I'm not a priest," the man said softly. "I'm a pastor, but please call me Oliver or Ollie."

"Um, that's kind of hard to do with the collar on." I realized that I was running my finger beneath my own collar.

"Does it make you uncomfortable?" He raised a brow. "I can take it off." Was he flirting with me? Surely not. Andy had staked his claim when he introduced me as his boyfriend. Then Pastor Ollie turned his soulful brown eyes on my guy, and I knew exactly where his interest was.

Hold up. Andy had specifically said that his Wednesday night rendezvous were strictly NA meetings and dinner afterward. This was the same group who brought a *pastor* to a drag show for his birthday. What was this world coming to, and was Andy truthful when he said there was never anything intimate between them?

"Uh, no. I'm just surprised."

"About what?" he asked sincerely.

What could I say without giving myself away? I couldn't ask if his congregation knew he liked cock, because how would I know that? I couldn't demand to know his real relationship with Andy because my boyfriend seemed clueless about the pastor's affection for him. "I honestly can't say, I just am," I managed to tell him. Eager to change the subject, I blurted the first thing that came to mind. "I got my blue ball. I'm ready to play."

"Just one blue ball?" Andy asked. "How does that even happen?"

"I guess I only emptied one chamber last night," I said with a shrug. Then I remembered we weren't alone. "Oh, um... I'm sorry, Father Ollie, Pastor Ollie. Fuck me! This is awkward."

Father-Pastor-Fuck-Me Ollie smiled broadly before he gave into hearty laughter. "I can see the collar is making you nervous, so I'll take it off."

"No," I said in a hurry. "Let's just start all over again." I stuck my hand toward the clergyman and offered a friendly smile. "I'm Milo Miracle. Andy has told me a lot about you, and I'm grateful to meet you." I wholeheartedly subscribed to the keep your friends close and your enemies closer theory. Make no mistake, I'd choke Father-Pastor-Fuck-Me Ollie with his own collar if he wasn't careful. I just got Andy back, and I wasn't giving him up again.

"Likewise," Ollie said cheerfully. "Andy has told me *a lot* about you too."

Something about his tone struck me funny, so I glanced toward Andy when I dropped his sponsor's hand. I'd hoped his smile would put me at ease, but he looked like he'd swallowed something that was a week past its expiration date.

"I'm just going to go change," Ollie said, seeing the tension rising between Andy and me.

"Seriously, Ollie," Andy said, wrapping his arm around the other man's bicep to prevent him from leaving. "It's not necessary."

Ollie looked from Andy to me before he offered a friendly smile to Andy. "Yes, I believe it is. Besides, I don't normally wear my collar when we go out. I just came from the hospital visiting members from my church. No worries, Andrew. I'll be right back." *Andrew?* Why did it sound more like a caress when Ollie said his name?

Okay, I felt like a big gaping asshole. Especially when he walked away and Andy turned disappointed eyes on me. This time, it was my bicep he gripped when he hauled me a few steps away from his group of friends.

"What's going on with you, Milo?"

"I don't know what you're talking about."

"Of course, you do," Andy replied. "You're acting weird around Ollie. I know damn well it's not his collar since you serve the local clergyman every morning when they stop in for coffee and pastries. What is it about Ollie that has you so worked up? Are you attracted to him?"

"What? Me? Not that it matters since he only has eyes for *you*?"

Andy shook his head in confusion. "You sound upset that Ollie isn't in to you." Oh, he was in to me the night I was dressed as Peach, but I wasn't about to blurt that one out.

"I'm upset because I think there's more between *you* and Ollie, not wishing that was the case for *me* and Ollie," I clarified.

"Oh," Andy said.

"What's that mean? Just 'oh' and nothing else?"

"It just means 'oh.' I told you that I haven't been with anyone else since I returned home, and I wasn't lying."

"There's something you're not telling me though, Andy."

"I mean, I could've had sex with him, but I didn't return Ollie's interest."

Was that supposed to make me feel better? On some level, I knew that my reaction was ridiculous, but I couldn't help my mind from wandering back to the night at Queen City Divas when they appeared closer than Andy was telling me. I remembered the way they leaned close to whisper in each other's ear, and the sexy smirk on Andy's face when I was singing happy birthday to Oliver. It wasn't a Wednesday night either, so they obviously hung out more than just on Wednesday evenings. What else wasn't Andy telling me?

"Look, it's obvious there's something bothering you, and we need to have a lengthy conversation. Can we do that privately? Ollie's sponsorship and friendship are important to me, and I'd really like for you to get to know him." Andy pressed a few sweet kisses against my lips, garnering catcalls from his buddies. "Please."

"I'm going to make you beg for other things later, Slugger," I whispered in his ear. The sparkle in his eyes eased the nerves making my stomach pitch and roll.

"I'm looking forward to it," Andy said before he kissed me once more.

"What'd I miss?" Ollie asked, as if he couldn't see that my lips were pressed against Andy's.

"Andy is sucking face with his boyfriend," one of the guys said.

I'd forgotten his name already. I think Andy called him Alec or Allen or something. He wore a goofy grin on his face like a perpetual frat boy. In fact, all three of the other guys looked like frat boys. I noticed that smile dimmed a little when Ollie didn't react to his remark. Exactly how did Frat-Boy-Alec-Allen think their sponsor would act? It seemed obvious to me that he knew about the connection Andy shared with Ollie. Was he jealous? Was he gay too? Were they all gay? Exactly what did they get up to during their meetings? *Whoa!* My brain was spinning out of control, but I blocked my mind from playing out a naked orgy in the basement of a church.

"This shouldn't come as a surprise to anyone since we knew how much Andy wanted to reconnect with Milo," Ollie said kindly. "I'm happy for you...both."

"Thanks," Andy said, rubbing the back of his neck like he did when he found himself in an awkward situation. Maybe he should've thought this through a little better.

"Are we going to bowl or what?" Bill, or maybe it was Bruce, asked.

"Let's do this," Ollie said. He walked over and entered our names into the computer. Adam, Brent, and Tyler were their names.

I was so happy that Oliver didn't make me go first. Perhaps he didn't hate me after all. Surely that was against his religion, right? Adam, Brent, and Tyler were on one team, and Andy, Oliver, and I were on the other.

Adam, Brent, and Tyler took their practice turns and all threw strikes or spares. *Fuck.* I hadn't bowled in a long time.

"Babe, just have fun with it," Andy said, clearly remembering how horrible I was when he bowled together in high school.

"Thanks," I said dryly, rolling my eyes as I turned away from him.

Channel the Peach. Channel the Peach. Channel the Peach.

"I saw that," Andy said.

I looked coyly over my shoulder. "You haven't seen anything yet, *darling.*"

Yep, I had an extra sway as I picked my ball up and walked up the steps. *Don't fall on your ass. Don't fall on your ass.*

"You got this, babe," Andy said cheerfully.

As I stood there looking down the lane, I had a choice to make. I could reveal to Andy that I had improved my game since we last played together, or I could keep that a secret right up until it counted. Hmmmm. *Like there was any real choice here.* I walked awkwardly, swung my ball out of rhythm, and let it fly so that it landed with a hard *thunk*, barely having enough energy to roll into the gutter.

142

I thought that maybe I overplayed my hand when it looked like it might roll to a stop before it cleared the lane.

"Oops," I said sassily, turning to face the five men who wore conflicting expressions on their faces. Adam, Brent, and Tyler grinned from ear to ear, knowing that victory for their team would be a sure thing. Andy looked embarrassed—for me or because of me, I couldn't be sure—while Oliver looked stunned. *Surely, he'd seen worse. No? Wait for it...*

My second practice throw was carefully orchestrated as well. I nearly dropped the ball on my foot, purposely, of course, and I managed to slowly roll the ball at the perfect angle so that it didn't hit the gutter until the last second. I wrapped my left hand around my right wrist like it was too frail to roll the little ole ball down that super long lane.

"I'm a little rusty," I said apologetically when I made my way back to Andy.

Andy pulled me onto his lap and whispered in my ear. "That's okay. I still love you."

Blink. Blink. Blink. I forgot to breathe. My eyes stung with unshed tears while Andy looked at me with a look of panic on his face.

"Uhhh," Andy said, spurring me into action.

"Oh no. You're not taking it back, Andy," I said boldly then kissed him on his mouth while I did a happy shimmy that would've made Peach proud.

"Is there something you'd like to say to me, Milo."

"Uh huh," I said coyly.

"And?"

"It's Ollie's turn to bowl."

Andy growled lightly in his throat and nipped my ear, but I wouldn't allow him to distract me from sizing up my competition. Ollie's first attempt knocked down eight pins but left a wide gap between the two remaining pins. Andy, and I suspected the goober triplets across the way, could've knocked them both down to pick up the spare in the situation, but Ollie wasn't up to their level. Hell, he wasn't even up to my level. He just didn't know it. *Yet.* His second practice bowl was much better because he picked up a spare. There was a touch of smugness in his smile when he looked at me.

"You're up, Slugger." I rose off his lap and gestured to where the rest of the guys were waiting. Adam, Brent, and Tyler wore matching dopey grins watching our exchange while Oliver looked resigned.

"Milo," Andy said in a warning growl when he stood up. "I want to hear the words later."

"If you force them out of me then how will you know they're sincere?"

"I'll take my chances," Andy quipped as he confidently approached the thingy with the bowling balls on it. I admired his swagger and the way his firm ass looked in his Levi's when he approached the lane. Andy's moves were smooth and well-practiced as he sent that ball speeding down the lane and crashing into the pins, knocking them all down with conviction.

"I'm damn good," he boasted then came to me for a celebration kiss.

I glanced over and caught the pastor struggling to peel his eyes off Andy's ass. Just what kind of godly man was he? Clearly one that ogles my guy and is cocky about his mediocre bowling technique. Wasn't he supposed to be humble, kind, and celibate? Oh wait. He's not a priest. Well, save himself for marriage at least? All right, I had ventured into Petty Town, and I didn't like it. I couldn't fault the guy for being attracted to Andy, and he obviously cared about the man I loved. Therefore, I would need to get over my unwarranted jealousy, fully embrace the fact that Andy Mason still loved me, and focus on kicking the shit out of Larry, Curly, and Mo across the lane.

"Let's get this party started," Adam said.

I sat quietly doing my best to look worried as I watched the three of them bowl strikes. They high-fived one another, pointed in our directions as if to say we were going down, and other juvenile antics.

144

Well, I had every intention of going down on Andy later, but it would be a freezing day in hell before this queen lost to them without a fight.

I could feel the difference in my demeanor as I approached the ball return thingy. I was confident of my ability; I was graceful and elegant. I was Peach. I held the ball in front of my chest and visualized where I wanted it to go then I did my graceful step sequence, releasing the ball with flourish. I kept my long leg stretched for balance as I watched the ball sail down the lane and knock down every-single-mother-fucking pin.

I stood up and faced the guys. "Oh my God!" I jumped up and down like a little kid. "Do you believe it? That's good right?" Five astonished faces stared back at me with gaping mouths and bulging eyes. "Must be a fluke."

"Yeah," Ollie said quietly as he rose to his feet.

"Don't I get another turn?" I questioned. "I thought we got two chances." I looked up at the scoreboard. "Hey, why don't we have any points?" Of course, I knew the answers, but it was better to keep up the charade as long as I could.

"We bowled strikes," Tyler explained patiently. "They'll add our score from the next two rolls to our first frame."

"Got it."

"I guess it's your turn, Oliver."

"Okay then," he said, shaking his head like he still couldn't believe it.

The other four men remained quiet when Oliver took his turn. Three men switched their attention to the bowling action, while the last man only had eyes for me. A slow grin spread across Andy's face.

"I think we've been played," my guy said, tugging me back down onto his lap. I loved that he couldn't seem to keep his hands off me regardless of where we were or who we were with.

"I don't know what you're talking about," I replied coyly.

"Liar."

"It wasn't lying, Andy," I told him. "It's called acting. You all expected me to bowl a certain way, and I met those expectations."

"And now?"

"And now, I show you what I'm really made of, lover." I sealed my promise with a lingering kiss. I was mindful of our setting and audience, so I kept my tongue to myself and let the warmth and firmness of his lips be enough for the moment.

"Andy, you're up," Ollie said from behind us.

"Not yet, but I think you're getting there," I whispered in Andy's ear.

"Later, I want you to show me all the other tricks you've been saving for a rainy day."

"Baby, I can't reveal that all in one night."

A throat cleared behind us in an annoying manner. *Go pray about something, Pastor Ollie.* I reminded myself that he was Andy's friend and sponsor. I rose from Andy's lap and gestured for Andy to take his turn.

"Go get 'em, Slugger." I clapped proudly when my man retrieved his ball and took his position in front of the lane. Like his practice run, Andy bowled a very convincing strike. I glanced up at the scoreboard to check out the cute graphics then noticed that the only score posted was Ollie's since the rest of us bowled strikes.

I could've been catty about the four pins that Ollie managed to knock down, especially since he was a better bowler than that. I knew my performance shook him up and took him out of his game. He was on my team, therefore I needed to lift him up while hoping I rattled the frat boys.

"You'll get them next time, Ollie."

The next round had similar results since the other team felt that my strike was luck or a fluke. I showed them they were wrong by rolling another perfect strike. By this time, Ollie was smiling because he realized that I'd been playing all of them during warmups. He bowled a respectable spare, and Andy was pure perfection once more.

Since we weren't professional bowlers, it was only a matter of time before we made mistakes. I started to see hashtag team frat boy lose a little steam in the seventh and eighth frames. I knew we could easily make up the difference if we stayed strong. We were neck and neck going into the final frame, so I motioned for our team to huddle up before we took our final turn since only one of the three frats bowled strikes.

"We can do this, guys. We don't have to bowl perfect frames. Let's just end strong."

We bumped fists, and I approached the lane with confidence. I hadn't bowled a strike in the last few frames, but I'd racked up respectable eights and nines. *Come on, Peach. Let's teach these boys a lesson in humility.* I released my breath at the same time I let go of the ball then held it as it rolled quickly down the lane. I couldn't resist doing a fun little shimmy when I knocked down all the pins.

"That's my guy!" Andy yelled proudly. I refrained from jumping into his arms, but just barely.

I had two bonus rolls, and I earned a strike on the first roll and nine on the second. That made my final frame worth twenty-nine out of thirty possible points.

"Oh my God," Adam groaned.

Ollie bowled a spare and earned an extra roll, earning a total of eighteen points. Then my guy got up and rolled a perfect frame with a total of thirty points. We beat hashtag team frat boy by six points. It wasn't an ass-whooping but might as well have been by the dejected looks on their faces.

"How much time do we have left?" Brent asked Tyler.

"Um, about forty-five minutes," Adam answered. "We won't get an entire game in, but we can declare a winner when the time is up."

"You guys think you can beat us again?" Brent asked.

"Uh, yeah," I said confidently. "I'll run and get us a pitcher of soda while you guys work on your comeback game plan."

"I'll go with you," Ollie offered.

"I can carry a pitcher of soda by myself," I teased. "Unless there's something else you would like to buy." *Or something you want to say to me.*

"Yeah, I'll buy some snacks for the group and a bottle of water for myself."

"Tag along then, friend."

I expected Ollie to speak his mind as soon as we were out of earshot, but he said nothing until we were standing off to the side waiting for our order. In fact, he might not have said anything without a little prompting from me.

"It's okay to say what you're thinking, Oliver."

"What am I thinking, Milo?"

"You're wondering if I'm good for Andy, or maybe if I'm good *enough* for Andy."

Oliver nodded his head subtly.

"It's okay that you doubt me since you don't really know me, or even all that much about Andy."

"I know Andy better than you think, Milo," he said softly. Then his eyes widened when he realized how that sounded. "Not in the biblical sense."

"You mean naked?" I clarified. "I know that. Andy already told me, and he wouldn't lie to me."

"You're right about that. He wouldn't lie."

"Can I ask why you're concerned about my relationship with Andy?"

"I'm afraid that stress from a relationship with you could cause him setbacks."

"Ouch," I said, rubbing my hand over my chest to alleviate the sting of his words. It would've been less painful if he twisted my nut sack. "Andy's happiness and sobriety are my top concerns." I wished like hell that his blunt words hadn't caused tears to well in my eyes and doubt to infiltrate my mind. Bad for Andy? Was that true?

"The past two years have been harder on him than you realize, Milo. In fact, I wasn't aware that the two of you had reconnected and was extremely worried when Andy missed the weekly meeting and didn't even call to check in with me. That is something that has never happened in the two years that I've known him, Milo."

"Things are good between us now. We've talked things through and—"

"Yes, it's all new and exciting again. But what happens if it doesn't work out between you? I don't want Andy to tumble into that dark hole like he did the last time you quit on him."

"Excuse me," I said angrily. "You know nothing about me or my past with Andy. You've heard one side of the story and feel like you know it all."

"What's your side then, Milo? You didn't just dump him at the first sign of trouble?"

"It's not that simple, Oliver, and let's not forget that I was sixteen years old. Quite frankly, I don't owe you an explanation. I appreciate that you're Andy's sponsor, and I do believe you want what is best for him. You and I will have to disagree that *you're* what's best for him and call it a day. I won't give him up, Ollie."

"Even if that's in his best interest?"

I looked over to our lane and saw Andy chatting, smiling, and laughing with his friends. He must've felt my gaze on his because he looked my way. That smile on his face turned from happy to delirious in a blink of an eye.

I blew him a kiss then turned back to Ollie who had watched the exchange. "If I thought for a second that I was a danger to Andy's sobriety, I would walk away. That is not the case. I love him, Ollie. I've always loved him. I admit I was young, brash, and brokenhearted when things didn't work out between us fourteen years ago when we were *kids,* but I'm a grown-ass man now who's head over heels for Andy Mason. This time around is very different. So, you can either get on board and support us, or continue deluding yourself that Andy will belong to you someday. If you can't be objective in your sponsorship, then you need to refer him to someone else. It's my belief that *your* relationship with him is potentially the unhealthy one."

Ollie didn't have a chance to respond because the pitcher of soda was slid in front of me.

"Sorry for the delay, fellas," the guy behind the counter said. "Your food will be right out."

I took the pitcher and left Ollie standing at the counter. I had nothing else to say, and there was nothing I wanted to hear out of his mouth, except an apology. I could see that he hadn't reached that point, and there was no reason for me to hang around. I returned to the only man who'd held my heart, the same one who smiled happily when I stopped in front of him.

"I love you too, Andy."

I didn't say it because I felt threatened by Ollie. I said it because it was the absolute truth, and I wanted to prove that we were done with childish games. Teasing was one thing, but toying with emotions was another.

"Now, let's whip some more ass."

seventeen

Andy

"**Y**OU HAVE A LOT OF EXPLAINING TO DO," I TOLD MILO AS soon as we were alone in my truck after winning the rematch. "Did *Tucker* teach you how to bowl like that?"

"Do you really want me to answer that question?" Milo countered.

"I wouldn't have asked it otherwise."

"Lots of people ask questions they either don't really want the answer to or when they already know the answer. Then there's you who falls into both camps."

"Do not," I countered, but he was right. I didn't really want to hear that Tucker was the one who taught Milo how to improve his aim, but knew he was the most likely culprit. Did Tuck press his body tight against Milo's and move with him as he went through the motions? Did that lead to other things when Milo felt the proof of how much Tucker wanted him?

"Oh, for fuck's sake," Milo groaned. "I can see that bowling porn is playing in your head right now. I assure you that the reality is a lot less sexier than what you're thinking." Milo released a dramatic sigh then crooked his finger so I would lean over the console and meet him halfway for a kiss. "I was going to tell you that I fucked the entire bowling team at Blissville High just to get pointers in case this day ever came, but we're past playing games…with each other."

"That's right. I'm a mature adult who can handle it."

"Yes, Tucker was the one who helped me improve my bowling game. Little did he know that it was just another way that I tried to stay connected to you. I never really let you go, Andy. No matter where I was, or who I was with, you were always there."

"That must've been a crowded bed," I replied dryly. "Sorry, that was a dickhead thing to say."

"Lucky for you, I like to give *your* dick head, so I'll give you a pass this once. However, I do think we should clear the air a bit more." Milo smiled wryly at me and his eyes twinkled with mirth in the darkness. "I wasn't as sexually active as I might've led on. All that flirting with the hunky superintendent and the others was for your benefit."

"You don't say," I deadpanned.

"I know, I'm quite the actor."

"Well, I wasn't as indifferent to the flirting as I let on. I might've wanted to smash some windows or slash tires," I confessed.

"You don't say," Milo repeated just as wryly.

"We're so mature and shit. I told you it would be different this time around. No more running and hiding behind pretense." I wasn't sure what I said to make Milo look uneasy. I opened my mouth to say something to him, but there was a knock on my truck window. I looked and saw that Ollie was standing next to my door.

"You left your phone on the table," Ollie said loud enough so I could hear him through the glass. He held my cell phone up for me to see. I rolled down my window, and he handed it to me.

"Thank you, Ollie. I hate how much I depend on that thing, but it's pretty vital for my business."

"You must've been really distracted to leave it behind then." Ollie's mouth turned up at one corner. "Or in a hurry to celebrate your victory." Oddly, it seemed like he aimed that last part at Milo. I'd gotten a weird vibe from them all damn night, and I needed to figure out what was going on between them.

"Uh, something like that," I replied. I mean, Ollie was cool and all, but he was still a pastor. Talking about sex or hinting that I'm about to be balls deep in Milo, or he in me, just felt *awkward*.

"Drive careful, guys."

"Will do. I'll be at the meeting on Wednesday," I assured him.

"I look forward to it. You can always reach me by phone should something come up and you need me before then."

I just blinked at him because I felt like his words had double meaning. Did Ollie think that my relationship with Milo was a fleeting thing? Did he still hold out hope that maybe we could be together? When Ollie confessed that his feelings for me extended beyond his sponsorship, he had assured me that he would find another sponsor for me if I returned his feelings, or if his interest made me feel uncomfortable.

Ollie was a beautiful person, inside and out, but I wasn't attracted to him in that way. He needed to accept that there could never be anything between us beyond friendship, regardless if Milo was in the picture or not.

"Your friendship means a lot to me, Ollie." It was the only thing I knew to say right then. I could tell it wasn't what he hoped to hear because I saw his inner light dim.

"Likewise," he said jovially, but it seemed forced. Then he looked at Milo once more and his smile turned brittle. "It was good to meet you, Milo. I meant to tell you that after the game ended, but you seemed eager to be someplace else."

I expected Milo to zing him with a snarky comeback, but he surprised me. "I look forward to getting to know you better, Ollie. Any friend of Andy's is also a friend of mine." I looked at Milo so fast I nearly got a crick in my neck. There wasn't a shred of sarcasm, boastfulness, or spite in his voice. He was sincere.

Ollie visibly relaxed, and I wondered exactly what they said to each other when they went to get drinks and snacks between games. "Goodnight, fellas."

I watched Ollie walk away for a few seconds before I rolled up my window and looked at Milo. He too was watching my friend depart and looked at me when he realized I was observing him. I would describe Milo's expression as speculative and maybe a little unsure, but about what? Did he still believe there was something between Ollie and me?

"I've never been involved in a relationship with him. I've never kissed him or was intimate with Ollie in any way."

"I know," Milo said softly. "I believe you, Andy." I wasn't expecting such a mild reaction from him.

"What exactly did you guys talk about?" I asked.

"That's between Ollie and me," Milo stated. Regardless of his words, I saw that something was weighing on his mind. I had to respect that he would talk to me about it when he was ready.

"Ready to get home?" I'd practically moved myself into his place, but it was the first time I'd implied it was my home too.

"Yes," Milo said breathlessly. "I'm sure Alli Cat will have found a way to show her displeasure at being left home all by herself this evening."

"You mean like barfing inside my work boots?" I asked.

"Yeah, or pissing on the jeans you left on my bedroom floor."

Alli Cat adored me at first, but that didn't last long once she was banned from the bedroom at night. "Why would your cat blame your absence on me? Surely you spent some nights away from home before I came back into your life."

"Not really," Milo said. "I never brought guys home, and I didn't date much. She knows you're the culprit."

"I need to make amends with her."

"You're a smart man, Andy. You can always surprise her with a few catnip toys from Brook's Pets."

"That's what I'll do."

The drive home was quiet. In fact, I expected Milo to be asleep when I glanced over, but he was pensively looking out his window, not that there was anything to see on dark country roads.

"Are you going to tell me what's on your mind?"

Milo jerked slightly in his seat like the sudden sound of my voice startled him. "I think it would be better to show you." He sounded worried, and that didn't bode well for me.

Alli Cat greeted us loudly when we arrived, expressing her displeasure at being abandoned for nearly an entire day since Milo only came home long enough to shower and feed her before we left on our date. She wove in and out of her daddy's legs until he picked her up and cuddled her against his chest.

"How much does that beast weigh?" I asked.

Milo and the cat both looked at me; one looked amused and the other looked annoyed. "Slugger, you never ask a lady about her weight or age."

"Oh, I thought that only applied to human ladies."

"Ladies are ladies, isn't that right, Alli Cat? She doesn't want to be shamed over her *twenty-six* pounds. It's taken her *five years* to achieve such amazingness, and it should be celebrated, not scorned."

"Forgive me," I said seriously, scratching beneath the cat's chin. "I'll never ask such personal details again."

"Well, this is a good segue into the thing I need to show you," Milo said after taking a deep breath and setting his cat down on the ground.

I couldn't imagine how we were segueing from his cat's sensitivity about her weight and age to whatever he wanted to show me, but both his feline and I followed him upstairs to his room.

"Get comfy on my bed. I'll be back in a few minutes after I've worked my courage up." His voice shook with nerves, and I hated to see him so upset.

"Milo, whatever you think you need to show or tell me isn't necessary unless you're ready."

"It really is, Andy. I should've confessed to this after that dinner with your family."

I realized then he was referring to his years as a drag queen. Did he still worry that it would be a turn-off or something? "I love you, Milo, and that won't change when you reveal your secret identity to me."

"You make it sound like I was a spy, and I assure you it was nothing that exciting. I'll be right back. Don't fall asleep."

"Fat chance of that."

"Freddy will get you if you do."

"Milo!" I shouted when he ducked out his door. "You know how much I hated those fucking movies. I didn't sleep for a week each time you talked me into watching them." Milo's laughter bounced off the walls of the hallway as he walked away from his room. "Have you ever notice that the strong, dumb jock is one of the first to die in horror movies?" I yelled. "I think those writers or movie producers use their jobs to get even at jocks that made their lives miserable in high school or something."

"You're not dumb, Andy," Milo yelled back. It sounded like he was in the bedroom next to his. I heard a lot of thumping around in what I assumed was the closet on the other side of the wall behind his bed. What did he keep in there? "You're the furthest thing from a dumb jock, but I can see how it's hard to shake that stigma. It doesn't help when you look the way you do."

"How's that exactly?" I prompted because I liked having my ego stroked on occasion.

"Sexy as fuck," Milo replied in a matter-of-fact tone. "People look at you and see your ripped muscles, athleticism, and good looks, and they can't imagine that God blessed you with a brain too. How fair would that be to the rest of the dudes?"

"Blessed, huh?"

"Well, God does love her rainbow babies the best."

I laughed because I thought Ollie would agree with Milo, except for the gender of the almighty. I would love to hear them debate why Milo thinks God is a she while Ollie sticks with masculine pronouns because that's what's in the bible. At least that's what I think Ollie's argument would be anyway. I opened my mouth to reply, but his bedroom door crashed open and there he stood in the doorway, wearing a sequined gown with a slit clear up to his thigh. The dress looked vaguely familiar, but I was distracted when he turned to the side and I could see the full length of his toned leg and that perky bubble butt that I... Something about the pose and the gown seemed really familiar, but blood was heading south in a hurry. I wanted him to lose that dress and ride my cock.

"I didn't bother to tuck the boys away since I'm not performing for you tonight. I just wanted to show you my favorite dress. I haven't worn it in a long time."

I finally glanced up and looked at Milo's face. His body language spoke of confidence, but his expression gave away his nervousness. Why? I already knew he'd performed drag. He acted like wearing this outfit should have special meaning or something. I looked at the blonde wig that reminded me of Marilyn Monroe. Then it hit me. I had seen this exact outfit on a drag queen, one who had honestly turned me inside out with a smoldering glance, and a provocative pout of luscious lips. I remember lusting after those long legs and wanting to feel them wrapped around my waist while I gripped that firm ass and fucked the man beneath the gown. Afterward, I felt guilty for wanting someone other than Milo.

Then I recalled the other dress Madame Something Peach wore to give Ollie a fucking lap dance for his birthday that nearly had him coming in his jeans along with the rest of the audience. I jackknifed off the bed and headed for the doorway. Milo jumped aside when I reached the door and followed me into the spare bedroom. I went straight for the large closet and began searching through hundreds of dresses and outfits until I found the one I was looking for. The white halter dress that looked just like the one in Marilyn's famous pictures. The one that he wore to flash Ollie his ass while the rest of us cheered him on. Or her? What the hell was I supposed to call Milo when he was in drag?

I held up the dress and turned to Milo. All color had leached from his face, and he looked scared. "No wonder you acted funny when I introduced you to Ollie. You had no idea you gave my NA sponsor and friend a boner."

"Oh, I knew I'd given him a boner, Andy. I did that on purpose to make you jealous. I didn't know that I'd given a *pastor* a boner! What the hell were you guys thinking when you set that up?"

"That a drag queen would sing him a little song. I didn't expect you to dry hump him until he creamed his jeans."

"Did he?" Milo asked. He took the dress from me and returned it to the closet then began removing the sequined number too.

"Is that important?" I fired back. "Would that make the scenario somehow less awkward?"

"I don't normally act that way," Milo said softly, hanging the shimmery dress up. "I'm sure you saw the difference in my performance for the grooms before I locked eyes with you when I rounded the table." He put his hands on his lean hips, and I tried to stay focused and not stare at his toned abs or the bulge in his boxer briefs.

"No, not really," I replied, crossing my arms over my chest. "I saw you straddle that guy's lap at the grooms' table and let him run his hand along the inside of your thigh."

"He slipped me a tip," Milo said, dismissing my jealousy.

"He wanted to slip the tip of his dick in your mouth." Milo didn't even bother trying to deny it. We both knew it was true.

"What about you, Andy? Were you seduced by my actions?"

I said nothing, working my jaw while I battled for composure. I had zero right to be so jealous, but I was.

"I saw the way you leaned into Ollie at the table, and kind of lost my mind a bit."

"*Kind of?*"

"Okay, I was insane with jealousy. I just knew he was the guy you were fucking every Wednesday night. And he could've been."

"I can't apologize for something I didn't do, Milo. We had to lean toward each other to be heard over the loud music and singing. I never once led Ollie on, not that night or any other time in our acquaintance."

"So, what did you fellas do after you left the show?" Milo asked. "I know for a fact that you didn't go straight home since you pulled in behind me at the gas station."

"We grabbed a late bite to eat before we all went home. Alone. Why were you out so late?"

"All the queens were hungry after a long night."

"I bet," I said dryly.

"What's that mean?" Milo demanded.

"I was referring to that backstage action that surely goes on."

"Are you asking if consenting adults find a convenient place to fuck, or are you asking if we give private dances or some shit?"

"Um…"

"Surely, you're not implying we queens were offering other services for a fee."

"No," I said quickly, shaking my head. "I meant that every man in that room wanted a chance at your ass."

"Is that so?" Milo asked, closing the distance between us. "Even you?" Milo licked his lower lip seductively, and I wanted to feel that pouty mouth wrapped around my cock.

"Especially me. My body recognized you, even if I didn't."

Milo snorted. "Andy, it's okay that someone other than me made you horny."

"But it *was* you," I told him. "You were just in drag at the time."

"So, what would you have done with Peach if you'd had the chance?" Milo placed his palm on my sternum then slowly slid it down until he cupped my erection through my clothes. Milo released my cock and walked backwards until he stood in front of a dressing table. "Say we were alone in the dressing room after the show or between performances."

Milo turned to face the mirror then bent over so that his perfectly round, biteable peach of an ass was thrust up in the air.

"Better hurry, Slugger. Someone might catch us."

I just stood there staring at his perfect offering. Did he doubt how much he tempted me? Did he think I needed more encouragement? He must have because he reached back with his right hand to pull his briefs down below one delicious ass cheek. His eyes dared me to take what he offered, to get lost in the fantasy with him.

I crossed to the vanity and dropped to my knees behind him. I kneaded and rubbed the exposed cheek with my right hand while revealing his other cheek with my left. Fuck, I wanted to bury my cock between the tight mounds, but first, I needed just a tiny bite of his peach. I sank my teeth hard enough into his right cheek to make him gasp, but not hard enough to hurt.

I pulled back and admired my handiwork, loving the slight indentations my teeth left behind. "Mmmmm, so sweet," I said before marking the left one in the same way.

Milo didn't pull away from me, he pushed his ass tighter against my face and reached back to grip my hair. My peach loved it rough and wanted to be bruised, so I marked him in ways that only we would see. Then I stood up, stripped down, suited up, and showed Milo exactly what I would've done had I been able to live out the fantasy playing in my mind when he teased Ollie and the guy at the groom's table.

I punched my hips forward, filling him fast and hard enough to knock over all the bottles on the vanity table. I had no idea what he used all that stuff for, but I didn't care. I locked eyes on his in the mirror over the table and watched his skin flush pink as passion and pleasure washed over his face.

Skin slapped against skin and masculine moans and whimpers echoed throughout the room as I set a swift pace that would guarantee a fast orgasm for both of us. Afterward, we clung to each other in the shower while hot water sprayed down on us.

"I love you, Andy," Milo whispered. "Welcome home."

I'd been home for two years, but that's not what he meant. Walls and roofs provided shelter, but Milo's heart was my real home.

"There's no place I'd rather be, Milo. I love you too."

After Milo had fallen asleep, I opened the bedroom door and went in search of his feisty feline. She looked up from the chair she'd curled up in and meowed. "Are you coming or not?" I asked her.

If I wanted a happy future with Milo, and I wanted it more than anything, then I'd need to find a way to make peace with his sidekick who felt slighted by my presence. Plus, it would reduce my risk of stepping in cat puke when I slid my foot inside my boot.

Milo turned into me when I climbed between the sheets again, and I held him in my arms in the center of the bed while I waited to see what Alli Cat decided to do. She jumped up on the bed and sat by our feet for a long time, long enough that I started to worry for my safety. Slowly, she walked up along the edge of the bed until she reached my pillow. I could feel her staring at me, and it was all I could do not to laugh. Finally, she somehow arranged her large body in a tight ball on the edge of the pillow.

I was lulled into a false sense of security by her heavy purring but was reminded that she was still in charge when I felt the faintest nip of sharp teeth on the outer rim of my ear before she rubbed her head against the back of mine.

"Truce," I whispered into the darkness.

eighteen

Milo

DIDN'T WAKE UP FEELING LIKE A NEW MAN JUST BECAUSE ANDY told me that he loved me the previous night, or because he didn't get angry when he learned about my alter ego. Well, he was a little angry, but only because he was jealous about the lap dance I gave Ollie. I still couldn't believe that I'd given the man a boner. Did he pray for forgiveness? How'd that even work. Ollie was unapologetically gay, but how did he feel about random boners and casual sex? *Hold up there, Peach. That's a rabbit hole we don't need to tumble down.*

I woke up feeling like the same man, just completed in ways I never dreamed would come true. It put a little extra sway in my hips while I fried bacon, eggs, and hash browns.

"I smell biscuits," Andy said, stumbling into the kitchen still half asleep. He was rubbing his eyes with one hand and scratching his chest with the other. "I'm so hungry after last night."

"Yeah, your stomach isn't the only thing making demands," Memphis piped up.

"Fuck!" Andy said, dropping his hands to try to cover his junk in such an adorable fashion. He needed more than two hands to cover up his morning wood. "Warn a guy next time, Milo," he grumbled as he turned and retreated to my bedroom.

I looked over my shoulder at Memphis who sat grinning from ear to ear. Our eyes met, and we burst into laughter.

"Stop!" I said, trying to catch my breath. "Andy's going to get a complex."

"Not with a dick like that," Memphis said. "You're one lucky bastard, Milo."

"I know," I agreed. As much as I loved Andy's cock, there was so much more to love about him.

Andy's face was slightly flushed with embarrassment when he returned to the kitchen wearing a T-shirt and loose shorts he'd left over earlier in the week. "I see I have a drawer already," he said gesturing to his clean clothes. "I like it."

"And I like you."

"Should I leave?" Memphis asked when Andy I stared into each other's eyes long enough to make him squirm. "Or grab a video camera. I can't tell which would be more appropriate at a time like this."

Andy looked over at him. "Stay but keep your video camera put away."

"Did I forget to mention that Memphis stops over for breakfast on Sundays?"

"Knock knock," Maegan said, coming through the back door.

"Maegan and Elijah too," I said.

"You failed to mention that, Milo," Andy replied, sending Memphis into another laughing fit.

"What did we miss?" Elijah said, looking between Andy and me. "Should we leave?"

"Hell no," Maegan said, pulling out a chair and plopping down. "There's a story here, and I want to hear it."

"Milo neglected to tell Andy that we come over for breakfast every Sunday morning."

"And they come over to my place on Wednesdays for a French toast brunch," Maegan said. "You're more than welcome to join us."

"I sense there's more to the story, Freckles," Elijah said, a wry grin spreading across his face.

"I saw Andy's dick," Memphis said then started laughing again.

"It's a good damn thing I'm a confident man," Andy said, pinning Memphis with a baleful look. To Maegan and Elijah he said, "I came down here buck-ass naked because I smelled biscuits. I was rubbing my eyes with one hand and—"

"I'm not sure we want to know," Elijah said, holding up his hand to stop Andy.

"I was scratching my chest, not my balls," Andy told Elijah.

"He's talking about how hungry he was after going at it with Milo all night long," Memphis said.

"I did not," Andy replied. "I just said I was hungry after last night. I'll have you know that Milo and I really—"

"I've lost my appetite," Maegan said. "There are things a twin sister doesn't need to know."

"Listen here, Miss Yes! Yes! Yes, Elijah! At least the neighbors haven't called the cops on us."

"I was going to say that we kicked ass at bowling, but yeah, we had a really good night once we got home. Didn't we, Peach?"

A little thrill snaked down my spine when I remembered the slight bruises on each butt cheek. Yeah, I checked as soon as I woke up. "You can say that again." I winked suggestively at him, not caring who the fuck was watching.

"I love being the fifth wheel," Memphis whined.

"Hey, there are plenty of nice guys around here," I told him. "You just have a taste for tatted-up bad boys."

"True." Memphis smirked. "I try going out on dates with squeaky clean ones, but I like them edgy."

"Wait," Maegan said. "Did he just call you Peach? As in…"

"Yeah, he knows now."

"*All* of it?" she asked.

"Yeah, he vividly remembers the performance," I told my wide-eyed sister.

"So does Pastor Ollie," Andy said smugly.

"Who's that?" Elijah asked.

"He's the guy Peach gave a boner-inducing lap dance to the night we went to the club to celebrate his birthday. He also happens to be my NA sponsor."

Maegan spat her coffee across the table.

"Gross, where the hell are your manners?" I asked.

"It was that or choke to death," she said defensively wiping her mouth with the towel Andy handed to her. "I think I made the best choice."

"Not so sure I agree," Memphis said. He had coffee splattered all over his face and T-shirt.

"Oh no, Memphis," Maegan said, rounding the table to wipe him up. "I'm so sorry." Maegan eased his glasses off his face and cleaned them before setting them on the table.

"Don't give me a spit bath," he teased when she started to wipe off his face.

"I figure you got enough of my saliva on you for one day," Maegan replied.

"Memphis, grab yourself a clean shirt from my bedroom and toss that in the laundry room on your way back. I have to do laundry in a bit anyway."

I checked my hash browns, and they were a perfect, crispy golden brown. I put them in the warming drawer with the cooked bacon and checked to see how my biscuits looked.

"Mmmmm. This time I'm not moaning about your ass," Andy whispered in my left ear. "Those look perfect."

"Just a few minutes longer," I told him. "Just enough time to make the eggs."

"Scrambled?"

"Fried," I answered. "Do you still like yours fried hard?"

"Yep, no runny yolk," Andy replied adamantly. "Cook them to death."

"Got it." I had just reached for the carton of eggs when my phone rang. I saw it was my mom and just couldn't send it to voicemail. "Good morning, Mama Miracle."

"Milo, make sure you bring Andy to dinner."

"I will ask him if he'd like to join us," I replied.

"What's she fixing?" Andy asked. I held the phone up so he could hear her.

"Braised short ribs in a wine sauce, herbed potatoes and carrots, and homemade bread," my mom said.

"I'll be there, Jackie. I'm looking forward to it."

"Peach cobbler for dessert with vanilla bean ice cream," she said just before I pulled the phone back. Andy waggled his brows.

"Mom, he already said he was coming to dinner."

"See you later, love. Make sure Memphis knows he's invited also."

"He knows," I assured her.

"I think I met someone that Memphis might like," she told me.

"Does he have tattoos?" I asked.

"Um, not that I know of," Mom said.

"How about piercings?"

"Milo, I didn't ask these things. He wore a leather jacket and looked like a 'bad boy.' I didn't ask a total stranger if he had tats, piercings, or if he wore briefs, boxers, or went commando. Let Memphis discover some things on his own."

"Don't forget jock straps."

"Excuse me?" I could picture her brows lifting.

"Mom, a lot of men prefer jock straps for convenience."

"Convenience for what? Do they worry they'll take a knee to the groin or something?"

"They don't tuck a cup in their jock, Mom. They just… Never mind."

"Anyway," she said cheerfully, "this guy was in town asking questions about Bliss House. I can't wait to talk to Maegan about it tonight."

"Where in town? When?"

"Books and Brew, of course. It was last night when I stopped in to pick up the books you ordered for me. He said he was in town doing some recon for a television show he produces. He has a friend who lives in town, and he'd mentioned possibly featuring Bliss House on his show. Something about ghosts and whispering."

"Paranormal Whisperer," I said into the phone. I couldn't keep the smirk off my face when Memphis nearly fainted at my table. He wanted to be the guy's cock whisperer.

"Mom, did you tell him that your daughter is in the process of buying that house and could grant him access once the closing is final?" By this time, Maegan and Elijah are just as alert as Memphis for different reasons. My sister wants to solve the Anthony Bliss mystery, and Elijah doesn't want any man around my sister. "He's unapologetically gay, E," I assured him.

"Yes, he is," Memphis sighed. I was pretty sure he came in his pants.

"Mom, why didn't you call Mae so she could come down to the bookstore to talk to him?"

"He was just passing through, so I showed him some books on the history of the town, which he bought, thank you. He seemed to be really interested after talking to his friend and looking at the books. He said he'd email Mae this upcoming week because, of course, I told him my *amazing* daughter was buying that house."

"What's she saying, Milo?" Maegan asked, coming to stand beside me.

"Here, you talk to her. See you tonight, Mom."

"Bye, darling."

I turned my attention back to frying eggs in the cast iron skillet. "Okay, so frying eggs in the leftover bacon grease isn't healthy, but it tastes so damn good."

"Bring it on," Andy said bravely.

I half listened to Mae's side of the conversation with Mom. She sounded so excited that she might be able to solve Anthony Bliss's disappearance. "I just know he never left the property alive. It's his ghost in the house."

"I think I should be jealous," Elijah said. "She was looking at old photos and fussing over how handsome he was."

"You can't be jealous of a ghost," Andy reasoned with him. "What could he possibly give Maegan that you can't?"

"Mystery and adventure?" Elijah asked with a shrug. "We're going to have big problems if he starts showing up during sexy times. All I need is a ghost who falls in love with Maegan and tries to knock me down the steps or some shit."

"Sounds to me like your problem could be solved really soon," I told him. "Maybe before you even move in."

Elijah raised crossed fingers up in the air.

Maegan's conversation with Mom didn't last long, and I fried eggs to order while the biscuits baked to golden perfection. We all sat around my kitchen table that was large enough for six people. I couldn't help but wish there was a sixth person there because I wanted Memphis happy. He deserved it. I knew he was attracted to leather and tattoos, but that didn't mean the guy with the bad boy exterior couldn't possess a kind heart.

After breakfast, everyone went home except for Andy. He pulled me onto his lap and kissed me soundly.

"What are our plans?" he asked.

"Besides a whole lot more of that?" I asked. Andy nodded. "Um, I have some boring-ass laundry to do. I'm set on groceries until Wednesday. I was going to lie around and read until dinnertime at my folks. Is there something you want to do?"

"I try not to do a lot of anything on Sunday," Andy replied. "I usually watch baseball or racing."

"You can do that while I read."

The afternoon that followed was the most relaxing and peaceful one I'd had since… I couldn't say. I cuddled with Andy on the couch and read Chaz's latest book while he flipped back and forth between the Braves and racing. Of course, I made sure Andy knew how disappointed I was that he still chose the Braves over the Reds.

"Go back to reading," he teased, nipping my ear. "Ouch!"

I looked up to see what made him yelp and saw Alli Cat sitting on the back of the couch. She was slowly retracting her paw like maybe she thought he needed another good swatting.

"I thought we declared a truce," Andy said to the feline. Alli Cat's response was to swish her fluffy tail. "Fickle females," Andy grumbled.

I turned my attention back to my paperback and was immediately sucked back into the story. It wasn't my favorite trope, but it was Chaz's creation, and I adored everything he wrote. This one was by far his best, and I felt my body react when things started to heat up in the story.

"Must be pretty hot stuff," Andy whispered in my ear, jolting me out of the sensual fog I'd found myself in.

I turned my head and looked at him out of the corner of my eye. "Excellent, but how would you know? Are you reading the book over my shoulder?"

"Don't need to," he replied. "You're practically grinding your ass against my dick. We're starting to get ideas."

"Oh," I said, feeling my cheeks heat. "It's definitely hotter than I expected."

"Is this Chaz's latest book that everyone is talking about?"

"Yeah," I replied. "It feels more sensual or risqué than his other books."

"Yeah? Read it out loud."

"This isn't elementary school where we take turn reading paragraphs," I told him. "Why are you so eager to hear the sexy words that Chaz wrote anyway?"

"No need to get salty," Andy told me then pinched my ass. "I don't want to hear them because Chaz wrote them; I want to hear what turns you on." Andy pulled me tighter into his embrace so that his erection nestled firmly against my ass then he slipped his hand under the hem of my T-shirt to tease the skin above the elastic waistband of my shorts. I was ready to say no until he slid his hand up to tease my nipple. "Tell me a story, baby."

I cleared my throat and began to read. "Marco dropped to his knees in front of Shamus and slowly caressed the back of his thighs with his skilled hands while staring at Shamus's proud, leaking cock."

"Oh, yeah. This is good," Andy said. "Suck his cock, Marco."

"Do you want to hear the story or not?" I asked.

"Sorry. Please continue."

"Marco leaned forward and licked the tip of Shamus's cock as a second set of hands joined Marco's on Shamus's body."

"Whoa!" Andy exclaimed, earning a playful jab to the gut.

"Rafe seemed every bit as eager as Marco to please their young lover. Rafe parted Shamus's ass cheeks and licked a path along his crack at the same time Marco sucked the full length of Shamus's cock into his mouth. The overstimulation made Shamus's knees buckle, but two sets of firm hands gripped his hips to steady him enough to receive the pleasure."

"Ever engaged in a threesome?" Andy asked before I could read further.

"No," I answered truthfully. "You?"

"No," he replied. "Is that something that you want? Is that why you've gone all wiggly?"

I set my book on the coffee table and rolled in the circle of his arms so I could look into his eyes. "I have everything I've ever wanted with you, Andy. Reading about something and finding it hot doesn't mean you want it for yourself."

"I'm glad you feel that way, Milo, because I would never share you. There will be no Rafe coming in here and rimming you while I suck you off. I might not be able to do both of those things at the same time, but I can do them so fucking good that you won't care that you have to suffer through enjoying one before I get to the other."

"Show me," I challenged. And he did.

My mother was resplendent in some sixties throwback dress complete with a scarf around her head. "She's channeling Jackie O again," I whispered to Andy.

"What's that mean? Hey, how does that work when you channel Marilyn?"

"She threatened to disown me," I said in mock horror. "Anyway, it means she's nervous. She wants everything to look perfect."

"Fuck!" my mom yelled from the kitchen.

"That didn't last long. Jackie O has left the building, folks," I announced. "She either burned our dinner or herself."

"I'll go check. It's good to see you, Andy," Dad said.

"You too, Dennis."

Maegan and Elijah arrived next with Memphis quickly on their heels.

"Did you have a chance to talk to Emory about the mysterious visitor in town?" I asked him.

"Yeah, he confirmed that Lyric was passing through and—"

"Blissville?" Andy asked. "Who the hell just passes through here?"

"Well, if you want to be technical, Andy," Memphis said, "he was driving south down I-71 from scoping out a possible film site in Columbus. He called Emory to see if he would be free for a short visit."

171

Memphis's cousin, Emory, moved to Blissville following a series of psychic visions. Emory was one of the country's most famous psychics, not for the work he did with law enforcement agencies helping them solve cold cases, but for the episodes he filmed with Paranormal Whisperer. The show, and all the cast members, had quite a following. Emory wasn't a series regular, but he was still popular.

"So, what did Em say about them filming here?"

"Lyric sounded interested. He drove by the house and was impressed by the outside. He's itching to see the interior as soon as Maegan can get that arranged." He nodded to Maegan. "Your mom wasn't exaggerating. Lyric called Emory on his way out of town and told him how excited he was to explore the Bliss House for possibilities.

"I have mixed feelings about it," Maegan confessed. "I'm excited to show the house to him, and I'd really like to solve the mystery of Anthony Bliss's disappearance."

"But with one T," I prompted.

"But, I don't like the idea of strangers tromping through my house. I don't think Anthony will like it either."

"Maybe that's what it will take to solve the mystery. You have to make him uncomfortable enough to take action."

I realized that everyone was looking at me with their mouths hanging open.

"What?"

"Peach, you practically ran out of that house like your ass was on fire," Andy said.

"How would you know? You were up in the attic."

"I heard about it from someone."

"There was only one 'someone' who witnessed me calmly walking out of the house." I narrowed my eyes at Memphis when he snorted. "Who are you to talk?" I asked him. "You were right beside me."

"Well, if that ghost had appeared, I would've knocked you down so that I could escape. I didn't have to be the fastest runner, I just had to be faster than you."

"You would sacrifice me like that?" I asked dramatically. "Your new best friend?"

"Hey, you know what it's like to be in love. Not all of us can say that." Memphis's cheeks turned red from embarrassment. He opened his mouth, and I could tell that he was going to try and laugh it off or walk it back, but he was saved when my parents came out of the kitchen carrying dishes.

"Who's ready to eat?" Dad asked.

"Me!" we all replied.

My mom's cooking was hit or miss; it would either be the best thing you ever had or the worst. Luckily for us, especially her since she went to a lot of trouble, the meal was exceptional. I saw how much it meant to my mom when Andy happily devoured her cooking in between praising her skills.

"Thank you, dear," she said. "Save room for dessert, Andy. I made peach cobbler from scratch. It's the one thing I never fuck up."

Andy wiped his mouth with his napkin. "I always have room for peach anything." He shot me a playful wink when no one was looking, and I nearly asked for ours to go. Instead I leaned forward for a quick kiss and settled into his side when he wrapped his big arm around my shoulder. I wouldn't deprive my mom of hearing Andy fuss over her dessert.

Later when we were leaving, Mom held me tight and whispered in my ear, "Fall is a lovely time for a wedding, Milo." When I pinned her with an incredulous look, she just smiled broadly and said, "You can't blame a mother for trying."

On the way home, I realized my mom was absolutely right. Fall was an amazing time to have a wedding.

nineteen

Andy

OVER THE COURSE OF THE NEXT MONTH, MY LIFE TOOK ON A dream-like state. I'm not talking nightmares; I mean the kind of perfect fantasyland where you want to stay forever. I started a dream project of rehabbing an old, mysterious home, nearly completed the apartment renovations for the Miracle twins, and fell deeper in love with Milo every single day.

As a horny teen, I was enthralled with all the physical things I liked about Milo. As an adult, our sexual chemistry burned hotter because I appreciated all the other aspects of his personality a lot more. I couldn't imagine a day without him zinging me or making snarky comments about something. I didn't want to spend a night that didn't include long, hot kisses and me wrapped around him while we slept. How had I lived fourteen years without him? The truth? I hadn't truly known what I lost until we reclaimed one another. He was the cinnamon in my French toast, the chipotle in my barbecue sauce, and the 7UP in my Captain Morgan—well, fruit punch these days. He was sparkly, sweet, spicy, and that extra something that made the ordinary extraordinary.

Everything was as it should be with one exception—Ollie. Things felt awkward between us since the bowling night, and I wasn't sure how to fix things, or even if I should. As the weeks passed, he seemed a little friendlier, but not the way he was before he met Milo. I suspected Ollie hadn't realized how serious I was about my boyfriend until he saw us interact together. Hurting my friend was never part of my plan, but he needed to know that Milo was it for me. I hated the rift between us, but I thought it was best to let things go. If our friendship was meant to be, we'd find a way to work it out.

"Pastor Ollie," Rebecca, a new member, said, "why do you hold weekly meetings?"

"Well, it's kind of like how people attend church every week. They do it to remind themselves of God's love, to feel refreshed and renewed, and to connect with people who think like them so that they don't feel alone," Ollie replied. "By coming to NA meetings each week, you meet with people who share your same struggles. They inspire, encourage, and lift you up when you need it. Now, some people have lived with their addiction longer and choose to meet bi-weekly or even monthly, which is fine. I've established a flexible program within the guidelines to meet a variety of needs. For those who are newly sober, I strongly recommend you attend as often as you can."

"Thank you, Pastor Ollie." She bit her lip nervously and looked down at her feet.

"You can just call me Ollie or Oliver if it makes you feel more comfortable," he said kindly. "I'm not here to convert any of you to religion, and I'm not here to judge you. I simply want to help you stay sober." He smiled when he looked around the room, but I noticed he didn't meet my eyes. "Who wants to go first this week?"

"I do," I said. Ollie looked surprised that I spoke up. I couldn't blame him since I never volunteered to speak first. "My name is Andy, and I've been sober for thirteen years now."

"Hello, Andy," they all said.

"What's going on with you this week?" Ollie asked. His tone was friendly, but his eyes lacked the warmth I was used to seeing.

"Nothing has changed since last week. I'm still working on the same projects, still in love with the same guy, and I feel happier than I've ever been in my life."

"Then why are you still coming?" Keeton asked. He was also attending for the first time. "If everything is so perfect, why come here? To brag and make us feel worse about ourselves?"

"Not at all, my friend."

"We're not friends," Keeton fired back.

"I'm not your enemy either, pal," I said peacefully. "I come here for the reasons Ollie mentioned. I've made lifelong friends who share this journey with me." I nodded to Adam, Tyler, Brent, and Ollie. "We've formed a tribe, if you will, and I'm stronger with them than without."

"Goodie for you," the younger guy said sullenly.

"Even when I'm feeling at my strongest, I show up because others might need to pull from that strength just like I did from them during some of my most difficult times. That's what we do here."

"That's nice. I could really use that in my life right now," Rebecca said softly, earning a glare from Keeton.

"We all can," Adam told her then winked at me. "Always got your back, Boo."

I smiled when I thought about Milo calling Adam, Brent, and Tyler the frat boys. They did come across as rowdy guys out for a good time, but they were incredibly smart men with careers that no one would have picked for them judging by their appearances. By day, they were an engineer, doctor, and CFO; by night they were jokesters who wore their ball caps backwards and said silly things like calling me Boo. Half the time I thought they did it to tease me, but maybe it's how they balanced their stressful careers. On the surface, we appeared to have nothing in common, but beneath the skin we were very similar. Each of us got involved with drugs during our college years for various reasons, and we wanted to live clean, happy lives.

"One of the reasons I think Ollie's meetings work so well is that they're geared to us in the rainbow community. We can sit and discuss the problems that every single one of us has dealt with. I can mention that I have a boyfriend and not worry that I'm going to be harassed for it."

"Dude, you're built like Johnny Fucking Bravo. No one is going to mess with you," Keeton said hostilely.

"You think that all threats come in the form of a physical attack?" I asked Keeton. "People don't have to be able to kick your ass to get you fired. Cyber bullies are every bit as threatening, maybe more so, than a physical threat because they can hide behind their computer screen. Sometimes the bullying comes from someone you love, and it's delivered in a way that makes you think that person is doing you a favor."

"Huh? Dude, you lost me."

"College baseball scouts started looking at me when I was only a freshman in high school. In addition to the school team, I played in a competitive traveling league that helped get my name out since scouts probably had never heard of Blissville High School. Rumors began circulating during my sophomore year that I could have my pick of colleges."

"You must've been really good," Keeton said, sounding a little more interested.

"I thought I was exceptional because that's what everyone told me," I said wryly. "Especially my high school coach, who expressed on numerous occasions that he only wanted what was best for me. I believed him too. I had no reason to doubt Coach when he suggested that I delete my social media accounts because they could be used against me when a school made a final decision on a scholarship. I thought he meant my grammar was shitty or something." The other members in the group chuckled, but not Keeton. He knew where this was going.

"Yeah, what he truly meant was that he didn't want the scouts to see that I was openly gay. It was something I had never tried to hide. Milo often came with my family when I traveled for games. He was my prom date for both my junior and senior years. It never occurred to me just how hateful the world could be. I was naïve to say the least."

"Did you do what the coach said?" Rebecca asked.

"I did. I was so excited about the possibility of playing ball for a Division I school that I didn't think through my actions. I didn't realize how much I hurt the person I loved. Milo stayed silent about his feelings because he wanted what was best for me and wanted to make me happy. Coach took me aside before graduation and told me that it would be best for me not to let on to my team that I was gay. He recommended that I get a feel for their attitude before I let them know. He worried that it would impact their acceptance of me, and my playing time."

"Did you tell him to shove his stupidity up his ass?" Keeton asked.

"No, I didn't. I listened to him. I explained the situation to Milo, and I knew it upset him, but he seemed to be on board with it. Looking back now," I told them, "I can see now that our relationship was doomed to fail under the circumstances I created."

"Because you were a dumbass," Keeton grumbled.

"Keeton, this is a judgment-free zone," Ollie reminded him. "Talking about these things is one of the ways we work through our urges to do drugs or drink booze."

"Or sell your body to buy the drugs and booze," Rebecca whispered. I just wanted to hug her.

"Don't expect me to open up and share my sob story with any of you," Keeton said somberly. I think we all felt like that when we first arrived, but Keeton would share when we earned his trust.

"Continue, Andy," Ollie encouraged. This time his smile was the genuine one I'd come to associate with him.

"I assume there's a point to this," Keeton prompted.

"There is a point to this story," I confirmed. "I didn't realize until much later that Coach's sage advice was really a form of bullying. He was telling me that it wasn't okay to be me and love who I love. He was telling me in a soft voice with a compassionate expression that my new team wouldn't accept me. He didn't beat me over the head with it, but he said it often enough that I started to believe it. Then I acted on it, and it sent me into a downward spiral."

"So, your high school baseball coach is to blame for your drug addiction?" Keeton asked.

"That's not what I was saying at all. The story was to show you that not all bullying is physical, as you suggested. My coach didn't have to beat me or verbally abuse me to cause emotional harm. My drug addiction is all on me. I accept full responsibility, and part of that is acknowledging the events that got me to the dark place in my life to avoid putting myself in that situation again."

Keeton nodded in response, which I accepted as a big victory.

"Anyway, we got off course from my original plan when I volunteered to speak first." I shot a teasing glance at Keeton, who flipped me off. I saw the faintest hint of a crooked smile, so I shook off Ollie before he could admonish him. "I had just wanted to say thank you, Ollie. These meetings with your leadership have made a huge difference in my life."

Ollie's cheeks turned pink like the praise embarrassed him, but then a different expression washed over his face. I thought it might be shame, but it disappeared so fast that I doubted myself.

The meeting went on for another ninety minutes while people shared stories of their past or what was happening in their lives. Neither Rebecca nor Keeton seemed ready to share, and Ollie never forced the issue. He wanted to build a foundation of trust, and my respect for him grew when he softly spoke to them individually after the meeting ended.

"I know you're eager to get back to Milo," Adam said, "but how about you join us for burgers and fries like old times."

"We miss hanging out with our friend," Brent said.

"Pretty please," Tyler said then playfully pouted and batted his eyelashes.

"Sure," I said. I missed hanging out with them too. I texted Milo to let him know I'd be home later than normal. I was half expecting a pithy remark, but instead he offered sexual favors for a burger, fries, and milkshake. Oh, how I loved him.

Ollie seemed surprised when I turned up at our favorite burger joint. Instead of commenting on my absence, he smiled and scooted over so I could sit next to him. We didn't talk about addictions and recovery over juicy burgers and crispy fries; we talked about our jobs and the people in our lives that made sobriety so important. I didn't linger as long as I normally would have prior to reconnecting with Milo, but I did stay to enjoy the amazing bond we'd formed.

Once Milo's to-go order was ready, I told the crew I was heading out. Adam, Brent, and Tyler made kissy faces and lewd gestures, not giving a damn that a pastor was among us. Silence descended on the table when the pastor in question said he wanted to have a private word with me. Like me, the frat boys didn't know what to make of it, so they just kept shoveling French fries in their mouths as Ollie followed me outside to my truck.

"Are you about to tell me what's been bothering you this past month?" I asked.

"You noticed, huh?"

"Of course. Do I make you uncomfortable? Would you like me to find another sponsor, Ollie?"

"Heavens, no." He shook his head as a pink flush crept up his neck. "I take it that Milo never shared the details of our conversation with you."

"No," I said slowly. "I knew something occurred between you, but I wasn't sure what. I thought maybe you recognized him as Madame O-Feel-Ya Peach or something."

"Shut up!" Ollie exclaimed. "No way!"

"Oh, yeah. He confessed to me that night, so that was the connection I made. I thought maybe you were sorry my boyfriend gave you a boner, even if he wasn't my boyfriend at the time. I also worried that maybe seeing me with Milo was just too awkward for you. I wasn't sure what to think of the sudden change."

"Oh my God!" Ollie said, and I could tell he was reliving Milo's lap dance.

"Hey!" I said. "Let's get back to the reason you followed me out here."

"Oh yeah," Ollie said, but it looked like he struggled to remember what he had planned to say. He grinned after I snapped my fingers when he started to zone out again. "Oh, um, I wanted to apologize to you for the way I behaved at the bowling alley."

"I don't understand, Ollie. You didn't act weird, and we didn't exchange harsh words. I assume this is about Milo."

"I said some foolish things to Milo out of jealousy. I realized how wrong I was, and that's why I've been so distant lately."

"What kind of foolish things?"

"Um, I implied that maybe your relationship wasn't healthy for you."

"Ollie!" I couldn't hide the shock I felt. "Why would you say that?"

"It just happened so fast, and it was obvious how much Milo had hurt you with his rejection after you returned home. I was worried that a breakup would cause big setbacks for you." Ollie swallowed hard. "That was a conversation I should've had with you, not Milo. Can you forgive me?"

I suspected this all came from a place of jealousy. It's easy to forget that Ollie was a man beneath the collar he wore, which meant he made mistakes. "Yeah, Ollie, I can forgive you." He released a huge sigh of relief. "But it's really not me you should be apologizing to."

"I was afraid you were going to say that," Ollie said. "Can I get Milo's number from you?"

"Yeah, as long as you don't try to steal him from me."

"That could never happen. Start paying attention to the way he looks at you, Andy."

I thought about what Ollie said on the way home. When I walked into the house, I paid attention to the smile that spread across Milo's face and the way his eyes lit up.

"You must be awfully hungry," I teased when he leaped over the back of the couch to get to me.

"Ravenous," he replied, but made no attempt to take the food from my hands. He stood on his tiptoes and kissed me long and sweet. "Welcome home, Slugger."

I decided to let Milo tell me about the conversation he had with Ollie, if he chose to divulge it. I would only worry if Milo thought for a second that he was bad for me. So far, he gave me no indication that was the issue. I watched Milo devour his treat with a huge smile on his face. After he was done, he set the empty bag on the coffee table and turned to me.

Milo whipped his shirt over his head and tossed it to the ground. "About those sexual favors…"

twenty

Milo

"HOW IN THE HELL DID WE GET TALKED INTO COMING BACK down here?" I asked out loud.

"Maegan must've put a spell in the coffees she brought us from Books and Brew," Memphis said.

"Oh hush," Mae said. "You love it down here and you know it."

Memphis snorted. "That's a stretch. At least Milo's boyfriend made sure the lighting is much improved from the last time we were in the dungeon of death."

"Well, it was actually Mike the electrician who made it happen, but it was Andy's suggestion." I looked around at the stacks of boxes all around the cellar. "I expected it to smell mustier."

"This house was built exceptionally well," Memphis said. "They don't make them like this anymore."

"I can't believe it's mine," my sister said dreamily.

"What exactly are we looking for?" Memphis asked. "It's doubtful I'll find comic books or vinyl records down here to sell in Vinyl and Villains."

"You never know," Mae said, pulling down one box and looking inside it. "It's doubtful that all of these boxes belonged to the Bliss family."

"Some guidance though, Sis?" I asked.

"Okay, well, I'm looking for unique things to set out as decorations." She pulled out an old candelabra from the box. "Like this! All it needs is some polish and TLC to restore it to its former glory." Maegan went back to looking in her box. "It's doubtful this is the only candelabra down here."

"Why couldn't they have boxed the sets together?" I asked. "Why put one candelabra in one box and another in a different box?"

"Maybe they didn't pack things in a rational fashion," Maegan said. "How familiar are you with the history of Blissville, the founder Anthony Bliss in particular?"

"Admittedly, not very," Memphis said absently. "Anything juicy?"

"Oh, just family curses, a sudden disappearance, and his widow's complete isolation afterward."

Of course, I'd heard this story numerous times over the years. One of the things I admired about Maegan was that she never embellished the story with each new telling like a lot of people would. She took the mysterious disappearance seriously and had wanted to solve it the first time we rode our bikes past this house as kids. She'd felt an immediate connection to the spooky-looking house while I couldn't pedal away from it fast enough. In school, the Bliss House had been a subject in her history projects and papers, as well as some fan fiction stories for English. This house was destined to belong to her.

I stood and watched her weave a tale that completely ensnared Memphis. "It was originally built by Anthony Bliss who founded this town in eighteen thirty. Anthony was a progressive railroad tycoon who believed that Blissville could be a thriving depot because of its central location to bigger cities like Cincinnati, Dayton, and Columbus. He believed railroads were the key for both shipping and traveling. People thought he was crazy when he laid out this tract of land and named it after himself. He built the home here and moved his family from New York City. His vision came true, and this tiny little community became a bustling trading town. At first, the railroads were used strictly for travel in Ohio, but eventually, they expanded to include national railways."

"Huh, that's cool," Memphis said.

"Rumor has it that Anthony Bliss had ulterior motives for relocating his family." Maegan leaned closer and dropped her voice. "It's believed that he was trying to outrun a curse."

"A curse?" Memphis sounded as skeptical as everyone else when they heard this part.

"There are different versions of who placed the curse on the family from gypsies to Native Americans, but it seems to have started with Anthony's father, John. He was reported to be a ruthless businessman who lied and manipulated to get his way. The curse was placed on him and his heirs because the sins of the father are passed along to their offspring and all that jazz."

"That seems to be the way it goes," Memphis said.

"Anyway, John Bliss died of a heart attack in his mistress's bed in upstate New York supposedly a week after he was cursed. He left behind a wife and four sons. Anthony was the youngest."

"Did his three older brothers die from mysterious causes?"

"One of them died in war, one of them died after falling from a horse and breaking his neck, and the third brother drowned in a river. Anthony was the last Bliss standing and decided to try and outrun the curse."

"I don't think that's how it works, but you can't blame a guy for trying," Memphis told her. "Then what?"

"Anthony Bliss disappeared without a trace in 1850."

"Huh."

"He went for a horse ride, like he normally did every day, regardless of the weather, and never returned."

"What happened to his family? Is that when they just got up and left without taking their things?"

"Well, Melanie Bliss was distraught and was never seen in public again. Too many years had passed since his last brother died for her to believe that he was a victim of the curse. She was convinced he left her to start a new life, so she was too ashamed to show her face in town. Her sister came to live with them and assumed care for the children until Melanie died of a broken heart."

"That's really sad."

Maegan nodded. "Melanie's sister packed up the children, sold the house to a prominent doctor in town, and moved back to New York. She shipped what she wanted to keep and left everything else behind. From what I've heard, Melanie held onto all of Anthony's things in case he returned, but her sister had no desire to drag his stuff back to New York after he left his family high and dry. Dr. Martin's family moved in and reported that inexplicable things kept happening. Doors slamming in parts of the house where no one was or the smell of pipe tobacco floating through the air when no one in the family smoked."

"Why are Bliss's things still here after all this time?" Memphis asked.

"The house remained in the doctor's family for many decades until the kids sold it to the Renzos after both their parents died. The caveat was that the Renzos took possession of the contents as well as the house. Which meant that they possibly inherited some of Anthony Bliss's possessions as well as the doctor's.

"I hired a cleaning company to haul away all of Renzo's stuff and anything that looked to belong to the doctor's family too," Maegan told us. "I recently found an old pipe carved out of ivory upstairs that I think belonged to Anthony Bliss. I'm pretty sure it's the source of the tobacco smell that floats randomly through the house."

"We," I gestured between Memphis and me, "smelled it the night the ghost locked me in the attic with Andy."

"Have you asked Emory to do a reading?"

"Not yet," Maegan said. "If it is Anthony Bliss, does that mean he never left the property and was killed here, or did his spirit return here after dying. Is Bliss House his purgatory?"

"I guess either could be true. I'm not an expert, but we know someone who is," Memphis told her. "What have you heard from Lyric?"

A month had passed since his visit. He'd sent one email to Maegan to let her know he was interested in touring the house once she purchased it. She'd contacted him after the sale went through but hadn't heard from him since. "I don't want to be a pest. He's either interested or he's not." Maegan shrugged, went back to digging through boxes, and we followed her lead. "I also found a pearl necklace I believe belonged to Melanie Bliss. She definitely died in the house, so she could be the entity we feel."

"I don't think so," I told my sister. "I'm not getting a scorned woman vibe from our friend. Besides, the pipe tobacco makes me think it's a male presence."

"Don't be sexist," Maegan said. "Plenty of women smoked tobacco back then. They were just discreet about it."

"Let me call Emory and see what he's doing. He can touch those items and see what he thinks." Memphis pulled his cell phone out of his pocket but didn't get service beneath the house. "I'll be right back."

I continued sorting through boxes with Maegan while Memphis went upstairs to call Emory. I hadn't found anything of interest in the stack of boxes I looked through. I was sure the historical society might like some of the clothes in the boxes, but I didn't think it was what Maegan was looking for. When I opened the final box on the bottom of the stack, I knew I'd found something special.

"Jackpot!" I said.

"Oh, you found another candelabra?" she asked.

"Better. Come check this out."

Maegan set down whatever was in her hands and walked over

187

to me. "Oh my God!" she said when she saw what was in the box. "Leather-bound journals that appear to be as old as the Bliss era. Look at the engravings on the covers," she said in awe. "Only the wealthiest men would've owned something like these."

"Let's take it upstairs and look through them," I said excitedly.

"Ha! The thrill of the hunt has finally caught you too."

It was true. I was ready to drink some sweet tea and look through these journals with Maegan until Andy was ready to go home. I should've felt guilty about not helping him, but I was more of a hindrance than a help when it came to that type of thing. I was great with a paint brush and roller and would gladly volunteer once we reached that phase of the project.

We met Memphis on the way up the stairs. "Oh," he said, coming to a halt. "Done already."

"Milo found something way cooler than candelabras," Maegan said excitedly.

"Old journals," I told him. "Really old. I bet there's all kinds of details in them."

Memphis pivoted on the steps and said, "Emory will be over in a few minutes. He was surprised that you hadn't heard from Lyric, Mae. He has talked to Lyric a few times after he visited, and each time he mentioned how interesting he found Anthony Bliss's story."

"Maybe there's something juicy we can use to lure him to town," I suggested.

"I only want him to visit this house if he truly wants to help me solve the mystery and send Anthony wherever it is he wants to go," Maegan told him. "I'm not about to nag or pressure him in any way."

"I'm going to order pizza," I said when we reached the first floor. "I know that Andy must be starved by now."

"Fine, but nobody touches these journals with greasy fingers."

I placed the order for pizza and went upstairs to check on Andy while Emory did his thing with the pearl necklace and pipe that Maegan found. It wasn't that I didn't find Emory's psychic ability fascinating, I just felt Andy's pull stronger. I found Andy upstairs in the largest of the extra bedrooms. He was sanding the window seat that was built in to the turret.

"What an amazing place to read a book," I said when I entered the room. "Any child of Maegan's will love that window." Built on both sides of the bay window were shelves for books, toys, dolls, or anything else a kid would want to place there. I knew that Maegan would make this a magical space.

"It's my favorite room in the house too," Andy said.

I crossed the room and handed him the bottle of water. "Pizza will be here in thirty minutes. You must be hungry."

"Starving actually. I have a really bad habit of getting caught up in my projects and losing track of time. I haven't eaten since I left Books and Brew this morning."

"Andy, you didn't stop to eat lunch?"

"I didn't feel all that hungry until you mentioned it," he said, shrugging his shoulders and taking another long drink. I watched the way his throat moved up and down while he drank. Who knew that could be sexy, but like always, my hormones got the best of me when he was near.

"What time is it anyway? Three o'clock?"

"Try six o'clock," I told him.

"Get out of here." He pulled his phone out of his pocket and checked the time. "Damn, I guess I really did lose track of time."

It would be the last time I allowed him to skip lunch if I could help it. "This room is looking amazing."

"I like the color scheme Maegan picked out for it," Andy said. "She's picked a rich, warm stain for the wood floor, trim, and the crown molding and a soft yellow for wall paint."

"That does sound pretty," I replied. "Kind of funny how she's suddenly good at that, isn't it?"

Andy met my gaze, and we both laughed. Maegan had looked for any excuse to shove us together, so it was only fitting that her ghost,

189

as I started to think of the apparition, was the one to finally force our hand.

"Get the idea out of your head, Milo. I stink." He stepped away from me when he saw the ornery gleam in my eyes.

"I never said I was going to shove my nose in your ball sack," I told Andy as I took the few steps that separated us. "I don't want to spunk up my future niece or nephew's room. I just want a little kiss."

"There's no such thing with you, Milo." I noticed that he stopped walking and let me catch him. "You only know how to give me a boner."

"I promise to be good," I said, sliding my hands slowly up his magnificent chest. "Sorta good."

"Yeah, right. Follow me."

Andy led me to the bathroom next door and closed us in. He might've thought he stunk, but I thought he smelled manly and delicious. I'd been downwind from him after a doubleheader in nearly a hundred-degree weather. *That* was stinky.

Long wet kisses, fumbled clothes, and a hand job later, I practically skipped down the steps. Damn, I loved Andy's big hands, and the way he could jack us off at the same time.

"Don't get any of that on my journals either," Maegan said when I re-entered the room I left them in. They'd set up two sawhorses and a piece of plywood to form a makeshift table.

"Any of what?" I asked, looking down at myself. Everything was all tucked away nice and neat. Maegan hadn't even looked up from her reading, so how did she even know?

"I don't need a twin link to know what took you so long upstairs," she said, answering my unspoken question. She looked up from the journal and raised one brow.

"What did Emory say?" I asked. "He wasn't here long."

"Twenty minutes," Memphis replied. "You were up there longer than you thought."

"This house is like a time vacuum or something," I told them.

"Andy thought it was only three o'clock. He didn't even stop for lunch today."

"That's not good," Mae said, sounding concerned. "I don't want Andy wearing himself out. I'm not on some tight deadline where I need this house fixed next week."

"He knows," I told her. "Andy said he got wrapped up in his projects and didn't realize how late it was." Kind of like how I lost track of time wrapped up in his arms in the upstairs bathroom. Maegan's smirk said she knew where my mind had gone. "Emory," I prompted.

"It's definitely a male presence, but he's not exactly sure if it belonged to Anthony or a different man," Maegan said almost absently as she returned her attention to the journal she had open. "Oh wow," she said then turned the page to continue reading the script.

"What is it?"

"These are Anthony Bliss's journals," she said. "I've discovered the real reason behind the curse placed on his family."

"Really?" Memphis and I said, stepping closer to her.

"He said that a woman, who was reported to be an enchantress, caught his father in bed with her husband. She put a curse on both men. John Bliss didn't die in his mistress's bed; he died in his male lover's bed."

"Ohhh," Memphis and I said.

"Of course, I don't think that has anything to do with Anthony's disappearance since he was a pretty young kid when his father died."

A door slammed somewhere from upstairs.

"Wasn't me," Andy hollered down.

Suddenly, a strong whiff of tobacco floated through the air.

"It's Anthony," Maegan said firmly. "No one will convince me otherwise. We're going to solve his death and set him at peace." She reached for her phone and started tapping keys.

"What are you doing?" I asked.

"Did I say I wouldn't nag?" she asked. "If so, I lied. There's an amazing story here, and Lyric Willows is the only man for the job. I'm sending him an email."

I looked over at Memphis who bit his lip nervously. "It won't be long before you get to cock whisper with the paranormal whisperer."

"Hush," Memphis teased. "We don't know he's coming."

"Ha! That was fast," Maegan said. "He said he's filming in Nashville right now but plans on coming here as soon as he wraps up."

Another door slammed loud enough to make us jump.

"Anthony sounds pissed," I said. The doorbell rang, and I nearly jumped out of my skin. "Pizza delivery," I told them breathlessly.

I left Maegan and Memphis laughing at my jittery reaction while I retrieved our food and drinks. When I got back, Andy had joined them.

"Gimme, I'm starved," he said when he locked eyes on the pizza.

"We know," Maegan and Memphis said at the same time.

I shrugged when Andy looked at me. "We're not as sneaky as we thought."

"Make sure you deduct your make-out sessions with my brother from the hours you put on your bill," Maegan teased.

"I smell pizza," Elijah said, coming through the door.

"Oh my," Maegan said with a mouthful of pizza. Elijah did have a very striking appearance. He was tall, strong, and looked damn good with a badge clipped to his belt and a shoulder harness strapped to his back and shoulders. "Babe, I need to show you something."

I expected her to show Elijah the journals, but instead she took him upstairs. I snorted and went about eating my pizza.

"Always the bridesmaid, never the bride," Memphis said wistfully.

"That's all about to change," I told my friend, earning a doubtful frown.

"Yeah, right. Lyric Willows isn't just going to roll in here, take one look at me, and fall in love." I looked at his messy, curly hair, big brown eyes framed by black-rimmed glasses, and firm lips that hid a breathtaking smile. I believed enough for both of us.

"You'll see."

twenty-one

Andy

WITH EVERYONE PITCHING IN TO HELP, MAEGAN'S DREAM home was ready for her to move into by mid-June. It wasn't fully renovated, but only a few rooms remained untouched. Maegan said she'd worry about them when she was ready to fill them with kids. All her main living spaces weren't just habitable, they shone like polished gems. Maegan truly had an eye for diamonds in the rough. As pleased as I was with the interior work I did, I was proudest of the exterior work.

Bliss House was once again an architectural feast for the eyes instead of being a dilapidated eyesore that leaned toward creepy. I admit that I didn't have Maegan's same vision when I first toured the house, but I quickly got on board with her plans. After finishing the interior, I focused all my energy on the exterior. I had inspected the cedar board siding, stone, stucco, and mortar looking for cracks and other concerning damage beyond the normal things you'd expect to find on a house that old. Beyond filling and sealing a few cracks, all the exterior issues were as cosmetic as the interior.

Ivy had covered the entire east side of the house, which actually looked natural on the stately home. Unfortunately, I had to cut it all away to inspect and repair portions before I could power wash the entire structure to prep for painting the stucco, cedar siding, and trim around the roof, windows, and ornate pieces fastened to the stucco sections.

Maegan chose an ivory paint for the stucco and a deep-brown color for the trim, which accented the diverse colors of stone on the rest of the house. Elijah helped me do all the exterior work while Maegan, Milo, Dennis, Jackie, and Memphis worked on the landscaping. I don't mean they simply cut the grass and cut a few shrubs either. They had to cut back decades of overgrowth before they could even see what they were working with. I learned that Milo had a green thumb and was passionate about landscaping. It was fun watching him take charge and oversee the grooming, relocating, and planting. I liked it even more when I glanced down and saw his perfect ass on display, until I nearly fell off the ladder.

We worked tirelessly as a unit to help make Maegan's dreams come true. When we were done, Maegan hosted a cookout to celebrate and thank us for all that we did. As much as I loved barbecued or smoked meats, my favorite things were the abundance of side dishes. I couldn't get enough of the potato salad, macaroni and cheese, baked beans, and seven-layer salad.

Once it got dark, we sat around the firepit and stared into the flames while roasting marshmallows for s'mores. I wasn't sure where I was going to put the gooey, chocolate treat after eating two helpings of strawberry shortcake, but I was going to give it my all.

The problem with making s'mores was that you had to be patient, and it took technique to make good ones. You needed to hold your marshmallow above the flame just so and let the heat toast the marshmallow, because if you just stuck it in the flame, it would catch fire. That meant the outside was charred while the inside remained firmer than I liked for my s'mores. Don't get me wrong, I liked the crunchy charred ones on occasion, but not for my s'mores. So, I kept rotating my metal stick until all sides were a golden brown then assembled the perfect s'more; graham cracker, section of Hershey's bar, marshmallow, another piece of chocolate, and the top graham cracker. Then I squeezed it together so the marshmallow would start to melt the chocolate.

"How do you do that?" Milo asked, pulling his stick out of the flames. His marshmallow was a raging ball of fire, sizzling as the sugary substance lost its form and plopped to the grass. "Well, damn."

"It takes patience," I told him. "Kind of like winning someone's heart back after you broke it." I leaned over and kissed his pouty lips. "I love you."

Milo smiled sweetly and said, "You know what you can do to prove it?"

"Teach you how to toast the marshmallows properly?" I asked.

"I guess that will work too," he groaned.

I crooked my finger at him, and Milo sprawled across my lap, making sure to wiggle a little extra to entice me into doing his work for him. I handed him my precious s'more and demonstrated my toasting technique.

"Mmmmm, so good," Milo said around a mouthful of s'more. "What?"

"You're supposed to be paying attention so that you can do this for yourself next time," I said then nipped his earlobe. I felt a tremor of awareness move through his body.

"I couldn't resist," Milo said then rotated the s'more so he could lick the marshmallow goo oozing out the side. He licked around the entire edge of the graham cracker sandwich.

"You're such a dirty boy," I whispered.

"What? Everyone does this." We both knew he was teasing me.

"Um, Slugger." Milo pointed to the end of my stick where my

marshmallow blazed hot enough to fall off the stick and into the fire. As a consolation, he held the s'more in front of my mouth so I could take a bite. I would've preferred to kiss him and taste the dessert on his tongue, but we had an audience.

"This backyard is stunning, Maegan," Jackie said.

"Thanks, Mom," her daughter replied happily from the chaise lounge she shared with Elijah, who looked like he was about ready to nod off.

"It would be a beautiful place for a wedding."

"Mom!" Maegan said in shock. Elijah's eyes opened wide, signaling he was wide awake after that comment. What did Milo do? He laughed at their discomfort.

Jackie fixed her gaze on her son and smiled smugly. "I was just telling Milo that fall weddings are so lovely."

Milo stilled and went completely silent. "Show me again how you make your marshmallows so perfect."

I thought his awkwardness was totally cute. Why was Milo so nervous? Was he afraid I would get scared away if I knew they were talking about weddings. Hell, my mom had already started calling him Milo Miracle-Mason and her future son-in-law. It was a foregone conclusion to everyone who knew us that we would get married someday. Fall was only a few months away, and I doubted they expected us to get married that quickly.

"Maegan, did you take a lot of before and after pictures for that paranormal guy that Memphis has the hots for?" Dennis asked, changing the subject. Milo visibly relaxed in my lap and went back to eating his s'more while he waited for the right time to jump into the conversation.

"I sure did, Dad. I'm not sure when, or if, he's really coming though," Maegan replied. "He said he was interested and would head here when he finished filming in Nashville, but then he kind of fell off the face of the earth. The network announced a temporary hiatus in filming, and he's kind of disappeared."

"Intriguing," Dad said. "What rumors are circulating? Personal crisis or network dispute?"

"No one knows enough about Lyric to really form a rumor," Memphis said softly. "He has this loner vibe about him, but his crew seems to genuinely like him. Emory respects the hell out of Lyric, but even Em doesn't know much about him." It was impossible to miss the disappointment in his voice.

"Lyric will arrive when the time is right," Milo said. "I just feel it."

"What are you going to do with all your free time now that this project is finished, Andy?" Dennis asked me. The correct answer was that I planned to spend as much time naked with his son as I could wrangle, but I very well couldn't tell him that.

"I'm not really sure yet, Dennis."

"I think I have the perfect solution," Elijah said suddenly. "We're putting a softball team together. Games won't start until late summer or early fall, but we're starting practices in a few weeks. Interested? A little birdie told me that you are a hell of a ballplayer."

Playing competitive ball again appealed to me, but it would cut into my time with Milo. Not only that, I wasn't sure how busy I would be over the next few months. I had a few jobs to start next week and another few to bid. One thing was clear, I needed to hire some help because my business kept growing. I loved my job, but I loved Milo more. I didn't mind working until nine or ten at night the past month for his sister because he often worked with me on various projects. Maegan would be family, so exceptions would be made for her, but I needed to be smarter about accepting jobs until I could hire a trustworthy crew.

"That was a long time ago," I said to Elijah.

"That's what Tucker said too," Elijah replied. A sly smile crept across his face. "He figured your ego wouldn't allow you to play with the likes of us." Maegan elbowed him, and he winced. "Or maybe he said you were an out-of-shape has-been who wouldn't be able to keep up with us." Maegan went in for another jab, but Elijah evaded her pointy blow. "Don't kill the messenger, Freckles."

"All lies," Maegan said. "Tucker wouldn't speak that way about Andy." Too bad Maegan didn't look as certain as she sounded. I suspected there was a bit of truth to Elijah's story, even if he did blow it way out of proportion.

"He'll do it," Milo said. "You'll show them that you still got it. I'd hazard to say that you're even better than you were back then because you're not as cocky."

"Um, thanks."

"Don't get me wrong, Slugger. I really liked your swagger, but I love the humbler version of you that came back to me."

"Aww," was heard all around the fire.

Milo leaned toward me and said, "And selfishly, I'm dying to see you in a jock strap again, or better yet, strip it off you."

"Yeah, I'm in," I told Elijah. "Just let me know when the first practice is, and I'll show up."

"Yes!" Elijah said happily. "The Blissville Bombers are totally going to kick everyone's ass this year."

"The only day I won't be able to commit to practice or games is Wednesday," I told Elijah. I was in a really great place in my life, and I hoped to be a beacon of hope to those who needed it. I couldn't help but think of the progress Keeton had made in a short time. While he wasn't laughing and joking it up, he had joined us for burgers on a few occasions, and I felt like he was on the cusp of sharing his story with us. Sadly, Rebecca was back in rehab after a relapse, but she was due for release soon. I wanted to be there to show my support when the time came.

"Games are on Tuesdays, Thursdays, or Sunday afternoons," Elijah said. "I think we're going to practice a few times a week up until games start then practice will depend on the number of games we have each week."

"Looking forward to it."

"This has been a fun time, but we need to go home. Alli Cat has probably shredded Andy's new work boots in a fit of rage." Milo stood up from my lap and stretched. "Oh my God! I hurt in places I never knew I had." He bent over to stretch the muscles in his back, and I suddenly had something I was looking forward to a lot more than my first softball practice with the guys.

One week later, I pulled around the back of the high school and drove to the furthest corner of the parking lot near the ball diamonds. The school had agreed to let us use their field for practice and home games if we maintained the diamond and grass. Tucker, who was our team captain, put together a practice, game, and field maintenance schedule for us all to follow.

I was the first to arrive for practice, but I went ahead and grabbed my gear and headed onto the field. That diamond wasn't just a place of memories; it was ingrained in me. I'd spent countless hours working to improve my skills, earn that scholarship, and help my team win a state championship. I glanced over at the dugout where Milo had kissed me the first time during a football game. Neither of us had cared about the outcome of the game and only wanted to be together, so we snuck off and hid in the dugout. That kiss changed everything for me.

"Hey there, Andy," a voice said from behind me. "Reliving fond memories?"

I turned and faced my high school coach. I wanted to believe that Red Baker was a good man, and that he hadn't set out to make me feel ashamed of myself all those years ago. The thing was, I had never planned to tell him the negative ways he impacted my life, but I realized that I owed it to the young, naïve Andy I used to be.

"You could say that again, Coach."

"What's your favorite memory? That grand slam to clinch a

playoff berth that eventually led to a state championship run?"

Now was my chance. I pointed to the dugout where the home team sat for every game and said, "I learned exactly who I was right there." Coach stood straighter like he was bracing himself to receive accolades. "It was the first time I kissed Milo and realized there was absolutely nothing wrong with me. What I felt for him was true and real and as much a part of me as my blue eyes. I was never ashamed of my feelings for him, and I didn't think you were either." Coach broke eye contact and looked down at his feet where one of them was leaving a line in the dirt as he moved it from side to side. "You were wrong to tell me to hide who I was, Coach."

Coach looked up and met my gaze after releasing a deep breath. "I thought I was looking out for your best interest. I truly believed that those colleges would take a pass on you if they knew you were gay."

"We'll never know, now will we?" I asked. "That wasn't a call you should've made."

"I've regretted it," Red Baker said slowly. "I'm truly sorry, Andy. I hope you can forgive me someday."

I wanted to tell him it was all water under the bridge, but I wasn't there yet. I hoped to arrive at that place eventually because holding a grudge and clinging to negative memories wasn't a conduit to sober living. It was better to acknowledge the pain, come to terms with it the best I could, and move on.

Not sure what else to say, Coach patted me on the shoulder and said he would see me around. The rest of the team showed up shortly after he left, and we got to work. I made sure to put any worries to rest that I was a dried-up has-been, or that I thought I was too good to play with the rest of the guys. By the time practice was over, we were all sweaty and filthy. As I made my way off the field, I noticed a certain handsome brunette sitting in the bleachers. The smile Milo sent my way made me feel a lot less tired and sore.

"I guess you showed them you still have it, Slugger," he said when I approached the bleachers. Milo climbed down and handed me a bottle of Gatorade. "Oh, look," Milo said, smiling wistfully. "It's our special spot."

I grabbed his hand and led him over to the dugout to show him that I indeed still had it.

twenty-two

Milo

WATCHING ANDY HAVE SO MUCH FUN DOING SOMETHING HE used to love made me realize how much I missed performing on stage. Some might say that I hid my sorrows when I put on those gowns and became Peach. I didn't see it that way. Sure, I was able to forget the things that bothered me while I performed, but Peach also taught me how to be more confident and graceful. A person could question just how those two traits helped me start successful businesses with my sister.

Well, I sat straight and proud to disguise the inner quaking when Maegan and I took that leap and applied for startup funds at our local bank. I called upon Peach's elegance when I had to go back and forth between coffee machines and pastry display cases to feed our ravenous customers. I used the confidence to settle disputes between employees and my flexibility to rock Andy's world. Peach wasn't my alter ego, she was well and truly part of me.

So, on Wednesdays while Andy was meeting with his NA chapter,

Peach returned to the stage. For my first performance, I put on a big blonde wig to make any fan of the eighties proud and sang Bonnie Tyler's "Total Eclipse of the Heart" with so much heart and feeling that the crowd gaped at me for several seconds before they cheered and whistled. The following week I performed "Shadows of the Night" by Pat Benatar, which had them on their feet throughout the entire performance. If I had a penny every time my mom blared that song in the car, I could've retired. I made sure it was recorded so I could show it to her and earn some brownie points.

I stayed for a few performances after mine then left so I could meet Andy and the gang for burgers, fries, and shakes. I didn't go the previous week because I worried that my presence would throw off the chemistry in the group. The other reason was Ollie. He'd apologized to me for what he said, and I accepted. I was still nervous that things would be awkward. I knew I couldn't avoid him forever, so I agreed to meet them after my Pat performance. I was still pretty high—for lack of a better word—from the crowd's reactions, so I was all smiles when I walked confident and proud to the table at the back of the restaurant. *Thank you, Peach.*

There was an extra guy, who I presumed was Keeton, sitting across from Andy. His eyes widened as I approached the table, alerting the rest of the gabbing guys of my arrival. As I got closer, I heard music and singing coming from one of their devices and recognized my own voice. Apparently, Andy decided to play the link I sent him for everyone to see. He quickly shut it off when he looked up and saw me coming. I could tell by the grin on his face that he really liked my performance.

"Hello, boys," I said dramatically.

"Wow, Peach," Andy said, sounding breathless. "Where the hell have you been hiding those leather pants?"

"You like?"

"I bet you'd know the answer to that if he stood up," the new guy said.

"Keeton, don't be crude," Ollie admonished. He offered an easy smile, but his cheeks were flushed from embarrassment.

"I heard all about how you *enjoyed* the private performance you got for your birthday that one time, Reverend."

"Keeton." Andy's tone held a stern warning that the younger guy was about to cross a line.

"Sorry, Padre."

Ollie just shook his head. Andy told me how Keeton liked to address Ollie by every title except the correct one. Hell, he was already a reverend and a padre in the two minutes since I arrived.

"What are you performing next week?" Adam asked me.

"Heart," I replied before digging in the food that Andy was nice enough to order for me. "I'm just not sure which songs."

Brent whipped out his phone and pulled up YouTube. "Let us help you, Peach."

"Which sister will you dress as?" Ollie asked me.

"Definitely Ann," I told him. "She is the one with the pipes."

"Oh! 'Alone' would be amazing," Tyler suggested. "That's a badass song. Filled with longing and lust." I raised a brow, and he just shrugged and grinned mischievously.

"That's a contender, although I don't quite have the range."

"What about 'All I Want to Do'? That's a newer song at least. Sexy too." Adam suggested, waggling his brows.

"Something more dramatic," I replied. "I'm thinking 'Magic Man' would be a fun one to perform."

"Nice," Andy said.

"Why don't you sing something a little more modern?" Keeton asked. "I've never heard of this band."

"Child," I said dramatically. "In a world where every Britney, Beyoncé, and Christina song has been performed a million times over, this queen wants to do something different for her time on the stage."

"Madonna or Cher then? They're kind of old, but still cool. Sorta."

The rest of us gasped around the table.

"Old?" Ollie asked in shock. "You mean timeless?"

"They were our allies long before Brit Brit and Queen B were," Andy pointed out.

"I've already done those two fabulous divas a dozen times," I said.

"Did you wear the pointy bra or pretend to masturbate in the center of a bed on stage?" Keeton asked. Was he trying to rattle me? *Pay attention and take notes, cutie pie.*

"Who was pretending?" I asked sassily, earning cheers from everyone but him. *Game. Set. Match.*

"So, when are we going to bowl again?" I asked the fellas, changing the subject.

They suddenly couldn't figure out when they would be available again. They had such busy lives and stuff.

"We can draw names so it levels out the playing field a little bit more," I suggested.

"It does sound fun," Adam admitted. "Do you bowl, Keeton?"

"I've bowled a few times. I'm not very good at it though." He shrugged like it wasn't a big deal, but it seemed to me he was bracing himself for rejection.

"Yeah, right," Adam said then snorted. "That's the same bullshit that Peach pulled with us the first time."

Brent and Tyler groaned while Adam laughed.

"Glad you thought it was funny," Brent said.

"I thought it was hilarious," Ollie told them.

"Yeah, because you were on the winning team," Tyler pointed out.

"What happened?" Keeton asked, looking around the table.

"I might've led them to think that my wrist was so limp that I could barely roll a ball," I explained. "They assumed I wasn't good at bowling, and I wanted them to continue thinking it until it counted. I deliberately bowled horribly during warmups."

"Andy was all 'it's okay, baby' and then BAM! Milo kicked our ass. Twice."

"I wish I could say that I was faking a lack of talent, but I'm seriously no good," Keeton said.

"We would still love to have you join us."

"Could I bring a friend to even the teams out?" Keeton asked, sounding both hopeful and anxious.

"Absolutely," Ollie said. "You guys email me with your open nights for the next few weeks, and I'll set something up."

"Can't wait," I said excitedly, rubbing my hands together. Look, I was a competitive person. Drag queen competitions could be ruthless, and I was no shrinking violet.

When we got home, Andy surrendered his dreams to me, and I made them come true in the end, just like the song said.

"Oh my God, could you be any perkier?" Maegan asked when she arrived at work fifteen minutes after I did. "Tone it down a little bit. The overhead lights are glaring off your teeth."

"Someone sounds awfully sour this morning," I said. "Is the ghost interfering with your sex life?"

Maegan snorted. "Only the world ending could keep me away from Elijah," she said wryly. "Even then, I'm going out with a bang."

"You mean during a bang?" I asked.

"There's nothing wrong between Elijah and me, or problems with my new lovely house."

"Then what is it?" Maegan wasn't one to get down about much, and she was clearly upset about something.

"It involves Elijah, but it's nothing that he's done wrong. I shouldn't even be upset about it."

I handed Maegan a chai vanilla latte and a blueberry scone. "Tell your big brother what's wrong. Maybe I can help you fix it."

"Older by a few minutes," she reminded me.

"Those few minutes made a significant difference though, didn't they?" I asked. "We don't even share a birth month, let alone a birthday."

"Well, I'm light years ahead of you in the maturity department," Maegan said smugly. Then her face fell. "Then again, maybe not when it comes to this."

"What 'this' are you referring to?"

"I closed Books and Brew last night while Bonnie closed Curious Things. Just before we were ready to leave, Katie from the animal shelter shows up. I'd forgotten to lock the door. She didn't want to buy anything, she had a favor to ask. Katie said that they were organizing the photoshoot for the annual calendar to raise money for the animal shelter."

"Oh, that's a big hit each year. I wonder what sexy men will appear?" I started growling playfully.

"Katie wanted to know if we would be willing to sell the calendars in our bookstore for them. I agreed, of course, and that's when she dropped the bomb on me."

"Bomb?" I thought I knew where this was heading, but for once I let Maegan get to the point at her own pace.

"Katie said it was great since Elijah agreed to do the shoot."

"And you're upset because you felt blindsided by it, not because Elijah is a grown-ass man and can make his own decisions," I said.

"Of course," Maegan scoffed. "I would've preferred to hear it from him, but he had *just* agreed to it. She caught him off guard when she approached him about it while he was picking up dinner at Emma and Edson's diner." A smile slowly crept across her face. "The best part is that he didn't know he would only be partially dressed in the photo."

"She asked him to pose for the animal shelter calendar and he agreed without asking questions?"

"Pretty much. Now he's wishing he had asked for time to think about it first." I suspected Mae meant talk to her about it first, but I didn't bring that up. "I won't pretend that I'm not a little hesitant for all the ladies to see what my guy rocks beneath his clothes, but I'm mature enough to handle it."

"As you should be, Mae. It's obvious to anyone who sees you together that Elijah is crazy about you. Have faith in your relationship, and it will all be okay."

"I'm so glad you feel that way, Big Brother." That wry smile became downright evil.

"What have you done, Maegan?"

"What's with the tone?" She laughed wickedly then. "Okay, I might've told Katie before she left that Andy would probably love to pose for the calendar too. I mean, it *is* for a great cause. You should've seen how big her eyes got. She was hearing the serious coins she was going to make off Beefcake Andy's hot body."

"You didn't."

"I did," Maegan said proudly. "I even told her that *you* had mentioned what a good idea it would be if the opportunity presented itself."

"That's just mean, Mae." I didn't want all those people objectifying my man. Andy was a humble guy, and I didn't think he'd like the attention. Young Andy would've, but not the Andy I shared a bed with each night.

"It's no big deal, Milo. You're secure in your relationship with Andy. Everyone can see how much he adores you. Believe in your relationship and just go with it."

"I will get you back for this," I assured her. "It might not be today, this week, this month, or even this year, but I will make you pay for this."

It wasn't long before the rest of our crew showed up, followed by our eager customers. I got so busy that I forgot all about the calendar debacle until Andy showed up late morning looking very unhappy with me.

208

"I'd like to speak to you in private," Andy said softly. It felt like the calm before the storm. "I'll just wait over there." He pointed to the empty table he used to watch me from when we were still in the hissing and spitting stage.

"You got me in trouble," I hissed at Maegan.

"Honey, that's your middle name. You don't need my help."

I had hoped for an abnormally busy Thursday, but it was the exact opposite. Too soon, Andy was heading around the counter and through the door to the kitchen. He didn't stop there but continued out the back door and over to the apartment entrance. Uh oh, he must've really been pissed if he didn't want witnesses.

"Why the fuck did you volunteer me for that calendar? How am I supposed to say no after you told her I'd love to do it?"

"I didn't tell her that, Andy. My troublemaking sister did after she found out Elijah agreed to it without speaking to her first. She got the last laugh though because he didn't realize that he would be posing bare-chested."

"Wait! What did you say? I have to take my clothes off for this thing? I don't fucking believe this."

Andy started pacing angrily in the nearly finished apartment. His biceps strained beneath his shirt, and his stomach looked tight from all the tension in his body. I couldn't let him go all day in that condition, so I perked him up the best way I knew how. Andy looked stunned when I dropped to my knees in front of him, but quickly got with the program when I reached for his belt. Blowing Andy ranked up in my top two favorite things to do in the whole world, but I didn't take my time to draw out his pleasure like I normally did.

Andy came down my throat after I let my teeth lightly graze the underside of his cock. Then he yanked me to my feet so he could return the favor. Afterward, we grinned at the blissed-out expressions we wore on our faces.

"Could we be any more obvious?" Andy asked then chuckled.

"Do you care?"

"Not in the least," he answered. "About this calendar thing. Are we okay with it? I mean, I'm not so big on strutting around shirtless unless it's to entice you to jump me."

"You'll get to cuddle an adorable animal, maybe one that you want to adopt."

"I'm not sure Alli Cat would like a brother or a sister," Andy told me.

"She'll quickly learn that the world doesn't always revolve around her."

"I'll be sure to tell her that you feel that way so it's your stuff she destroys," Andy said. "Oh, and by the way, Maegan's future kid is getting the most obnoxious drum set on his or her birthday."

"Sounds perfect."

When I returned downstairs, Maegan rightfully assumed the reason for my good mood, but she didn't know all of it. I'd warned her I would get even, and my guy seemed eager to aid me.

twenty-three

Andy

"WELL, WHAT DO YOU THINK?" BECKER ASKED AFTER I'D had a chance to look around the house by myself.

"It needs work," I told him, looking around the kitchen that was covered with God only knows how many layers of wallpaper. "A lot of work."

"I think it's mostly cosmetic," the realtor said. "Of course, you know how it works. You can make an offer contingent on the outcome of an inspection. You're more qualified than most of the home inspectors in this area, but you can always have Mike, Chris, and Simon take a look at the electric, plumbing, and evaluate the heating and air conditioning."

I had worked with Becker before when I bought the small house across the street from Wren and Dare. The house only needed cosmetic work, and I really needed to stay busy so that I didn't continue to make an ass of myself over Milo. Only part of the plan worked, and anyone could probably accurately guess which one I failed miserably at. I spent a little over a month remodeling the interior and hired Dare upon Becker's recommendation to stage the house when I put it on the market. I'd never heard of that before but took the realtor's advice. Dare came through for me big-time, and the house sold the first time Becker showed it. The three of us made a good team, and I appreciated Becker giving me the inside scoop on this house before he listed it.

When I first saw the house on Lover's Lane, I thought it could be a great house to flip. Once I got inside, the house appealed to me on a different level. Instead of seeing dollar signs, I saw a house that could become a home I shared with Milo. I didn't hear fictional cash register sounds tallying up the profit I could make; instead, I heard little feet running across the hardwood floors. They might've been scuffed and damaged, but they would be as good as new once they were sanded and stained.

I heard a tiny *woof* then felt a rough tongue lick across my chin.

"Bull likes it," Becker said.

I looked down at the ridiculously tiny, black and white dog I took with me almost everywhere except work or places where dogs weren't permitted. I hadn't taken Milo seriously when he first suggested we adopt another pet, but then I met Bull. I took one look at that tiny little body shaking from fear and the big, sorrowful eyes that said the world had let him down time and time again, and I knew he was meant to be my dog. My nemesis, Tucker, thought I would throw a fit about taking a photo with such a tiny dog while he and some of the others got bigger dogs. The photographer, Scotty, said he liked the contrast of a big guy like me cradling a tiny dog safely in my hands.

You know who else found it appealing? Milo. I was the one who got the last laugh when I took home that tiny dog who didn't threaten my masculinity in the least because my guy found my gentleness to be sexy and hot. He said he knew then that I wouldn't drop the babies when they came. *Take that, Tucker!*

Bull became my shadow everywhere I went, so I had to be careful about where I stepped. He went with us to ballgames and family dinners. Milo started dressing him in silly sweaters or tied tiny bandanas around his neck. I usually took that stuff off him as soon as we were a safe distance from home, at least until the weather turned colder. Bull loved to ride in my truck, and he brought a lot of joy to people everywhere we went. He was especially a big hit on the nights I took him to NA meetings with me. Hell, even hard-ass Keeton couldn't resist his charms.

One of my favorite things was that he kept Queen Alli Cat on her toes. She wasn't to be outdone though. Milo felt horrible that Bull could go places with us while Alli Cat stayed home. Not only was he concerned about the safety of our belongings, but the emotional stress it could have on the cat. She was so used to being number one with both of us. Milo decided to try a harness on Alli so she could take walks with us. I laughed, but Alli Cat gave me a baleful look and went willingly with Milo.

Alli Cat might've resented Bull's presence at first, but I noticed a big shift in her behavior a few weeks after I brought him home. She seemed less needy and stressed about being left by herself. I worried it was because she picked on Bull, but the way that he curled up next to her during naps made me realize I was wrong. He wouldn't seek her out if she was causing him stress. We'd found harmony in our household, so why was I suddenly eager to cause another upheaval?

"Bull likes the big, fenced-in yard. Daddy likes that part too." I just needed to decide how and when to approach Milo with the prospect of moving. I mean, it didn't get any better than living on Lover's Lane. Even if Milo didn't like it, the house was a damn good investment because I would be able to nearly double my money after some sweat equity. "How much time do you need? I would like Chris, Mike, and Simon to take a look at the mechanicals, and I want to closely inspect the roof when it's not raining.

"Tell you what," Becker said. "Let's write up an offer that allows you ten days to get the house inspected and obtain conditional approval from the bank for a mortgage. I think the owners will be satisfied with that."

"Deal."

Bull and I followed Becker to his office and filled out the necessary paperwork. He phoned the owners with my offer while I was there, and they verbally accepted it. Becker would email a copy to both parties for electronic signatures, and we'd be good to move forward.

"Did you want to bring Milo by later to look at the house? I can either meet you or I would trust you with the lockbox code. It's up to you."

"How'd you know I was looking at this property for myself and not to flip it?"

"Your demeanor was totally different than the last house you bought to rehab and flip. You kind of had this dopey grin on your face when you met me in the kitchen after touring the upstairs. It seemed like maybe you were picturing your future there." I had done just that, especially when I saw an adorable picture window in one of the spare bedrooms. It wasn't quite as grand as the one in Maegan's house *yet*, but it had a lot of potential.

"You're not wrong," I told him, "but I don't know when I'm going to show it to Milo. I think I want the house to put its best foot forward. That wallpaper in the kitchen is scary, man."

"I can't recall a time when wallpaper with dancing peppers was popular, but to each their own. Right?"

I snickered. "Yeah, but I have a feeling that the previous owners didn't removed the other layers of wallpaper before they added the jazzy peppers. All I know is that it has to come down before Milo can picture himself living here."

Becker laughed. "I understand. I tried to hide my horrified reaction when I saw it, but I think I failed miserably. The husband pulled me aside and told me it was all his wife's doing. He was really stressed that the wallpaper would prevent people from buying the house."

"I've seen much worse," I told Becker. "Not sure Milo has though." I knew how he'd react to the ghastly print. Once I got the keys and started working on it, I couldn't very well ban him from stopping by the jobsite since he brought me lunch nearly every day, so I'd just have to wing it based on his first impression. If he saw the diamond beneath the dust, then I'd tell him my plans. If he was indifferent, I'd wait until it was nearly ready to put on the market.

Before I left Becker's, I reached out to Chris, Mike, and Simon to see when they could inspect the property so Becker could check their availability against his calendar. The guys all agreed to inspect the mechanicals the next day, which meant I could start working with my banker to secure financing. I had turned a huge profit on the last house I flipped and could almost pay cash for this one, but I didn't want to use all my capital. I'd see what the loan officer recommended, but I didn't want to put more than fifty percent down.

I shook hands with Becker and headed home, but Maegan called me just as I pulled onto our street. "What's up, Mae?"

"Lyric Willows is what's up."

"Hmmm. I didn't think you were his type," I teased.

"He's arriving in town later tonight to see the house in person. Would you mind coming over in case he has questions about your experiences while remodeling the house?"

"Sure," I said. The rain had completely screwed up my workday. "What time?"

"He said he'd be there by six o'clock. He sounded like the entire world was riding on his shoulders. I figured he could use a friend, so I invited Emory and Jon over. Thought we could do a little backyard barbecue if the rain goes away, or I'll fix a lasagna or something if it doesn't. I even offered the use of one of my guest rooms to him."

"And did he accept?" I wasn't as big of a fan of the show as Milo and Memphis, but Lyric came across as a loner on the episodes I watched. I expected Maegan to say that he politely turned her down.

"He did."

"Wow," I said.

"I was surprised also, but I'm telling you, Andy, the guy needs to be around people right now."

"Then he'll be around people," I told her. "Probably more people than he can stomach." I chuckled then asked, "You are inviting Memphis, right?"

"He is baulking at the idea, but I know he won't be able to resist meeting Lyric."

"You mean Milo wouldn't allow him to miss the opportunity."

"That too," she agreed.

"Is there anything you want us to bring for dinner?" Years of watching my mom taught me you didn't show up to dinner without asking if the host wanted you to bring something.

"I can't think of anything, but I'll let you know."

"Why don't you let me pick up a couple of pies from the diner at least," I suggested.

"Perfect. See you guys tonight."

I glanced sideways at Milo when we pulled into Maegan's driveway. He'd spent an extraordinary amount of time getting ready to meet Memphis's dream lover. One could argue that he didn't put that much effort into getting ready for our dates or even work for that matter.

"Is that shirt new?" I asked.

Milo looked down at the short-sleeved, button-up shirt in a navy-blue color that matched his midnight eyes. I hadn't seen those snug, white jeans before either. "Maegan got it for me for my birthday last year. I think this is the first time I've worn it though." Just how far had he dug in the closet to find the perfect thing to wear. At least he hadn't worn the leather pants.

"Your hair looks nice," I said.

"What's going on?" he asked suspiciously. "You never comment

216

on my clothes or hair. I wasn't sure you ever noticed."

"I'm pretty sure I notice that you wear clothes since I strip them off you as often as I can."

"You can't be worried about me meeting Lyric."

Actually, I wasn't worried, because I knew that I had Milo's heart. That didn't mean I wouldn't work him a little. "I've seen the expression on your face sometimes when the dude does something you feel is brave or exciting."

"That's sheer terror," Milo replied with an exaggerated eye roll. "I don't think he's brave; I think he's freaking nuts."

"I'm just yanking your leg," I told him.

"Save your energy to yank on something else later, will you?"

"I'll always have energy for that, Peach."

Everyone had arrived by the time we got there, but we got held up at the diner during dinner rush. Luckily, the weather cleared enough for us to have a barbecue and enjoy the backyard. Lyric was sitting at the patio table with Maegan, looking through the album of remodeling photos when we stepped onto the veranda.

There was something substantially different about Lyric when Maegan introduced me as the contractor who handled the renovations and her brother's boyfriend. I was proudest of the last part.

"It's good to meet you, Andy," Lyric said, shaking my hand. "You did a phenomenal job on this house."

"Thank you. It was truly a labor of love."

Maegan's assessment about the man was right. I recognized a man who was trying to outrun demons when I looked into his gray eyes. As empathetic as I felt toward his struggle, I wanted to be sure the people I cared about weren't caught up in the aftermath of his battle.

Elijah manned the grill while the rest of us talked about our experiences at the house. Lyric felt it was important to document what was happening in the house when the paranormal activity occurred.

"Renovations really seem to upset the order," Lyric said. "If the apparition had violent tendencies, they would've shown them while the house was under construction."

"Anthony made his displeasure known a few times, didn't he, Mae?" I asked. "It could've been coincidence, but I suspect the slamming doors indicated a big ole nay when we were picking out paint colors."

"It's very possible, especially with the care he put into building this house." Lyric looked up at Emory. "You're pretty sure it's Anthony's ghost, Em?"

"I am," Emory said. "I'm picking up a lot of residual energy from the pipe that's identical to the one in documented photos of Anthony Bliss. It could be a family heirloom and the energy belongs to someone else, but I don't think so. It's definitely male, and I've picked it up in other places in the house like the ivory mantel above the fireplace or the banister of the grand staircase. I can't be one hundred percent sure it's him, but I am positive there is a ghost in this house."

"I felt it too. He's not sure he wants me here. Not all ghosts willingly cross over, so he might not give us the information we need to solve his disappearance." Lyric patted his thighs, which was the first animated thing I saw out of him since I arrived. "We won't know until we try."

I heard playful barking and growling coming from the yard and went to see what Lulu, Maegan's French bulldog, and Bull were up to. They were engaged in a battle of tug of war over a stuffed toy. The hair on the back of my neck stood up, and I had this eerie feeling of being watched. I looked up to the second story just as a curtain fluttered shut in the master bedroom. I looked at the veranda and everyone was still sitting in the exact same place chatting about their experiences in the house.

"I can't give you an exact film date yet," Lyric told Maegan. "I'm in between things right now, and I actually think I'd like to stick around town and do some research. Is there a bed and breakfast or a boarding house where I can rent a room?"

"I have a spare room you can use," Memphis said softly. A pink flush spread up his neck and face like he couldn't believe he spoke up. "Um…"

"Okay," Lyric said with a casual shrug, but I saw the hint of a smile tugging at the right side of his mouth.

I looked over at Milo and saw that he was smiling smugly. I didn't want to add to his swelled ego, but maybe Milo's belief that Lyric belonged in Blissville with Memphis wasn't as much wishful thinking as I'd thought.

twenty-four

Milo

OVER THE NEXT MONTH, A LOT CHANGED IN OUR LIVES. THE renovations for the apartments over the shops were completed, and they were ready to rent. Andy finalized the loan on the house he purchased to "flip." I'm not sure who he thought he was fooling, or maybe he didn't realize how much he loved the house on Lover's Lane yet. I hadn't seen the inside since he just got the keys the day before, but he looked downright smitten every time he talked about it. I'd driven by the house plenty of times, and it was an adorable house with a big, fenced-in yard. He bought the house for a song, so I suspected the interior was pretty rough. I'd find out when I took his lunch to him.

"Morning, Milo," Memphis said when he approached the counter.

"Is that your shirt that Lyric is wearing?" I blurted out. I know damn well Memphis has worn that vintage Rolling Stones T-shirt before. "It looks quite a bit tighter on him, but I know that's your shirt."

Memphis leaned forward, his fair skin a vibrant pink. "Lower your voice, will ya? He needed a shirt to wear while he washed his clothes."

Lyric had left town for a month, presumably to wrap up some personal things, and had only returned the previous weekend. Memphis vacillated the entire time he was away between thinking he wasn't coming back and excitement that he would.

"Is he a big enough jerk for you? Are you head over heels in love yet?"

"Milo," Memphis groaned.

"Or is that bad boy, tatted image just a façade for a sweetheart?"

"It's not like we've had any heart-to-heart chats about anything other than Bliss House. He does admire my vinyl records and comic book collection."

"Hey, I think relationships have been formed over less things in common."

"Cut it out," Memphis said. "I don't know what his deal is, but it's obvious he's not in a good place. A relationship is the last thing on his mind right now."

"What's at the forefront? A certain dark-haired guy with the cutest chin dimple?" I leaned forward. "Tell the truth, Memphis. Have you seen him walk out of the bathroom wrapped in a towel?"

"I hate you," Memphis hissed before he left with two coffees.

I watched as he handed one to Lyric then got busy looking on his laptop for some *must have* record or comic. If Memphis had glanced up or paid the slightest bit of attention, he would've noticed Lyric's intense focus on him. How could he not feel the sexual tension in the man's gaze. Lordy, I was ready to fan myself, and he wasn't looking at me.

At lunchtime, I headed over to Lover's Lane to make sure Andy kept up his strength for the sex I would demand from him later. If I hadn't been convinced before that Andy was in love with the house, I would've known it when I saw that he took Bull with him to work.

Our dog was curled up on his doggie bed with his stuffed bunny. Both my boys looked at home in this house.

"I see you brought your attack dog with you to work today," I said when I walked inside the kitchen door at the side of the house. Then I got a load of the wallpaper and cringed. "I'm not living in a house with that kind of wallpaper, Andrew Mason-Miracle."

Andy dropped the scraper he was using to remove said ugliness. "I don't know what you're talking about, Milo."

"What part? The one where you take my name and not the other way around or that you've bought this house for us to live in?" I tilted my head to the side. "Come to think of it, shouldn't I have paid for half of the house too?"

"Well, I—"

"Wasn't sure if I would like it so you didn't bring it up," I said looking around the kitchen. "Tell me what you envision for this room, Slugger."

"Obviously, the dancing peppers have to go. These cabinets are still in excellent condition, but they've probably been painted a few dozen times. Stripping off the paint probably isn't feasible at this point, so I either sand and repaint them or replace them altogether."

"What about this wall here between the kitchen and what I presume is the living room. Can it come down to open up the space?"

"It's not a structural wall, so yes."

"Show me the rest, Slugger. Tell me what you see that appeals to you so much."

"It's not so much the looks but the feeling I have when I'm here. It just feels…"

"Right," I finished for him.

"Yeah."

"Eat your lunch then you can give me the grand tour." Bull suddenly looked alert once he got a whiff of the bacon in Andy's BLT sandwich. "What do you think about the house, little man?" Bull wagged his tail and barked. "I bet he loves that big backyard."

"He really does. Alli Cat would love the big windows with wide sills all throughout this house."

"Are you saying my cat is fat?"

"I'm saying your twenty-six-pound cat needs sturdy window sills for squirrel and bird watching. You can take from that whatever you want, but it's the truth."

The enthusiasm in Andy's voice was endearing as fuck, but I tried to play it cool. The truth was, I'd most likely live in a tent if it meant sleeping beside him each night. I mean, it would need to be a lavish fucker with silk pillows and plush bedding, but still.

"Show me the good stuff," I said after Andy threw our empty lunch wrappers and cartons away.

"You don't have much time left on your lunch break, so I need you to pick between the good stuff dangling between my legs or the house."

"House now, sex later."

As much as I teased Andy, I knew exactly what he was talking about when he said the house felt right. I liked the house I bought a few years ago, but it never felt like a forever home. Of course, that might've had a lot to do with a certain man missing from my life.

"This is my favorite room," Andy said then opened the door to a decent-sized guest room. "The window seat isn't as grand as the one in Maegan's house."

"Yet," I stressed. "I have complete faith in your ability to make this window even better than hers."

"Are you always so competitive with your sister?" Andy asked teasingly.

"Always, Slugger. Maegan's mini mansion is going to be tough to beat, but I believe in you." I raised up and kissed his mouth. "Show me the rest of the good stuff."

Andy showed me the master bedroom and a smaller bedroom next to it that he wanted to convert into a master bathroom. "It will have a large walk-in closet for your vast wardrobe over here," he said

223

walking over to the left of the room. "And over here, I see a large soaker tub big enough for two and one of those fancy walk-in showers, also big enough for two."

"I like the way you think, Slugger," I said, looking around the room and seeing exactly what he described. "What about the rest of the rooms?"

"Well, there are two more bedrooms and a Jack and Jill bathroom between them."

"Awww, Mae and I shared one of those when we were kids."

"The first floor is a living room, kitchen, dining area, and a half bath for guests to use instead of having to traipse up the steps."

"Or piss off the porch," I mumbled.

"I'll need an engineer to double-check that this isn't a support wall," Andy said when we returned to the first floor. If it is, we can still take down the wall, but we'd have to put beams across the ceiling, and there'd need to be support posts. There are plenty of ways to do that without it looking as tacky as you might imagine. I can show you pictures of the various options."

"This fireplace," I said as I walked into the living room. "It's beautiful. I love the old, weathered mantle just the way it is."

"I do too," Andy agreed. "And what about that big bow window? Won't Alli Cat love that?"

"Yeah, she'll have a blast watching birds, rabbits, and squirrels from that window. That front yard has a lot of potential for beautiful landscaping. I can have this looking like the prettiest house on the block in no time." I turned toward the love of my life standing in a shaft of sunlight pouring through the window. "I love it too."

"Really?" Andy asked hopefully.

"Yes, but that dancing pepper wallpaper must go, Andy. I'm not even playing right now."

"You have my word."

"Kiss me then," I told him. "I need to finish my shift and then I need to get to Queen City Divas to get ready for the big event. I can't wait for you to meet Archie."

"The guys and I will be there as soon as our meeting is over," Andy said. "You're not going to give Ollie a boner again are you?"

"Not on purpose," I replied sassily. "Kiss me."

And he did. Not some little peck on the lips but a full on I-can't-wait-to-get-you-home-tonight kind of kiss with tongues and feelings. It made me want to be late returning to work, but Andy shooed me out the door so he could get back to removing the tacky-ass wallpaper.

I couldn't keep the grin off my face when I drove away from the house on Lover's Lane. I snorted at the name of the street. The only thing cornier would've been if Blissville had an Easy Street.

"I wonder what Andy will think about this outfit?" I asked Archie.

"I don't think he'll be able to do much thinking at all with the way your ass looks in those shorty shorts and those fishnet stockings making your legs look a mile long. Damn, Peach, how many squats does it take to get an ass like that?" Archie swatted my butt for emphasis. "That little peekaboo cleavage you got popping out of your lacy corset is perfect. This drag mother is so damn proud of you."

"I miss Dame Alotta Bang Bang," I told him. "Are you sure you don't want to reprise that role?"

"Baby doll, my drag days are behind me."

"You're thirty-five not ninety-five," I argued. "So start acting like it."

"I just don't have the time anymore, even *if* I was interested. I have a new calling in life, one that I'm so proud of." Archie had hung up his stilettos after his best friend died of AIDS. He spent all his time running a transition home that provided people with HIV and AIDS a safe place to live, recuperative care, and even hospice in a compassionate environment. "With the latest cuts to the HOPWA

225

federal grants, I'm not even sure if I'm going to be able to keep Ryan's Place open much longer."

"I have an idea," I said. "Why not hold a charity event here where a percentage of the money goes to Ryan's Place? The ownership adores you and the crowds still ask for you."

"I don't know, Peach. I'm so out of practice."

"This isn't the confident person I know and love. Sometimes you just gotta tuck and strut until you feel that confidence return. Come on, Arch. Let's ask around and see if we can set something up."

"Okay, Peach. Don't get your hopes up."

"Peach, you're up in five," Tony said.

"Please don't run off before I can introduce you to Andy."

"I wouldn't miss it, Peach."

That night, I performed "Lady Marmalade" with a group of queens. Of course, we did the P!nk, Christina, Lil' Kim, and Mya version. I felt Andy's eyes on me as I worked the stage and sang my heart out. I loved performing, but it meant even more to me knowing that Andy not only tolerated it but encouraged me to be myself. Hell, he would randomly send me clips of songs he thought I should perform. That was an amazing gift, and I vowed never to take it for granted.

After I changed into my street clothes and removed my makeup, Archie followed me out to the VIP section where my guy and his friends sat.

Brent, Adam, Tyler, and Keeton stared at me like they still couldn't believe it had been me up on that stage. "I know, boys. I was amazing tonight."

"You sure were," Andy said, greeting me with a possessive kiss.

"Andy, I want you to meet Archie. He's my dear friend and used to be my drag mother extraordinaire."

"It's so good to meet you, Andy." Archie kissed both of his cheeks. "I've heard so much about you that I feel like I know you already."

"Uh oh," Andy said. "Only believe the good stuff."

"Of course, sugar. I know what a drama drag queen this one,"

Archie pointed at me, "can be." Archie wrapped his arm around my neck and said, "Introduce me to the rest of your friends, darling."

I introduced the frat boys and Keeton first, saving the best for last. I don't know how I knew, but I just had a feeling that Archie needed someone like Ollie in his life. I noticed the way Ollie's eyes widened and Archie's lips lingered on the pastor's cheeks. I sighed happily and plopped down in Andy's lap.

"I see the wheels turning, Peach."

"Everyone deserves to be as happy as we are, Slugger."

"Don't push," Andy said. "It will happen if it's meant to be."

"Sometimes we just need a gentle push."

"Or a ghost to lock us in a room together," Andy suggested.

"That too." I looked over at Ollie and saw he was deep in conversation with Archie while the rest of the table watched the activity on stage. I hadn't seen Archie smile like that in a very long time, and I desperately wanted to see my friend happy. Except, Andy was right. People had to find their way to one another.

I just hoped it didn't take twelve years for them to see each other again, and then another two years of acting stupid on top of that before they figured it out.

"I'd like to propose a toast," I said to the table. Everyone lifted their glasses of soda or water. "To serendipity."

"Serendipity," they all said then bumped glasses.

227

epilogue

Andy

"I DON'T KNOW, FAITH," I SAID LOOKING INTO THE MIRROR IN the dressing room. "I think I look like the lovechild of Burt Reynolds and Evel Knievel, not Kenny Rogers." I stroked my hand over my fake beard and took in my leisure suit. "I don't think I ever saw Kenny wear a leisure suit."

"It was the best I could find on short notice," my sister said.

"Uh," said a masculine voice from behind me.

"Just Andy," I told Tony when I could see he didn't know how to address me. I'd been behind the scenes enough to know he called the queens by their stage name.

"Okay, Just Andy. You're up in five minutes."

"Oh, Faith. I'm not sure I can do this."

"Knock it off," she said. "You're going to be amazing, and Milo will be so surprised." She smiled at me and tears swam in her eyes. "I love you so much, Andy."

"Damn it, now I definitely have to go through with this

harebrained plan."

"It was your idea," she reminded me. "I'm just helping you out."

When Milo told me Peach was going to perform a few songs as Dolly Parton, I came up with the idea of joining Peach on stage dressed as Kenny to sing a duet before I dropped to one knee and proposed marriage. What better time than when both our families were in attendance to raise money for Ryan's Place? I sure as hell couldn't back down now after I asked for Dennis and Jackie's blessing.

"Are you sure Milo knows the words to this song?" I asked.

"Positive," Faith replied with a laugh. "We used to sing it in the car all the time."

"Was that before or after you became Linda the cheating whore?" I asked.

"Before, duh. How could I be Kenny after Milo blew my ass up on that boat? That dude wasn't good enough in bed to die for either."

Her antics relieved my tension until Tony said, "Okay, Just Andy, Peach is wrapping up '9 to 5' so you're up."

"Wish me luck."

"Break a leg," Faith said. I gave her the evil eye. "That's what they say in show business."

I walked out from behind the curtain as soon as the music for "9 to 5" ended. The crowd hooted and hollered when they saw my ridiculous outfit. Peach turned around to see what the commotion was about and clutched her chest when she saw me walking toward her. The grin on her face was enough to melt my fear, and the music for "Islands in the Stream" began playing when I reached her.

I couldn't carry a tune in a bucket, but my Peach didn't give a damn. Whatever I lacked in musical talent, I made up for with swaying hips and emotion. We made one hell of a fucking team, Peach and I. When the song ended, I slowly lowered myself to one knee, careful not to rip a hole in the crotch of the leisure suit and reached for Peach's hand.

"I told you this time around would be different. What do you say, Peach? Will you share your life with me?"

"There's no one else I'd rather spend it with, Slugger."

After we soaked up the adoration from the crowd, I slipped Tony a fifty-dollar bill to play lookout while I lived out my dressing room fantasy with Milo.

The End!

Want to be the first to know about my book releases and have access to extra content? You can sign up for my newsletter here: eepurl.com/dlhPYj

My favorite place to hang out and chat with my readers is my Facebook group. Would you like to be a member of Aimee's Dye Hards? We'd love to have you! Click here: www.facebook.com/groups/AimeesDyeHards

other books by
Aimee Nicole Walker

Only You

The Fated Hearts Series

Chasing Mr. Wright, Book 1
Rhythm of Us, Book 2
Surrender Your Heart, Book 3
Perfect Fit, Book 4
Return to Me, Book 5
Always You, Book 6
Any Means Necessary, Book 7

Curl Up and Dye Mysteries

Dyeing to be Loved
Something to Dye For
Dyed and Gone to Heaven
I Do, or Dye Trying
A Dye Hard Holiday

Road to Blissville Series

Unscripted Love
Someone to Call My Own
Nobody's Prince Charming

The Lady is Mine Series

The Lady is a Thief

Coauthored with Nicholas Bella

Undisputed
Circle of Darkness (Genesis Circle, Book 1)

Standalone Novels

Second Wind

acknowledgments

First, I need to thank my husband and children for their constant support and encouragement. It's not easy living with a writer who often disappears into a fictional world for long periods of time. They do so many things to help me out so that I can realize my dream. I love you guys more than words can ever express.

To my creative dream team, thanks seem hardly enough for all that you do. Miranda Vescio of V8 Editing and Proofreading, thank you for your tireless work, feedback, and many laughs while editing. Jay Aheer of Simply Defined art is an incredible artist, and I love how she brings my words to life. Stacey Blake of Champagne Formats is also an amazing artist who does incredible interior formatting, illustrating, and designing for e-books and paperbacks. Let's not forget Judy Zweifel of Judy's' Proofreading. She does an amazing job of finding the tiniest details that make a book shine.

To my lovely PA, Michelle Slagan. I'm not sure how I ever did this without you. I love you to the moon and back!

Lastly, I am so grateful for my beta readers and the honest feedback they provide me. Thank you for all that you do, Racheal, Kim, Laurel, Michael, Brittany, and Jodie.

about
Aimee Nicole Walker

Ever since she was a little girl, Aimee Nicole Walker entertained herself with stories that popped into her head. Now she gets paid to tell those stories to other people. She wears many titles—wife, mom, and animal lover are just a few of them. Her absolute favorite title is champion of the happily ever after. Love inspires everything she does, music keeps her sane, and coffee is the magic elixir that fuels her day.

I'd love to hear from you.

You can reach me at:

Twitter—twitter.com/AimeeNWalker

Facebook—www.facebook.com/aimeenicole.walker

Blog—AimeeNicoleWalker.blogspot.com

www.ingramcontent.com/pod-product-compliance
Lightning Source LLC
Chambersburg PA
CBHW072229170626
46813CB00003B/1148